The Day after Death

Also by Lynn C. Miller

The Fool's Journey: A Romance
Death of a Department Chair: A Novel

The Day after Death

a novel

Lynn C. Miller

University of New Mexico Press | Albuquerque

© 2016 by Lynn C. Miller
All rights reserved. Published 2016
Printed in the United States of America
21 20 19 18 17 16   1 2 3 4 5 6

Library of Congress Cataloging-in-Publication Data
Miller, Lynn, 1951–
  The day after death : a novel / Lynn C. Miller. — First edition.
     pages ; cm
  ISBN 978-0-8263-5668-0 (softcover : acid-free paper) —
  ISBN 978-0-8263-5669-7 (electronic)
  I. Title.
  PS3613.I544D39 2016
  813'.6—dc23
                              2015025666

Cover photograph adapted from
photograph by Carla Cometto
Designed by Felicia Cedillos
Composed in ScalaOT 10.25/14
Display font is Univers LT Std

In memory of Carol Bly

1

Deep in sleep and shadow, the house stirs as the moon rises. Amanda wakes, aware of night sounds—the humidifier whines in the hall, the blinds *tap-tap* against the window in the breeze, the dreaming dog's nails click against the wood floor. When she hears her brother Adrian fidgeting in the room next to hers, she turns uneasily in bed.

She hears the rude scrape of his headboard hitting the wall—a sound she's heard many times—and she pictures him flinging aside the blankets on his bed, pushing himself upright. Her chest hurts and she coughs, even though she tries not to. She hopes he will go back to sleep. Amanda fears what Adrian might do and where he might go during his night walks. Every muscle tenses with dread as she tries to breathe quietly through clogged sinuses: *Don't come in here.*

Amanda's coughing goes on and on, and even though she cannot put it into words, she senses how the sound grates against the thin membrane of his patience. Adrian has no patience.

She imagines her brother in his bed, one hand clutching at the crotch of his pajama bottoms. Then, as if her body hovers near the ceiling in his room, she watches him slipping from the bed into a springy crouch. He sneaks into the hall, knees bent, ready to leap back into his room if either of their parents appears. She sees his scary shadow moving down the narrow corridor, listens to the soft slide of steps in the hall.

Back in her room, she hears the footsteps in the hall creep closer. Feverish with a cold, she feels weak and exposed. She blinks furiously, wishing for her parents who are sleeping three doors away. *Please come. Now.*

Her room crackles with energy as Adrian crosses the threshold. His right hand brushes the varnished molding around the door, his fingertips inch down the wall and detect the light switch, but he doesn't flip the lights on. He never does. The moon's glow spreads through the room, highlighting her narrow bed, her body the small mound at its center.

He glides closer in his gladiator's crouch. She's seen the covers of the books he reads, stories about ancient arenas, grand and ghostly in the moonlight. He steps toward her, one arm rising in front of his hairless chest like a shield. Gray eyes alert, he circles her.

Amanda's thin neck cranes upward, her anxious blue eyes track his motion. Her brother's shadow on the wall is huge and menacing. Tears leak in a crooked stream down her cheeks. Her small chest heaves up and down. When she tries to speak, her voice croaks. "What are you . . ."

He growls low in his throat. "Be quiet. Listen. There's a monster in here. It'll get you."

She draws in a ragged, shaky breath, too scared to speak yet afraid to be silent. A hoarse breath: "What?"

"The monster. You know it." Adrian squints down at her. "You've seen its shadow already."

"Ohhh," she says. Dark-blonde hair clings to Amanda's head in clumps, as if unevenly plastered. Her breath snags in her throat. She manages a bare whisper: "You mean the snake?"

Adrian chants: "A huge snake, green and red, with jaggy scales. Its skin is wet and slimy and slippery. It wraps around your neck. Then it puffs up, coiling tighter and tighter until you can't breathe at all . . ."

Amanda pulls the blue blanket up to her eyes. "Stop it," she says. "I hate that snake." But even if he could stop, it's too late—with his words the snake rears into her mind. Its body slithers toward her, the head curving back to strike.

Adrian raises his arm in a sinewy motion and hisses. He steps closer and jerks the blanket down to her waist. Amanda blinks and shivers. She tugs at the blanket.

Her brother pushes his knotty fists hard against her bony chest. "It hates you, too." His voice sharpens: "Look, it's crawling at the end of the bed and starting to slide up your leg. See it—there! It's under the covers now. It's wet and cold and its tongue is licking your feet."

"No, don't. No, no, no . . ." Amanda gasps for breath and starts to cry. Her brother frightens her even more than the snake.

Adrian's twelve-year-old arms are strong from helping their father on the farm. He clamps a calloused hand over her moist lips. "Be still!" he hisses. "If you move, it'll get you faster. The poison will go straight to your heart and kill you. Your only chance to live is if you're totally still and quiet."

Amanda squirms under his grip, chest heaving. Each breath is a struggle. She tries to call out, her voice a tiny croak: "Dad . . ." Mucus clogs her throat, prompting another eruption of coughing.

"Stop it, you baby." Adrian presses his hand down against her lips, grinding the soft flesh against her teeth.

Her eyes, wide and glassy, scan his face frantically. Her face glistens with tears and sweat.

His voice breaks: "Jesus, stop looking at me!"

Amanda sees only hardness in his face. She squeezes her eyes shut as her lungs fight for air—she never wants to see him again. She stops breathing.

Behind her closed eyes she feels the heat of his eyes upon her. He taps her breastbone. "Manda?" Nothing. "Hey," he says. "Wake up."

Amanda's eyes open just a sliver, enough to see him looking over his shoulder. He waits, hesitating.

A moment later, Amanda draws in a painful breath and holds it. A low buzzing moan of despair bursts from her mouth, an ugly, desperate sound. Adrian snaps his hand away as if he's been stung.

Just then a harsh light fills the room. "What's the matter?" Their mother, Eva, stands blinking in the doorway. Her grayish-blonde hair swirls around her high forehead in uneven peaks.

Adrian slips his hands from his sister's chest and grips her armpits; he scoots her upright. He moves the sides of his hands up and down her spine in a short chopping motion, as if tenderizing meat. "It's Manda. She's having an attack or something. She can't breathe."

Amanda recoils from him. Adrian always lies. She begins to wail. "He was choking me!" Her arms reach out for her mother.

Foggy from sleep, Eva picks up her daughter. "Shhhh," she says. "It's nothing. Adrian was just trying to help."

"No! I was okay before. He woke me up. He scared me, he was hurting me . . ."

Eva touches Amanda's forehead. "Honey, you're okay. You have a cold, that's all." She turns to Adrian. "Go back to bed. Next time, wake me up."

"She's such a baby," he says. "'He was choking me,'" he mimics in a high voice. "That's crap."

Eva pries Amanda's sticky fingers from her neck where they burrow for safety. "You're too hot. Don't hold so tight." She takes a step toward Adrian. "She doesn't feel good. You know she's not a baby. But she's still small, so be nice to her."

"I am nice to her." Adrian's voice is fierce. "Everyone's so nice to her it makes me sick."

"Adrian," Eva's voice is weary. "Go back to bed. Now."

"Okay, I'm going."

Amanda knows he's waiting for her to meet his eyes. When she does, he says softly, "I'll see you in the morning. Goodnight, Manda."

She doesn't say anything. He folds his arms across his bare chest. His narrow eyes bore into her far-spaced ones. "Sleep tight." His lips thin into a hard little smile that fades as he turns to leave the room.

Eva's tired face brightens as she watches Adrian walk away. She yawns and replaces Amanda in the crumpled sheets.

"Mom?" Amanda pipes up in a small voice. "Adrian is scary. He's—"

"Adrian is just a boy, that's all. We'll talk tomorrow. Let's try and get some sleep, okay?"

"But, Mom . . ."

"We'll talk about it tomorrow, honey." Eva pats the blanket around her daughter's shoulders and slips out of the room.

Amanda's congested chest makes her feel like she is underwater, straining to breathe through a thin straw. She imagines Adrian's snake trailing tepid ooze over her legs; her feet twitch and itch.

She isn't sure if Adrian will return or not. The rapid ticking of her heartbeat, the constant drumbeat of her fear, keeps Amanda awake. Pressed against the pillow, her ears pulse with her heart's panic. Rigid, alert to the sound of footfalls, she waits. Her body jolts upright when a gust of air blows through the room and the window shade slaps against the frame.

After thirty minutes pass, she struggles to stay vigilant. Adrian might sneak up on her again.

She focuses on a patch of torn wallpaper near the ceiling and slowly counts to five, over and over again, tapping each finger against the sheets in a steady marching rhythm as she ticks off the numbers. The repetition pacifies her. Her heartbeat starts to slow, and she turns onto her side. Exhaustion subdues her cough.

The silent house lulls her. She wraps her arms tightly around her torso and sinks into an unsettled slumber, dreaming of Adrian pouncing or evaporating in a random whirl. She never knows when she walks down a hallway if he'll leap out at her, blocking her way, or if the corridor will be clear. Sometimes he'll let her pass. Even in her sleep, the only thing she can count on is that she can't count on anything.

2

The voice of a small girl counting to five faded in my ears as I woke in my bed. Across the room, the clock flashed 2:30 in amber numerals, before advancing to 2:31, then 2:32. The digital display tumbled on as my mind went blank, my body slack. Then every part of me—brain, muscles, heart—collided in a nameless panic. The feel of Adrian's breath on my face, of his hands pressing down on my neck, of his voice hissing into the small oval of my ear, was not a dream. Every detail had the hard, clear focus of memory.

The warm body of my sleeping cat curled around my feet nudged me into the present. By the bed was the familiar rosewood nightstand, a pair of glasses, a pile of books. I was in my own bedroom, many years and states away from the midwestern house of my childhood. Yet the force of this memory vaporized the intervening thirty-five years of my life as if I'd never lived them.

The images had surfaced two weeks ago after a pickup rear-ended me on a commercial stretch of road in Austin, Texas. The accident was minor, barely an "accident" at all. It was only a shove from a truck at a traffic light in broad daylight that barely smudged my back bumper. But its impact lingered, leaving me alarmed by sharp noises and in dread of the dark.

At first the truck bump, while startling and unpleasant, seemed to have no adverse effects. Three nights later came the episodes that I'd assumed were dreams. Had the abrasion of metal upon metal stimulated a long-buried pathway in my psyche, or had the memory been waiting, a fissure that cracked open at the slightest pressure?

A fog of exhaustion lapped at my brain. Too many nights of broken sleep left me nervy but dull. The dreams kept me awake, knocked at the edge of my consciousness. The sequences varied: I saw myself at various ages, from five to thirteen, and in several settings, bedrooms, closets, hallways, the woods, and once, in an open field of ripe wheat. In each I saw a relentless Adrian closing the distance between us, the weight of his solid male body anchoring my childhood. Had the nightly visitations from Adrian really occurred? There was no one left from that time to ask. Only Adrian, and I couldn't ask him.

My rib cage ached. I touched it with the barest pressure, as if it housed a frail creature. On the ceiling a cobweb bloomed in the shape of a butterfly. My head rolled as my eyes traced it over and over. The safe harbor of my life receded amid a squall of rising fear. I coached myself to breathe into the pain as I kneaded a persistent knot in my left shoulder. My breathing stayed rapid and shallow. I focused on the ceiling again. If I looked away, the cobweb, like my life, might become unmoored and float away. Maybe the dream, like the butterfly, signaled transformation. Right now, it didn't feel that way. I didn't sense a positive change coming. I just felt afraid.

———

The next day I sat in my therapist's small wood-paneled office. The snug space was comforting, and some of my tension leaked away as I talked.

"When did the dream that isn't a dream first begin?" Helen's voice was probing and yet soothing at the same time. Her square glasses accentuated her serious expression.

"A pickup truck hit my rear bumper at a stoplight two weeks ago. It seemed like nothing, although it was hard enough to give me a crick in my neck." I found my hand straying to my left shoulder. "And then I've had this deep ache in my shoulder ever since."

"A collision," Helen said.

"Yes."

"It's just that sometimes our consciousness can crack open from the slightest pressure. Our nervous systems have compartments. This accident pierced a boundary and the memory emerged."

I saw the red truck loom too close in the car mirror, felt again the jolt of its bumper against the trunk of my Toyota. "Why this kind of accident, I wonder. A truck bump seems like a small thing, but it shook something loose. Adrian used to say for every action, there is an equal and opposite reaction. That's it. I've been jumpy ever since it happened." I attempted a laugh, but the sound came out like a sigh. "And tired."

A black circular clock ticked loudly in the small, carpeted room. For a moment I couldn't hear anything else, even though I could see Helen's lips moving, her chin tilting downward as she spoke. A fog of lethargy settled in with the monotonous clacking from the wall. "What?"

Helen wrote something down. Her wrists were large-boned and strong looking. "It's nothing. I was just thinking about how parts of our past are fortified for a long time. Then one day they just break off. The more painful the memory, the more deeply buried it can be. Sometimes."

I saw my childhood self as a captive in the small bedroom, waiting for the door to open. "I've never felt safe around Adrian. But I haven't been able to remember much about what did happen exactly. I . . . I haven't thought this much about Adrian for years." I managed a shaky laugh. "I thought maybe I'd forgotten him."

Helen looked at me soberly. "Let's talk about him. Who was Adrian in your life?"

"My older brother," I said absently. Could Helen be asking a trick question? Adrian had been fond of those.

"Yes, I know that. But what does he represent?"

The question seemed simple on the surface, but the more I considered it, the possibilities were exhausting. Everything and nothing came to mind.

"Amanda." Helen brushed fine strands of dark hair from her face.

"I feel tired. I can't think."

"Don't think."

I picked up the glass of water from the table beside my chair and drank half of it. The leather chair was chestnut brown, like Helen's hair. "He was the chosen one," I said. "My mother adored him. She didn't see anyone else."

"Did you adore him?"

"Sometimes. He fascinated me. He was a beautiful creature, in a way.

You know how cold things can be beautiful. Chiseled things. All edges and planes."

"Well, you're an artist. Of course you are dazzled by surfaces."

Was Helen criticizing me? I decided I didn't care. Not today. "You make me sound very superficial."

"Not at all. That's your work. The way things look, the way they appear. Their color and shape and texture."

"I couldn't feel Adrian's texture. He had that air, you know—look but don't touch."

"Oh, but I think he wanted to be touched."

My sleepiness was almost painful; Helen's face wavered in and out of focus. I blinked to stay awake. If only we could stop talking. "My mother touched him all the time. Her body melted toward him."

"And his?"

"I don't know. I don't remember. I think I was watching her."

"Did you like being a girl?"

"What? I guess. Well, no, actually. It didn't seem a very strong thing to be. My two brothers took up more space. I envied them that. The way their bodies seemed to expand indoors. The house came alive with their voices. I don't think anyone saw me when the boys were around."

Helen was quiet for a moment. "Do you remember what you typically did when they came inside from wherever they were?"

"It's funny. I remember that I was always reading, or hiding upstairs. I don't see myself in the room with them at all. But I can see the way they'd come in the doorway, Adrian as if the passage was made just for him. He'd look straight ahead, focused on something—my mother, getting something to eat. Duncan, so much younger, tagged behind."

"You haven't said much about Duncan lately."

"No? I think of him all the time."

Helen's face rarely reflected surprise and I found that reassuring. "Where was Duncan when Adrian came into your room at night?"

My twin brother Duncan and I had slept together until we were four. Then we'd been given separate rooms. I had often wished in those years that Duncan had been in the room with me when Adrian would come calling, but now I felt only relief—Adrian would have hurt him too.

"His room was downstairs." Even though Duncan hadn't been there, he hadn't been spared. I looked at my watch; the hour was almost gone. The pressure of tears made my vision blur. "I'd give a lot to see him again." I gathered my appointment diary and checkbook and reached for a pen. The pen slipped from my grasp, and as I leaned over to find it, my hair swept across my face like a curtain. "I dream about him, but when I wake up, everything is gone."

"Think about keeping a journal. Jot down any impressions." Helen watched me open my checkbook. "Do you want another appointment?"

I imagined my body receding from Helen until she was a small blip on the margins of the room. Then the feeling vanished. "You know I do. I'm just like a horse and this is my watering hole." I scribbled on a check and handed it to Helen.

"Same time next week then?" Helen stood as I rose from my chair.

I nodded as I moved toward the door. I turned to smile at her. "Thank you."

"Bye now. Good to see you."

As I walked down the corridor toward the elevator, I was aware that Helen was watching me as she stood in the open doorway of her office. I fluttered my fingers at her, and she returned the wave. As the elevator doors slid open to swallow me whole, I saw her still standing in the hall, waiting, as if seeing a child off to school.

When I arrived home, I unlocked the kitchen door, and my cat, Holloway, appeared and twined around my ankles. A light rain glazed her tortoiseshell coat with a halo of mist. I'd never known a cat before who liked water.

I grabbed a yogurt from the fridge and took it to my office in the back of the house. Next to my desk was a small bookcase of knotty pine. I squatted on the bare wood floor in front of it and ran my fingers over the spines of three old photo albums at one end of the bottom row. They were thick notebooks with cracked green covers and rigid black pages. My hands came away coated with dust.

I paged through the first album. Midway through I found a portrait of the three of us—Adrian about to be fifteen, standing behind Duncan and me. We had just celebrated our tenth birthday. Tow-headed and pale, eyes large, lips unsmiling, we aimed a frozen stare at the camera. Adrian had a hand on each of our shoulders. I knew all about the weight of those hands. Adrian's smile was possessive: *Mine*, he seemed to be saying.

I studied the photo. It might have been a derisive smile, one that said, *They don't count for much.* Adrian's eyes were at half-mast and emphasized his aloof air. We were much smaller; we didn't signify.

I closed the book, the pages so stiff they creaked. I wiped the cover with a tissue and put it back on the shelf. How much had I seen versus how much had I imagined? Maybe all older brothers were like Adrian, bored by their younger siblings, annoyed at how much they were in the way, how many resources they diverted from the important things—in this case Adrian, his well-being, his life. Adrian didn't like to share, that I knew absolutely.

I opened the middle album. There we were in class photos from first and second grade. I sat in the front row, cross-legged, while Duncan stood rigidly in the back. After we'd gone to Chicago to see our mother's brother who'd been a sergeant major in the air force, I remembered how Duncan's posture had gotten stiffer. Duncan had found someone he could look up to, and in our uncle's straight back and calm competence, someone to imitate.

When we were eleven, I asked Duncan if he admired me. "I don't think of things like that with you. You just are." His blue eyes were patient. "You're my sister," he said.

"I know. And you're my brother. I think you're pretty special."

"Well, yeah, you're special to me too." He squinted at me, a shy smile on his face. "So," his smile spread. "I'm supposed to look up to you because you were born two minutes before me?"

"No. I don't know. I guess that was just luck, being older than you." I felt sad when I said this. I hadn't wanted to be different from Duncan, not in any way. We were born at the same time. We belonged together.

But my life wasn't part of Duncan's. Not just because I was a girl and he a boy. We were separated because one day Duncan lived with us and one day he didn't. One day he was a part of our family and one day he was gone.

3

Duncan died in December, one month after our twelfth birthday. We were born on November 21, on the cusp of Scorpio and Sagittarius. Is it possible for fraternal twins in that configuration to lean in astrologically opposite directions—me tending toward the secretive traits of the scorpion, seeking dark mysteries, while Duncan evolved into the curious archer, always questing for adventure? Maybe it's not likely, but it happened.

The winter solstice that year was a cold day in a very cold month. Winter had begun early in rural North Dakota with snow falling by mid-October. We had a brief return to milder fall temperatures until November, but by the end of the month, ice covered the shallow sloughs in the pasture by our farm.

My brothers and I often skated together. Those were the days before other winter sports, like cross-country skiing or curling, had become popular in the upper Midwest. A barnlike structure in town housed an indoor ice rink. Unheated, of course, but at least the walls kept out the harsh winds that regularly scoured the prairie in midwinter.

I loved the movement of skating, the fluid motion of legs and hips and shoulders, my body angled forward as I glided across the ice. But I didn't like the cold, especially the wind that penetrated through my clothes and left my fingers icy. I had a recurring dream at that time of being left by my parents at an outdoor rink at dusk, of circling around and around as the ice emptied of other people and darkness came. Until there was only me, a small figure turning slowly into a frozen statue as my limbs stiffened in the deepening cold.

And so that day, the twenty-first of December, I stayed inside while Adrian and Duncan shouldered their skates and hiked to a nearby pond in the afternoon. I've learned since that ancient peoples celebrated that time of the year, the winter solstice, with a ritual called the Saturnalia. The reputation of the god Saturn, fierce and stern, colors the word, making the event sound like a fearsome pagan rite, but really it simply ushers in the arrival of Capricorn, the sign of boundaries and definition. And it was true, that day came to define my life more than any other. It was the day that part of me broke off and disappeared beneath the ice.

Of course later I wished I had gone with my brothers. When I replay that afternoon, I fervently wish that instead of reading in the old maroon upholstered chair in a corner of what my father still called the parlor, I had swathed myself in sweaters and gloves and trailed behind them. If only I had trudged on in their wake, kicking at the dirty crust of snow and ice at the top of the hill where the pasture began, dreading the wind as I tumbled down the slope.

I knew just where they'd gone. In the field bordering the slough, as big as a real pond that year from a wet summer, Adrian had hauled a makeshift bench from the ruins of our great-grandfather's barn. That dilapidated structure had collapsed long ago. Hidden in a tangle of juneberry bushes, the rubble provided raw material for dramas played out in castles and forts. But once Adrian resurrected the bench for skating purposes, we'd sit on its splintery slab, our fingers numb and clumsy in the sub-zero weather as we'd lace our skates. I'd wear leather gloves under my mittens, then take off the mittens, skilled at using my gloved fingers to weave the laces through the metal-encased openings, the leather hardened in the cold.

When I looked back on that day, I easily saw myself out with them— falling and sliding on the steep hill, cheeks rough and red, nose running Because if I had been there, watching his back, Duncan wouldn't have skated to the center of the slough where the ice barely covered the water with a brittle sheet. We'd had a couple of thirty-five-degree days that week, and the center of that slough was deep. The ice glittered there, black and shiny, but really it was whisper thin. It only looked solid. If I'd been there, he might have teased me for being a wimp, but I would have nagged Duncan off the ice.

Adrian didn't nag Duncan, not that day. He couldn't have. Because at three thirty I heard a strangled sound outside the window, then a hoarse bleating. I couldn't tell if the sound signified fury or sorrow. And then came the slap of boots against the linoleum on the back porch. The heavy feet tramping into the house, pushing through the back door with the force of a blizzard slamming into the side of a car, spinning it around full circle.

As I leaped out of my chair, the book I was reading toppled onto the floor. In a few steps I reached the kitchen. I braced myself in the doorway. Adrian was slumped on a chair by the table, my mother standing over him, cradling his head against her stomach. Eva's breathing, harsh and ragged, filled the room as she held Adrian. Adrian's clothes and hands were wet; he was covered with a glaze of ice. Eva's arms and hands were wet too, the front of her jacket and the knees of her pants streaked with dirt. When she shifted her weight, the folds of her coat, ice encrusted, cracked.

They didn't notice me; they could see only each other. "What's going on?" I said, a sickening wave of dread making me light-headed.

The two of them stared at me. My mother gasped as if she'd seen a ghost. One of her arms beckoned to me, but she didn't move from Adrian's side.

My mother's stunned look suspended time in a bloodless freeze. The ghost she'd summoned brushed by me in a whisper of cold air. "Where's Duncan?"

Adrian jerked his head out of Eva's grasp, coughing and sputtering as though he'd been brought up from the deep. Like a startled bird flushed from its nest, his head bobbled on his neck. "I couldn't get him out," he said, his voice raw, rising and falling in an eerie kind of keening.

He didn't look at me. My eyes bored into him, though. I wanted to penetrate his skull, to steal the evidence of what really happened.

"I tried." Adrian's voice rose in a panic. A prickling rash of red crept up his neck and onto his cheeks.

"Shhhh," Eva said, the skin between her eyebrows furrowed. Her eyes looked wild and she kept blinking, as if to refresh what she was seeing. Or what she had seen. She left Adrian then and came to me, encircling me in her arms. I wanted to lean into her but I was too frightened. My shoulders ached from the weight of her embrace. I held my breath until my lungs threatened to pop like an overstretched balloon.

"I did," Adrian said, his voice pleading—with me, with himself? "I tried. He fell through the ice and I went after him." He covered his face with his hands. They were big hands, the fingers thick and red, the nails crusted with dirt.

"He fell?" I repeated those two innocent words. I didn't believe him. Duncan moved like a dream on the ice, by far the most skilled skater of the three of us. I imagined the ice cracking beneath him. "You mean he broke through and drowned?"

"He didn't drown." Adrian shook his head, and a single drop of gray water coursed down his forehead. His hair looked as if it were melting.

I tried to take this in. "He didn't drown," I repeated. "Then why isn't he here?"

Eva left me and rushed back to her son. She looked frantically from him to me. I saw a mute appeal in her face that confused me. Adrian struggled to stand, but Eva pressed his head tighter to her body. She held him as if she'd never let him out of her arms again.

Adrian's voice was muffled. "I couldn't get to him in time. Then Mom came and we dragged him out."

I didn't understand. Both of them were there, but they couldn't help Duncan?

"His heart stopped. The cold," Eva said. "The shock of the water." Her eyes turned inward. I couldn't read her expression.

Did twelve-year-old hearts stop just because they were cold? Mine was bursting in the hot room. "How can you know that?" My voice sounded shrill in my ears. "I don't believe you. He's still alive. I'm going down there!"

"No!" Adrian's lips trembled around the word. "Don't go down there! I won't let you!" Adrian's gray eyes glanced crazily around the room as he broke away from Eva's grasp.

"It's not safe," Eva said dully and then began to croon to Adrian, "You're safe. You're safe now, baby." She motioned for me to come closer, to nestle under her other arm. I hung back. "You too, baby," she said to me. "You're safe."

I watched the two of them together until I felt the room beginning to tilt. Her arm was still outstretched and I imagined it as the crooked wing of a dark bird of prey, one that would pierce rather than comfort.

My skin prickled. I forced myself to breathe but inhaling irritated my dry throat. "No one is safe," I muttered. "Not now." Where was Dad? I had to find him, but the room seemed suddenly too big to cross.

"Manda, listen." Adrian's voice was urgent. "I want to tell you something."

"Shhhh," Eva said. Tears were running down her face and she was breathing in jagged gulps. "It's not your fault, sweet boy," she said over and over again. "You did all you could. Amanda, come here."

I didn't say anything. What they were saying was unspeakable. And unbearable. My head swam as my mind turned off.

In the long silence, Eva abruptly left Adrian and stepped into the space between us. She put a hot hand in the middle of my back. I felt a gentle pressure and then her voice in my ear: "Honey, I'm so sorry. You mustn't think we didn't try. We did everything we could. You weren't there. Honey?"

I shook my head and backed away from them, noticing Adrian's hands again, their bulky clumsiness, yet their hardness and strength. Adrian could have saved Duncan if he'd wanted to.

I ran toward him and threw myself at him. "You bastard! You pushed him!" I pummeled his shoulder with my fists. "You did it, you finally did it. And you're glad you did!"

Eva turned to me and her hand came toward me. I didn't know if she wanted to console me or slap me and so I ducked. I kicked Adrian and then ran out of the room. My heart bumped and skipped as I staggered up the stairs and into the hall bathroom just in time to vomit on the floor. Bile scalded the back of my mouth. But it woke me up too. I went into my parents' bedroom and lifted up the phone. Had anyone called an ambulance? Just then I heard a siren as a van slid around the corner and chugged up the short road to our house.

And that was when I looked out the window toward the back of the house and saw a slight shape lying under a blanket on the snow-covered lawn: Duncan's body, thin and bony. Someone had carried him to the house. Adrian? Or maybe he and Eva together had hauled him that half mile up the hill and across the yard. Duncan didn't weigh a lot at twelve, but still, a hundred and five pounds was a lot to carry in the cold when you were exhausted yourself.

Had they left Duncan alone in the cold yard? But then I noticed my father's car parked at a crazy angle—a deep skid mark by the rear tires scarred the yard. Dad, bundled in a parka and gloves, appeared in the frame of the window; he bent over and said something to the ambulance attendants as they emerged from the van. My father had gone to town for the afternoon. I'd thought my mother had been with him. When had she come home and gone down to the pasture? And who had called Dad? I felt the day dissolving inside me, my insides a mash of snow and ice and fear.

I ran downstairs, tore out of the house, and threw myself against my father. He looked at me, his eyes wide and staring. "Manda?" He pressed me to him for a few seconds, but then he set me aside.

"Don't look, honey," he said while my body cried out for his comfort. Then, he dropped to his knees beside Duncan and pulled aside the blanket. "Take her inside," he said to one of the medics.

But I didn't go inside. I wriggled away from the attendant and watched my father pull Duncan to him, saw him lay the small head tenderly on his lap. He touched Duncan's lips, which were blue and yet translucent like alabaster. Duncan's mouth was curved up in a small smile, his forehead smooth, his face beautiful, as if he were a prince in a trance.

Duncan! I wanted to whisper, *Wake up! Stop playing. . . . Are you playing?* But Duncan didn't stir and I watched my father's body slowly lowering to his son's. He rested there a moment and then his face turned toward the sky. But Dad's eyes were closed and his mouth stretched open in a ragged oval like the entrance to a dark cave. I waited for the scream I knew would come, but he made no sound. *This is how the world will end,* I thought—in silence, my father frozen in grief and Duncan dead. And both of them lost to me.

4

The day after Duncan's death my life started over. Duncan, my true brother, was dead. Adrian, the shadow brother, remained. But he had become something besides a sibling. Someone to watch, to track, to avoid. By any measure, he was a person I couldn't predict, a person with two faces. One face—or was it a mask?—appeared around our father. In his presence, Adrian was fearful, filled with regret. *I did all I could*, his every gesture said. "I would have died instead," his counterfeit voice insisted. He kept a physical distance from our dad, watchful of getting too close. Only when Eva was present did the tension release from his shoulders. *He can share his burden with her*, I thought.

Another face came out when Adrian thought no one was observing him. But I saw it. I watched from the upstairs windows when he set out across the fields for walks. In his jerky movements and fevered running I saw panic and guilt. For months, Adrian's nervous system was pitched as high as a constant scream. I heard him pacing in the room next to mine. Back and forth, up and back, around the perimeter. I counted seventeen steps between the walls at the widest point.

Once, I caught Adrian crying in the woods near the pasture. When he saw me, I started to walk quickly in the other direction. "Wait, Manda," he said.

I willed myself to stand my ground. He came up to within a foot of me. "Look, I know how you must feel."

"He was my twin," I said. "You can't know." *He was part of my body*, I wanted to scream. Is this what my mother felt too, I wondered briefly, when she lost Duncan? But no, having a twin deposits you in a different universe. You didn't bring someone into the world. They came in with you. You belonged together. Forever. Duncan might have been a boy, and I a girl. But I knew that I was the girl inside of Duncan, and he was the boy inside of me. Adrian didn't know it yet, but Duncan was still here. Duncan would live as long as I lived on the earth, and I intended to stay. I'd stay alive as long as it took.

Adrian bowed his head. "You don't know how I feel," he said.

"No." I looked at him and saw a traitor, a brute. And a killer.

"You think I'm a monster," he said.

In my mind I smiled at his rightness. But I had to live with Adrian. He was seventeen and much stronger and tougher than I was. And so I kept my face blank and told him: "I don't think anything. I'm too miserable to think. I loved Duncan."

For a moment, Adrian looked wistful. Did he wish I'd told him that I loved him? Not that he needed anyone as inconsequential as I was to love and adore him. He had Eva, after all. All of Eva, the very thing I'd imagined he'd always wanted.

"I know," he said. "I loved him too."

If he hadn't said that, if he hadn't lied about loving Duncan, I might have one day forgiven Adrian. Or at least forgotten him. But for the destroyer to claim affection for his victim—that proved too much for me. I felt heat rise from my neck to my eyes. I wanted to launch myself at him and batter him until he sank to the ground. But daylight was fading and the woods were lonely. I took off in a run, away from Adrian and the dark trees. As I passed him, I said, "But you let him die."

"Manda . . ." He swiveled toward me as I ran. "I never wanted him to die. You have to believe me!" His voice twisted in the wind like a slim reed swaying over water. I could barely hear it. *Save your breath*, I thought. *One day you'll need it.*

5

At the end of the week that I'd talked to Helen about Adrian, a woman walked into my office. Tall, with brunette hair cut short around her small-featured face, she propped her sunglasses on top of her head and studied the two abstract prints on the wall before looking at me. Her stride, long and loose, and her toned figure gave her a youthful aura. Only a loosening of the skin around her jaw suggested to me the markings of middle age. *Forty-five?* I wondered. *A well-preserved fifty?*

Though it was only March, heat had already descended on central Texas and the earth simmered under a blanket of humidity. Sunlight flooded the room from a bank of windows behind my desk, bleaching all color from Teresa Baron's face. "Amanda Ferguson?"

"Please take a seat, Ms. Baron."

We shook hands before we sat down at a small, round table. Her skin was soft and dry and very white. It was hard not to stare. She reminded me powerfully of a friend of my mother's when I was young, a woman who appeared to have a past and a life less transparent than my mother's. Sophia became my favorite aunt, even though we shared no ancestry. The two women were then only in their early forties as I am now, but then I'd viewed them as impossibly old. In my mind, the five miles that separated our two houses might as well have been the border between two countries; on one side was a mundane world preoccupied with habit and surface, and on the other a foreign land inlaid with depth and subtlety. With the cruelty of the adolescent daughter regarding her parent's flaws, I'd thought my adopted aunt Sophia much too elegant—in her bearing, her sensibility, her sleekness—to be my mother's friend.

In front of me, Teresa cleared her throat. "I'm sorry," I said. "You remind me of someone. I don't suppose you have any relatives in North Dakota or Minnesota?"

Teresa shook her head. A pink tinge creeping up her throat caused me to wonder why my remark had startled her—too familiar perhaps?—yet she leaned back comfortably, her laugh indulgent. Perhaps she only found the room warm. "I'm afraid I have the kind of face that reminds people of someone."

Oh no, I thought immediately. *I don't think so.* For Teresa Baron was as lovely as a meadow after a spring shower: skin rose-petal perfect, a well-molded face tipped forward on a graceful stalk of a neck. Her hazel eyes absorbed the colors around her like a chameleon's skin. She had the gift of seeming to belong to the room itself.

Teresa swiveled in her chair and looked at the two prints on the wall again. "A local artist?"

I nodded and mentioned a name. "He exhibited in a gallery I used to run that went out of business recently."

The gallery had closed the year before in one of the Texas bust cycles that followed each boom as regularly as the bluebonnets bloomed in March.

"I'm sorry to hear that," she said. "When bubbles burst, artists are the first to suffer. Do you paint?"

"I do, but no longer for public consumption."

Teresa smiled. "I suspect you're being modest." She gestured at the office. "This then isn't your only career."

"I trained first as a stage director." I resisted the impulse to tell her that I considered financial planning merely a job. My role, after all, was to inspire confidence in the task at hand.

She looked pleased. "We have something in common. Not that I was a director, but I was, well I guess I still am, an actor. Even though I make my living as a professor."

I picked up her folder at her reference to her livelihood. "Most of my friends in the theater world teach."

My eyes swept over Teresa's hands, noting the short, unpolished nails. I half expected her to remove a pair of wrist-length, white gloves. The gloves were another legacy of my mother and Sophia. A picture of the two of them—posed in the early sixties for a day in the city, wearing hats and gloves—had rested on the bureau in my parents' room. *Look at us,* the photo shouted. *We're young and pretty and worth watching.*

"John said you are interested in making some adjustments to your financial plan."

She looked grateful. "That's right. As I told him, my father died three months ago. There's some money I didn't expect . . ." She paused, staring at the window, her eyes narrowing against the bright sun. "I'd like to invest it."

"Let's take a look," I said. I glanced down at the few details in the file and noted her birthdate. I'd been right about her youthful appearance belying her age; she was fifty-one.

In my current job I assist John Walsh, a financial planner. A brilliant strategist, John has minimized his face time with clients. The pedestrian view—the questions most people asked, that the typical client simply needed to know—had ceased to interest him years ago. I'd discovered I have a talent for doing initial assessments, mostly taking vital financial statistics, answering the frequently asked questions, entering data into the computer, that kind of thing. Then he makes the plan, spends his time on the hair-trigger adjustments he excels at, keeps his clients' portfolios nicely tuned, and leaves me to answer the broad questions. Most people never get beyond those; those who do, John wants to see. Those are the clients who, like him, see more than a bit of poetry in the ebb and flow of markets and mania.

I began to take a standard inventory of her financial condition—allocation of cash, mutual funds, real estate investment trusts, individual stocks. Teresa willingly supplied statements and summaries. We talked over fee structures and timetables. It was all very polite, professional, and ordinary, but all the while I was racking my brain. No, it wasn't the likeness to my mother's friend, which, on close inspection, faded rapidly. As I said good-bye to Teresa and watched her walk out the door, it came to me: she reminded me of the kind of woman Adrian was often attracted to, one in particular.

I returned to my desk. In that falling-off-the-cliff way in which the past can ambush us, I saw myself sitting on the lawn of the commons of Amherst College with Adrian over twenty years ago. It was June and we were finishing a picnic, drinking champagne to celebrate the end of his first year as an assistant professor there. Adrian, the smooth planes of his face mottled with two weeks' worth of beard, had seemed carefree that day, his forehead relaxed, his eyes bright. That afternoon, he behaved well; he was the affable Adrian.

"Manda, what do you say we spend the weekend in Boston? Go out for dinner, shop for some wine, maybe go see a play. You'd like that, wouldn't you?" Adrian's voice, slightly higher than baritone, had a comfortable hoarseness. I'd noticed this quality since he went away to school and I wondered if it was some kind of affectation, or just the effect of the humid Northeast climate on his sinuses.

I'd arrived in Massachusetts expressly to see Adrian. I had no other plans, as he well knew. I'd just graduated from college in Minnesota. At twenty-one, not having lived in the same house as Adrian for eight years, I'd walled away my most difficult feelings about him. I didn't choose to do this. It happened gradually, brick by brick. Looking back, I realized that after Duncan's death I suffered a kind of amnesia. A veil had been cast over the past that I had no power to lift.

Adrian's opinion and attention still mattered to me. A thread still connected us. Duncan had died almost ten years before. Adrian was my only sibling now, my sole family touchstone to the past anywhere close to my age or to my experience. He fascinated me more than he repelled me. I didn't trust him but I wasn't ready to banish him completely from my life.

"Okay," I said, dazzled as the sun set aflame the canopy of a copper beech. The breeze ruffled the full leaves of the mature maples, and day-lilies and hollyhocks burst with bright blooms. New England was aglow with the beginning of summer and its ripeness, from the established plantings to the meticulously preserved spires and Queen Anne houses, made me nostalgic for the neat and ordered childhood we hadn't had.

"I think *Long Day's Journey into Night* is playing at Harvard," he said. Adrian had just finished his PhD in anthropology from MIT.

I felt hot at the mention of Eugene O'Neill's classic. "I'm not sure I'm in the mood for that much distress. It's such a complicated play. So dark," is all I said, but I was thinking that just being with Adrian slaked any desire for family drama I might have had. Until today, our visit had bumped and jolted along. I was thinking I'd go back home early.

"Is it?" He smiled. "Dark and complex sounds like your style. You thought the musicals at home too simple. What did you call them? Mindless."

"Well . . . in this play the family is just so tortured . . ."

His face clouded a bit. "How? I really don't know much about it."

"Very Irish, very colorfully and fascinatingly tortured." I laughed uncomfortably. "You know, the old 'it feels so good to hurt so bad' . . ."

Adrian's face took on a stubborn cast as if he didn't want to know what I meant so I continued more soberly: "The father is depressed and killing himself with alcohol, and taking everyone else down in his misery, and the mother has worn herself into a shrieking parody trying to keep everything together."

Adrian turned his gray eyes at me, ones so like Mother's, changeable and murky. "Sounds familiar."

"It's the old story," I said lightly. But I suspected both of us were thinking of our mother, of Eva Ferguson, not because of the drinking but the denying, the desperate smile in the face of misery. My mind turned readily to Tennessee Williams's plays. I had just played Laura, the physically and emotionally crippled daughter in *The Glass Menagerie*. Her mother, by coincidence named Amanda, the tireless Southern belle who pushes her daughter relentlessly and hopelessly toward charm and joie de vivre, was another permutation of the maternal figure beloved by playwrights—the mother who lives slavishly through her children. The "gentleman caller" she so treasured, for herself and her daughter, was an agent of unfulfilled desire. There would never be enough "gentleman callers," never enough flattery to make up for the fact that she had traded her youth and looks for a life of dependence.

Adrian sat in the grass, leaning on a thrust-out arm. The arm, rigid at the elbow, began to tremble. As he abruptly shifted his weight, his wrist collapsed and his fingers flailed out like the striking head of a snake. I ducked my head, reflexively. Adrian's tension was infecting me, but I said what I was thinking anyway: "Our mother belongs to a generation of women who too often gave everything away. They lived through their sons. And forgot about their daughters."

"You don't know what you're talking about." His voice was tight.

I drank the last of the wine in my glass. The bubbles had effervesced into the air a long time ago; the champagne had gone as flat as the afternoon. "My world is different from yours."

Adrian's lips stretched into a half smile. He leaned forward and brushed a twig from his jeans. "I'll say. I don't understand what point you're making most of the time."

But Adrian knew exactly what I was talking about, that's what he really couldn't tolerate. I didn't have to close my eyes to see our mother's face raised to Adrian, drinking in his words, drinking him in. He was the sun to her moon. My father and I were in eclipse when he walked into the room. If Adrian accomplished something—top honors in his class, fellowships to college, praise from neighbors or friends—my mother shared in the achievement. As long as she stood beside him, Adrian's glow reflected on her skin as well. He thought it was merely loyalty that brought forth her praise at these times. But I knew the truth lay somewhere else, that my mother knew she had worked for what he had achieved. Eva may have labored indirectly, with Adrian as her agent, but she had paid for his success just the same. Whatever he did belonged to her. Was I jealous? Oh, yes, I was.

I was about to call a truce to our deteriorating exchange when a tall, thin woman with brunette hair hurried by. Adrian turned to watch her walk, transfixed. For the moment, I was forgotten.

With a sudden catlike movement, Adrian leaped to his feet and ran after her. He called out something I couldn't quite hear as he reached her side. A minute later, she walked on and Adrian returned.

"Who's that?" I asked, admiring the easy stride the woman had, the way the light sweater she wore hugged the contours of her slender waist and hips.

"No one," he said impatiently. "Another faculty member here. I don't really know her."

But as I saw him track her movements until she disappeared entirely from view, I didn't believe him. The receding woman wasn't just a passing figure in my brother's scheme of things. His eyes followed her as if she represented the site of an uncharted archaeological find and he couldn't wait to examine the remains in microscopic detail. And her good looks ensured more than scientific interest as well.

Subject to his whims, object of his frustrations, I had honed my instincts as an interpreter of Adrian over the years; he became my project. Call it survival if you like or call it obsession. Both apply. But of one thing I'm certain: he was my creature every bit as much as I was his. Our neurological pathways shared some of the same synapses, and I fancied I could predict his behavior even before he felt the urge to act.

Recalling his gaze riveted on the woman who walked past us, I had no doubt he had finagled an opportunity to satisfy his curiosity. Once Adrian focused on something, it transmogrified into his prey: he pursued it with the tireless fixation of a tracking hound. You remember the famed beast that haunted the Yorkshire moors in *The Hound of the Baskervilles*? Even while Watson and Holmes disproved the supernatural powers of the mastiff, the chilling fact remained that just one whiff of the scent provided all the incentive the creature required. The hunt itself required only discipline and tenacity, two of my brother's most intense qualities.

My Adrian antennae still functioned across the years, and as I sat in my office I experienced a sensory flash as improbable as it was certain: Teresa Baron was uncannily like the woman who walked so easily, so fluidly, past us that day. Her ease, if nothing else, had attracted me as I'd sat on the grass with my brother, who was, for me, the most difficult person in my life. I envied her that grace, that I-don't-care-if-you-look-at-me confidence. She walked as if she enjoyed the movement, for herself and in herself. Her very lack of awareness of the attention paid to her by others guaranteed that she would attract the eye of almost anyone who saw her. She displayed what so many people worked so hard, so futilely, to attain: effortlessness.

At home that evening, I poured a glass of wine and wandered back to my study. Helen had suggested keeping a journal, and the meeting with Teresa Baron inspired me to buy a notebook for that purpose. I set the wine on one side of the oak worktable and cracked open the notebook. Always a slow writer, I stopped frequently to think and to have a sip of wine, then to cross out phrases and scribble in new ones. I wasn't sure that I could capture the complex feelings of the day. As I made notes of my impressions with words that seemed inadequate, I heard Helen urging me to continue the attempt. I took a break and sketched for a while, trying to capture Teresa's bone structure. And then, turning to a new page, I refined what I'd written with the intention of reading it to Helen when I next saw her:

The facts of a fractured life are often mundane; people toss them off in café conversation, read them in the newspaper. They're as care-worn and uninspiring as a rumpled beige raincoat on a day of drear and drizzle: childhood difficult, mother overworked, father distracted. This list seems shallow and yet perplexing. It doesn't reveal the grinding paranoia that haunts a life spent racing from its psyche. A life spent running in place.

I drew a line through what I'd written. Maybe I would share it with Helen, maybe not. Underneath that paragraph I wrote:

Today I met someone. That's all. It happens every day. It doesn't usually change your life. But sometimes it does.

———

On the day I met Teresa in my office, more than two decades after that incident on the lawn with Adrian, five years had passed since I'd seen or spoken to my brother. Five years, one month, and two days. But in the moment that Teresa seemed so very familiar, I was certain that she would lead me—as much as I didn't wish it, as much as I would try to avoid it—back to Adrian.

6

Five weeks after our first meeting, Teresa sent a note to my office to tell me she was performing in a play and enclosed two complimentary tickets. We'd met twice to discuss strategies and implement changes to her portfolio, and had coffee once as an extension of the second meeting. Our acquaintanceship remained professional, but we'd talked more about our common background in theater. She was in the cast of a new production of Harold Pinter's *Betrayal*, which opened in a converted warehouse just north of the river. A friend and I decided to go on a Friday. But the day of the performance, my friend had emergency root canal surgery, so I ended up attending by myself.

It was a beautiful April evening following a day of rain and damp. Just before I locked the back door, Holloway sniffed the clearing air and fled out on a hunting expedition. Across the street, her sleek, multihued body skulked under the neighbor's hedge of primrose jasmine. The joy and focus of a female cat in search of prey is a wonder of nature.

Deciphering *Betrayal* demands a similar concentration. The play requires that the audience member become a hunter—puzzling over clues and stalking the intricacies of the plot with feline persistence. The action of *Betrayal* unfolds—or rather unravels—in reverse chronology. In nine scenes, covering nine years, Pinter takes us from an epilogue that occurs two years after a love affair ends, back to its beginnings: we start with hollow cynicism and spool back to romantic delirium. Written over two decades before movies like *Memento* and *21 Grams*, the play's unusual structure forces audiences into active participation. Even so, for the theater enthusiast determined to follow all the clues, it's a workout.

I had the advantage of knowing the play well. I'd majored in theater studies as an undergraduate at a small university in Minnesota. The director intrigued me and I'd auditioned. But there are only three principal roles in this disturbing story of a love triangle and only one for a female. I didn't get the part but signed on to help design and run sound.

The program indicated that in the Austin production Teresa Baron would perform the role of Emma, the wife of one man and lover of another. I didn't know the male actors who played Robert, Emma's husband, and Jerry, Robert's best friend and the subject of Emma's passion. I put the playbill aside for a moment and thought back to the few office consultations I'd had with Teresa. She'd told me she was a new faculty member at the University of Texas in the English Department and had just moved to Austin last fall. A number of professors in that department had ties to community theater, and I knew several of them. Teresa hadn't shared details of her professional acting career.

In the minutes before the play started I fought a strong urge to leave the theater. Teresa's presence in the program troubled me. I didn't understand my unease, but I felt it so strongly—my hands became hot and moist as I gripped the program, and a familiar foggy, light-headed feeling assailed me—that I froze for a moment. Just then, the house lights faded. Feeling too conspicuous in my seat in the middle of the third row to exit gracefully, I remained in place. My indecisiveness rooted me to my seat and to my place in the drama that would follow. You might say that several dark recesses in my own life came into focus from that moment when the stage lights came up and the play began.

———

The production of *Betrayal* when I was in college became notorious at a time when the word *shock* had lost its value for a culture steeped in numbness. It was the very end of the seventies, just before the euphoric Reagan years—the horrors of Vietnam still incited ripples of outrage and despair, drugs flowed freely, experimental sex was routine. That was the rap anyway. It wasn't true, of course. If anything, the omnipresence of a counterculture created tremendous social insecurity: if you weren't happy or if you were bored, you assumed it had to be your own damned fault.

The theme of the play wasn't what made the production famous in

St. Cloud. After all, President Richard Nixon had resigned not many years before, impeached and disgraced. Betrayal hovered in the national consciousness. Nor was it the charisma of its young faculty director, Sarah Moore—although the rumors about her filtered through campus regularly: what was her story? Was she with women, bi, straight? With that marvelous melodic voice, the big persona welded onto the petite figure, was she a failed actress, resigned to teaching instead of professional theater? Mostly, the campus rumor mill centered around one thing: what was the secret passion/disappointment/despair (each circulated in its own time) that had brought her to a smallish university in St. Cloud, Minnesota?

The three actors in the play were all attractive in their way, each one famous on campus. The two men, Seth Anderson and my boyfriend Kirk Reid, were regulars on campus stages and both articulate, successful students. The lone female trumped them both on the infamous scale, though: ex-president of the student body, a charismatic subversive who'd resigned in protest of the antediluvian practice of selecting a homecoming queen. Now, if this ritual had resulted in a cross-gendered (or gay or campy) "queen," Jamie Stout would probably have applauded and stayed on in student government.

While all of these things—the glamorous cast and director, the focus on sex and betrayal, the backward construction of the plot, the embedded threesome (*the character of Jerry is not only Emma's lover but her husband Robert's best friend!*)—possessed great gossip value all by themselves, the psychosexual contortions of the cast and crew guaranteed the production would live on in the collective memory. While working on *Betrayal* for two months, marriages and liaisons fell into disrepair, sexualities crossed new boundaries, affairs blossomed, and friendships developed strains. One spouse—the wife of the assistant director—suffered a nervous breakdown and ended up on the fifth floor of Mercy Hospital.

The melodrama began after the first week of rehearsal when the marvelous Dr. Moore decided to expand the possibilities of the play by double-casting it—each of the six actors was then allowed to perform all of the characters, which added themes of homosexuality and bisexuality to the mix. Jerry, the lover, might be female in one scene with a female Emma, allowing lesbian overtones to enter the drama, while in another scene, with a female Jerry and a male Emma, the scene still contained heterosexual dimensions but issues of power and dominance were laid bare. The rotation of Emmas, Jerrys, and Roberts tossed and tumbled the play's dimensions into an intriguing, sometimes overwhelming, smorgasbord of flavors.

Like the rest of the cast and crew, my life experienced a transformation. The parade of sexual combinations onstage served up a heady brew that made us all punch-drunk on seduction. Most of us working on the show had a crush on Sarah Moore to complicate our own lives further—and make us critical of our relationships, if we had one. When rehearsals started, Kirk and I flirted with the notion of getting engaged. Two weeks later, Kirk packed up and left my apartment and moved into Jamie's, displacing her lesbian lover in the shuffle. My heartbreak over the decamping Kirk had barely escalated into despair and self-doubt when Ellen, Jamie's lover, seduced me at a weekend party. I had never had a female lover before Ellen, and to say that I found the experience revelatory was an understatement. Gone were my feelings that Kirk was a capricious shit; instead, it was good riddance to the monotony of his ego, his orgasms, his, well, you know the story. He was a year younger than I was, and I chalked up his behavior to craven immaturity.

Looking back, my relationships with men—and there were many of them—possessed a certain strained quality. I suspect I tried so hard and so often to find the perfect man in an attempt to overrun my own inhibitions. I couldn't admit it then, but men made me feel small and fragile. At the time, I always blamed the man I was with. He wasn't sensitive enough, didn't demonstrate enough interest in me, assumed everything was all about him: choose any of the above or a combination. But after Ellen, I admitted that I was the one who'd held myself back from intimacy. *Held back* actually meant *hiding*. I was like a weak-eyed creature lurking in a cave, darting away from the light of day at the slightest provocation. I couldn't let go. Male bodies weighed on my chest, and I struggled to breathe. Heavier than mere physical pounds, they had a leaden psychology all their own. The sound of my boyfriend's breath in my ear either gave me an urge to laugh or to get up and run. Often, I'd smoke pot or drink a lot beforehand to bury the fear beneath the sexy glow both drugs gave me.

———

"I disappeared with men," I confessed to Teresa Baron on the evening I attended her performance. When I'd gone backstage after the show to congratulate her, she'd invited me out for a late supper. "I pretended to be someone else, someone who responded 'normally.' And since I didn't know what normal meant, of course I failed."

Why was I revealing these details so easily? It was another offshoot of the effects of *Betrayal*: after ninety minutes or so witnessing the step-by-step dissolution of trust among three people, intimacy becomes the only subject. Betrayal is right there on the surface—as well as in the deep subtext—of every action in the play. Teresa, I knew, had been steeped in it for weeks of rehearsal.

She assumed a sober expression as I talked about uncovering my sexuality in the university production of *Betrayal*. In the silence that followed, I thought she hesitated as if weighing whether or not to disclose something about herself.

The moment passed. I rushed on, recounting the production of more than twenty years ago and the explosion of sex and angst around it. Apparently finding drama itself a more secure subject, she responded energetically: "Certain plays seem to trigger the very behaviors found in their plots. Or raise the possibility of its happening enough to spook their casts. *Betrayal*, it seems to me, is as alarming as *Macbeth*. You know how actors call it 'The Scottish Play' because there's apparently such a curse of disaster that follows it they're afraid to utter its name? Calling it something else is like whistling in the dark . . . in the hope of warding off the savage evil at the heart of the play."

I looked down at the tablecloth, white with a pattern of woven eyelets at the border. "Yes . . ." I said as a prickling sensation swept over my scalp. Sarah Moore had delivered a similar discourse during the first reading of the play around a table in the theater.

Teresa continued to expound on her theory: "The very practice of rehearsing such brutal evidence of human nature makes the behavior seem more plausible. And ordinary. It could happen anywhere, anytime. Mayhem becomes demystified." She sat back, her eyes dreamy. "The power of the theater."

"There are several mystery novels based on that very thing," I said, still encased in the ripple in time that had erupted around encountering the play again. "The plot revolves around a stage production and of course the very thing in the internal play happens in the world of the novel. I don't know if you're an addict of the genre, but Webster's play about incest and murder, *The Duchess of Malfi*, shows up regularly. Of course, it's particularly gruesome. Attractive when you're writing about death and deceit, I suspect."

"The old parallel plotline." Teresa's mercurial eyes, an unnerving gray-green at the moment, swept the room. "Murder and betrayal," she said thoughtfully. "Those are probably the most fearsome themes. What else do people fear as much?"

I put my fork down after helping myself to another bite of the shrimp quesadilla we were sharing. "I don't know. Maybe love?"

Teresa lifted the bottle of Sauvignon Blanc from its ice bucket near the table. She refilled her glass and added to mine. "Maybe. You can't really have betrayal without love, can you? You have to care deeply to feel deceived on that scale. I don't know. We were lucky in this production. None of us knew each other before working together."

"And now?" Across from me, Teresa's soft green scarf bloomed against the bare, off-white stone walls of the restaurant. The old building had been a warehouse of some kind in the 1920s when Austin had been a small dot on the Texas map.

"Oh, we know each other now," she said. "I considered going out with Dale, the actor who plays Robert. But, you know his character in the play is so despicable, and Dale plays it with such relish, that I didn't, and don't, trust him. I told myself it was unfair but deep down I'm not so sure. After all, the only experience I have with this man is the play. That's his history as far as I know."

I nodded, thinking that actors were probably more suspicious than most people about the hidden motives of others. Motive was an actor's stock in trade, after all. And since most could easily manipulate his or her own intentions for the sake of a script, how could actors not be suspicious of one another? Authenticity was a rare commodity in the world of artifice that made up the theater. "You see? It's the curse of the play. If you're involved with it, you either fall into bed or out of love, run away in paranoia, freeze in terror, or—"

"Or look somewhere else entirely," she said. She dipped the thumb and forefinger of one hand into her water glass and snuffed out the sputtering candle on our table.

I felt a sudden wave of shyness. "What do you mean?" I managed to ask.

Teresa laughed. "Oh, I just meant that a play like the one I'm in is enough to put you off relationships. For a while."

She didn't wear a ring; I'd already noticed that. She must have noticed the sweep of my eyes toward her hand. "I'm divorced," she said abruptly. "Two years ago." Her hand went to her neck, rested there, and then drifted down to her silverware. She picked up her dinner fork and then put it back down. "It wasn't amicable. I thought I'd recovered."

Her eyes roamed the room before resting on my face. "But, you know, doing this play, I find myself feeling rage at times."

She was silent for a moment. "At men?" I prompted, when she seemed to be waiting for a response.

"At human nature," she smiled grimly.

Our waiter came at that moment to take the rest of our order, and after he left, we drifted onto other subjects.

———

I didn't see Teresa for a week after that. Though April 15 had already come and gone, calculating and paying taxes often causes people to rethink their financial health, and our office's phones, faxes, and conferences frothed with tension. The financial business, like the acquiring and spending of money itself, has an inherent churning motion. Styles of investing come and go and return; advice proliferates, hot funds skyrocket and disappear. People are largely happy when they make money. If they don't make enough of it, they're tempted to take it elsewhere or manage it themselves.

I liked the work. The logic of money soothed me. I found the mechanics of how dollars shrank or grew, of debits and credits, far less stressful than being alone with a blank canvas on a day when stray smudges were all I had to show for hours of work. Along the way, John helped me to demystify the business of investing. He managed my moderate inheritance from my maternal grandmother, the one that had allowed me to study theater and art in the first place.

It was 2001 and the markets were continuing the declines they'd begun the year before. Teresa was not one of the panicked callers; in fact, she'd received my financial report weeks earlier with definite stoicism. She'd assured me that since the money under management was a windfall— and not something she currently lived on—she was committed to her investments for the long term.

When I read the local paper's review of *Betrayal*, I learned, in the laudatory assessment of Teresa's performance, that she had been a professional actress in New York for five years before going to graduate school at the University of Illinois to get her PhD in English literature. That she'd lived in the Midwest seemed another connection between us.

On the way home from the office near the end of that week, I wandered into a florist. On impulse, I sent Teresa a dozen yellow roses. Besides my name, I wrote just one word on the card: "Congratulations." Even with this generic message, it occurred to me after I left the shop that Teresa might wonder about my intentions in sending the flowers. When I'd revealed my sexual history with women at dinner that night, she had seemed noncommittal. Although it's hard with a subject like sexual orientation to appear neutral, that's what she had done. Well, she was an actress, after all. When the evening had ended, with a nightcap at the Four Seasons on the river, I still didn't have a sense of where her romantic interests might lie. She appeared friendly, inquisitive about my life, but ambiguous. I assumed she was straight. Surely I'd given her the opening to tell me otherwise.

Was I making a pass? Flirting? I can't say I'm sure even now.

When Teresa received the flowers, she called to thank me. And suggested dinner at her house the following Wednesday when she had no performance of the play.

7

A s I drove across the river and toward Teresa's house in north-central Austin, the three- and four-bedroom ranch houses I passed in that relatively flattish part of town reminded me of the suburban developments in the Midwest. Once again, I found myself submerged back in the time when *Betrayal*—and betrayal—had taken over my life. As I pulled away from a red light, I realized it wasn't just the houses that made the connection. Teresa had catalyzed my memories as well, and not only by the coincidence of her involvement in the same play that had so marked an intense time in my life. The slight uplift of her chin as she listened reminded me of Sarah Moore. I calculated that the two women were the same age, "of a generation," as my father used to say.

When I was a university senior, Dr. Moore modeled that elusive sense of mastery that to me belonged to a future adulthood. I've said that she stirred speculation. She also inspired adoration. Her five foot three frame exuded confidence and a certain daring. Her stock in trade, though, it turned out, was a gift for intimacy. Good directors often have it. It allows them to bond easily with actors. If a director engages you in a primal way, it encourages you to dig deep and take risks as a performer. It's hard to describe this quality. You have to see it in action. There, I've said it: some good directors are even better actors, especially when they're playing their own lives.

When Sarah coached an actor, she might toss off a suggestion from the back of the theater, as if she were merely an interested observer. Or, she'd walk onstage, put her face an inch from the actor's nose, and demand a response. She kept the actors slightly off guard and wary. One night Kirk and Jamie rehearsed the first scene of the play, where Emma and Jerry meet in a pub for a drink two years after their affair ended. Emma's life has turned to ash—she finds her husband has betrayed her and the cycle that began with the corrosion of her affair with Jerry is complete. For an hour, the actors were mired in the first page of scene 1; each time, Sarah halted them and made them start again. Finally, she threw her script on a chair.

"These two people haven't been alone together for two years." She bounded onto the stage, her voice bristling with controlled energy. "After spending seven years of afternoons together. Think about that—all those years of intimacy, and then . . . nothing. Two years of absence and their failed love affair stand between them. What they *were* to each other and would never be again is the elephant in the room. But the point is that Emma needs to tell Jerry that she and her husband are divorcing and that she's told him *everything*."

"But the first line of the play is so simple. Jerry just says, 'Well . . .'" Kirk said, his voice weak. "How much can I do with that?"

Sarah smiled, not patiently. "I'm not talking about spoken language. Rather, the language of their bodies. How they look at each other given their history after two years of not being alone together. The scene begins long before the first line. It begins with heavy freight—she's been up all night and he's been wondering for hours why she chose to call him now, after two years. It's *what they don't say* that you need to capture."

"I—I . . ." Kirk stammered.

"Just think about the weight of all that's unspoken." Sarah swiveled to face Jamie. "And when you say, 'How are you?' in response to Jerry's 'Well . . . ,' it's a huge line. She doesn't mean conversationally, conventionally. She means how was his life during those two years *without her*. She's asking him an unanswerable question, but she desperately wants an answer."

The two young people just stared at her. Sarah pressed on. "Okay, let's read through the last scene of the play, when Jerry tells Emma he's infatuated with her. And then let's try this again. And you—" she touched Kirk's shoulder with the barest pressure and he jumped—"I want you to show in your face and your body *before* your opening 'Well . . .' a strong hint of the intrigue and adoration you felt for her back at the beginning of their intimacy. Your awareness of her sensual power has to be there from the first instant you bring those drinks to the table and face her."

When they didn't immediately respond, Sarah pushed up her sleeves and tucked in her chin. In a brisk walk that signaled *watch me*, she mimed going to the bar, picking up two drinks, and then, much more deliberately, strode toward Jamie. And the whole time she moved, her face reflected a war between eagerness and dread, attraction and relief so that by the time she put the glass down in front of Jamie, Kirk breathed a tense "Well . . ." under his breath, and for the first time it had a punch behind it.

If she hadn't been so professionally productive, Sarah Moore might have been labeled an artist manqué. Her life went beyond the theatrical: it was a perpetual high-wire act. I don't know how she kept her feet, for at least during the brief time I was in her orbit, bodies lost their balance and fell all around her. As we would have said then, they crashed and burned. The high wire had no safety net.

Like Teresa, she was a brunette with creamy skin. Another English rose. In 1979, her tailored, classic look appeared slightly old-fashioned and therefore even more captivating. From my first class with her, I speculated that she read Henry James and Kierkegaard late at night and sipped single malt whiskey. She had an old-world quality that spoke of prosperity, a good education, and a clear idea of a life well lived. Coming from the rural Midwest, I found all of this very attractive. I hadn't grown up in a fertile intellectual culture; I had to till that ground myself. Sarah helped me to make up for lost years. She made me her pupil and I was grateful for it.

In many ways she played the part of a mentor admirably, generous with her time and her fine mind. She had only one major flaw: she coveted the youth she tutored. When I first met her she lived with another woman, Marta Conway, also a professor. They were obviously very close; later, we realized with fascination that they were romantically intimate. In small-town Minnesota in the 1970s lesbian couples were rare; they shocked even when little else had the power to shock.

Both very striking women, they displayed a dramatic flair from the way they talked—in complete, eloquent sentences—down to the rakish way they held their cigarettes, between thumb and forefinger. They were the same height, with dark hair cut short and framing their faces in a similar way. Like many people who live and work together, their mannerisms often reflected one another and created a synchrony that increased an impression of togetherness and likeness.

Young women—and men—flocked to their classes, lurked about during office hours. Wherever they were, the two women held court, casting an exclusive aura like a soft spotlight around their chairs. For a while we all inhaled the heady atmosphere, feeling witty and gifted just by virtue of sharing their presence.

Kirk, he of the faithless loyalties, hung on every word either of them uttered. One night at a party at Sarah and Marta's he leaned over and whispered to me, "These women are too cool. Is there a handy term like fag hag for a guy like me who's attracted to gay women?"

But in September during early rehearsals for *Betrayal*, Sarah and Marta broke up. The word filtered down slowly; no one appeared to know the cause. Outward appearances remained the same: they still kept house together, they continued to share an office at the U. I think I might have remained in ignorance of my professors' personal cataclysm if I hadn't gotten snared in its rippling effects. I was twenty after all, and my own life was providing more than enough fireworks to dazzle me.

The memory of the night I auditioned haunted me. In the front row was Sarah, wearing a black button-down shirt and blue jeans. Sitting with her was her assistant director, Alan. A sprinkling of other actors occupied the theater. I was in the third row, scrunching down so that I could barely see over the seats in front of me. Two young men with scripts in their hands had just exited the stage.

Sarah stood up. "Let's stop there. We'll take a five-minute break now."

One of the actors had frozen up at the end of the scene. He looked sheepish then went to the edge of the stage, grabbed his jacket, and left. I followed him outside. "Jess, wait a minute."

"God," he groaned. "I completely blew that."

"No, you did great."

"I don't want to talk about it. You reading tonight?"

"I thought I would, though I don't have a prayer." I looked down at my thin frame. "Emma has to be both very intelligent and earthy. That's tough. I'm pretty sure Jamie has the role cinched."

Jess squinted at me, his dark hair falling in streaks across his forehead. "Well, give it a try. I've gotta go. See you in class tomorrow."

I went through the side door, painted a splashy shade of green, and back into the auditorium. Sarah was bent over the script with Alan. She had a hand on his shoulder. He looked flustered. I looked around; no one else was in the theater.

Sarah's hand patted Alan's shoulder and then fell as she stepped away. She looked up and saw me. A smile crossed her face. I imagined her wondering what I'd seen, but I hadn't seen anything, that was the thing. "Are you reading for Emma?" she asked in a low voice.

"I . . . I thought I might."

She laughed then. "Be definite, Amanda. Either you are or you're not."

I picked up my script and clutched it. "I am," I said.

By then, other students had filed back in and Sarah called me up onstage. I read the opening scene with Jerry and Emma. It went okay. Emma is nervy in this scene, she's been up all night, and that mix of anxiety and neediness felt easy to play.

"I'll post the callbacks tomorrow," Sarah said after another half hour of readings.

Alan asked me if I felt like going out for a drink and I said I would. "Me too," said James, who had just read with me. The three of us rode over to The Depot and snagged a booth in the rear of the restaurant. Five minutes later, just as we ordered drinks, Sarah came in and Alan waved her over.

He leaned toward me. "We sometimes go out after auditions just to decompress," he said. Sarah joined us before I could ask for more details.

"Johnnie Walker Black, water on the side," she told the waiter. She had on a pair of square glasses, a black shirt, blue jeans, and white K-Swiss tennis shoes. I had a pair just like them that I actually wore on the tennis court.

I sat back, nursing a Michelob while Alan, Sarah, and James talked about Pinter and the play.

"What do you think, Amanda?" Sarah asked me directly. I hadn't heard James's comment; the room had erupted in laughter just then and I was at the end of the table. It was something about whether Robert was the immoral center of the play or if it was Jerry's desire to please that poisoned everything.

I stuttered for a moment and then said, "I think they're all addicts. Emma and Jerry are obsessed with each other. Robert has compulsive affairs with other women but is furious when Emma has one."

"Exactly," Sarah said, relishing the three syllables of the word by drawing them out. "Any one of them could have opted out. But they don't."

"Too much at stake?" I said.

Sarah turned her gray eyes on me. "That's usually the problem."

I flinched and was at a loss for words. Fortunately, Alan jumped in. "That's how it works. The shifting balance of the threesome makes everything ratchet up, until . . ." He downed the rest of his beer.

Sarah looked at him approvingly. "Until one of them snaps. But it's that tension—the balls in the air, almost falling, but precariously staying up, that keeps the audience glued to the action."

I could only nod. The conversation felt too competitive and heady and I was about to leave when I remembered I'd driven over with Alan and was too far from my apartment to walk. "I have a big test tomorrow," Alan said, zipping up his jacket. "I gotta go."

"Me too," said James.

Before I could say anything, Sarah said, "Go ahead. I'll drop Amanda off." And in an instant, we were alone.

We both took a sip of our drinks. Sarah's eyes met mine. "Do you have a test tomorrow too?"

"I have a lot to do tonight," I said.

Sarah paid the check and we walked out to her car. Inside, she leaned toward me. "Why don't you come to my place for another drink?"

Heat emanated toward me. It drew me in but fear moved me away. I didn't move. "I . . ."

After a moment, Sarah nodded and pulled away. "We'd better get you home."

8

The drama of the trio enacted onstage spawned triangles all around it. Freud called the triangle a classic unit of interaction. It's also classically imbalanced—let's call it disharmonious—as two legs ally and oppose the singleton, often on a rotating basis. First, Kirk fell in love with Jamie who left her girlfriend Ellen. Ellen attached herself to me but also attracted Sarah. Marta appealed to Kirk and Jamie in her distress over Sarah. Especially given the extended rehearsal time (nine weeks instead of six) occasioned by the double casting of the play, the merry-go-round turned more tortuously than the bare facts suggest.

Early in the fall, Ellen, who had no role in the production, started haunting rehearsals so that she could monitor Jamie's love affair with Kirk. That's how we grew closer: together we enviously watched our exes' growing infatuation with each other.

Soon, Ellen and I were inseparable, regularly sharing those delicious 2:00 a.m. binges of fries and Cokes after rehearsals—prefaced and followed by a round of drinking—that marked my senior year. Studying happened after these bouts or right before class, if at all.

Ellen, a great mimic, had charm and humor. Of medium height, with a former cheerleader's curvy figure, she was pretty and unaffected. She suffered painful blitzes of anxiety about being liked, which I didn't understand given her looks and personality. But that, and her frankness about it, engaged me as well—I'd struggled for years to hide my own feelings of inadequacy. Her obsession with Sarah and Marta mirrored my own, leading to endless rounds of confidences.

"I've seen their apartment," Ellen told me early on. "There's a room that's always open—it has two twin beds in it. But then there's another room that's always closed. Do you think they just put the guest bedroom on display?"

"I guess. I can't believe you didn't go in the other bedroom to find out if that was the one they shared."

"Well, yeah, but I was only in the apartment for two seconds when Dr. Moore needed a ride home. She didn't really let me out of her sight."

"Then how did you see the open bedroom?"

A dimple appeared in Ellen's cheek. "It's on the way to her study. She gave me some photos to take to the newspaper."

"Oh. Was Ms. Conway there too?"

Ellen leaned in closer, her hand poised above a slice of pizza. We were sitting in a café about two miles from campus. She looked over her shoulder. "Yeah, but she didn't say anything. She looked pissed off. I mean I guess she said hello to me but that was it. What do you think that's about?"

"God, who knows? They're breaking up, right? Of course she's pissed. But they're still living together, right?"

Ellen nodded, her cheeks flushed.

"And I heard Dr. Moore told her to leave you alone."

"No! Oh God, you're kidding." Ellen made a face as if this news was beyond the pale, but she looked thrilled. "You think Marta Conway is interested in me?" And then quickly, "But wait. How would you know?"

"Kirk told us after a rehearsal last week that he'd heard them arguing backstage. It was late. They thought everyone was gone. But Kirk was in the men's room. You know how close it is to the green room? Well, that's how."

"No way."

I shrugged. "Just thought you should know."

"Look." Ellen's full face grew sober. "If anyone should watch out, I think it's you. I think Dr. Moore thinks you're amazing."

I changed the subject. "Look, I've got to get out of here. I have a test tomorrow. A big one. And I've missed some classes. Have to ace this one."

Ellen's easy sympathy and quick admissions of her neuroses appealed to me. I felt understood and appreciated. I grew addicted to the confidences we exchanged during these sessions. So much so that when Ellen first kissed me and I drew away, frightened, all she had to say was "Then we can't be friends anymore" to change my mind. Or perhaps just to switch my mind off entirely.

My initial misgivings evaporated as our bodies became familiar; I felt natural in bed with another person for the first time. I felt a sense of fit with Ellen and our affair progressed with startling intensity. While we were oblivious to others for several weeks, our friends noticed our single-minded devotion to each other. In particular, one woman looking to replace her lover cast her eyes our way—Sarah Moore, perhaps aware of her own aging in the midst of her young, hormonally charged actors.

Any attention from the vaunted Dr. Moore was prized. Sarah lavished it on Ellen by asking for favors. When she spoke to her—at the end of a class, in the hallway—her striking face focused on Ellen as if she were the only person worth talking to. It was the way Sarah spoke to everyone, but Ellen looked entranced at her most pedestrian requests. "Ellen, do you have time to pick up the gels from the lighting company?" she might ask, or "Ellen, could you drive my car home? I'm catching a ride with Kirk to Abel's after rehearsal."

Flattered, Ellen complied. With no role in the production, she became Sarah's personal assistant, privy to Sarah's charm, receptacle for her occasional moody outbursts. Ellen relished that Sarah needed her. Moreover, as her assistant, Ellen sat next to the center of power. Around Sarah sparks flew, intellects clashed, creative juices ran. Only the unpredictable was predictable. Heady days for a twenty-year-old from a small farming town on the northern plains where the main games in town for teenagers were sports, drinking, and moping around at the drive-in.

"She's just using you," I'd say, annoyed, and apprehensive too. How could Ellen be so gullible? Or Sarah so transparent?

I watched as Ellen got drawn into Sarah's life—and Marta's. For when Ellen would drop something off at their house, Marta would often be there, thirsting for details of Sarah's life. Often Ellen stayed on drinking with Marta, listening to her stories of bitterness, of trust betrayed, while I waited for her at our apartment. Marta had not yet completed her PhD, and Ellen theorized that the lack of the "Dr." in front of her name affected the power balance between her and Sarah.

"So, what was Marta's big complaint tonight?" I asked one night when she came home at one in the morning.

"Oh, honey, come on. She's just lonely. She feels out of the loop."

"I don't trust her. I don't trust either of them." I slumped against the stereo cabinet; its cheap veneer creaked against my weight.

"I dunno. I feel kind of sorry for her. For both of them, really. Did you know they've been together seven years?" Ellen's dark brown eyes glistened in wonder. To her, seven years went beyond eternity. In those days, a relationship of three months was considered long-standing.

Seven weeks turned out to be the duration of our time together. A week before our relationship fractured, Ellen and I traveled in a car with Sarah and Marta. It was late September, with iron-gray skies. At that time of year, snow was possible but the weather held to a mild low fifties. Our professors had invited us to participate in a guest stint at an out-of-town high school to talk about the play. Three of the actors, driving separately, joined us in the classroom.

The session was engaging, if a bit predictable. Sarah and Marta had an easy back-and-forth mode in giving presentations, their compact bodies and close-cropped heads moving in tandem. I rarely saw the two women side-by-side in quite this way—I was able to just watch, not react or take notes as I habitually did around them. They completed each other's thoughts and sentences so smoothly that they appeared to enter a liminal zone, a blurring of the border where their individual selves began and ended. Their dance together reminded me of a film we'd just seen in my cinema class—Bergman's *Persona*, with its striking opening sequence where the contours of the two actresses' faces overlap and then merge into one.

Marta gave a mini-lecture about Pinter and contemporary drama, Kirk and Jamie enacted a cross-gender scene, and the students asked questions. The tenor of the questions indicated discomfort from a few of the students at the fluidity of gender in the performance, but I was too distracted by Ellen's frequent sidelong smiles in Sarah's direction to pay close attention.

On the way back to campus, a rainstorm broke loose. We'd driven all the way to the state line, to Moorhead. The plains around the Red River, the land flat with few trees, provided little barrier for storms, and the rain came at us in heavy sheets. When the skies opened up, the land and the air melted together into a thick murky stew. It hurt my eyes to peer through the gloom and glare. Marta drove the car, a Honda Civic, too cautiously. Other cars sped around us, splashing currents of water against our windshield. The wipers whipped against the glass in a crazy syncopation. That and thunder were the only sounds as we made our unsteady way east.

Head craned forward to peer through the streaming windshield, Marta asked Sarah for a cigarette. "Light it for me, will you? God, I've never seen a storm like this." From the backseat, I could see the tendons straining in her neck.

"Hang on just a second." Sarah sounded irritable as she fished a crumpled pack of Pall Malls out of Marta's trench coat pocket. She put the cigarette in her mouth, lit it, and passed it over.

In the exchange, the cigarette got flipped around so that Marta jammed the lit end of the cigarette into her mouth. "Christ!" She expelled the cigarette with a cry. The rear wheels hydroplaned before Marta pulled the car out of its skid and over onto the shoulder. The car slid to a stop in a trough of water and gravel.

The front seat erupted in a flurry of slapping hands and arms until the burning cigarette was located and tossed out the window. Ellen and I, muffled in a cloak of shock in the backseat, exchanged an acute look. Should we say something? Try to help? We remained mute.

But our presence didn't even register to the two women in the front seat. Their own drama, so old and so practiced, absorbed them. To our horror, Marta burst into tears. "You're always hurting me!" she cried. Her voice—constricted and hoarse—telegraphed misery.

Sarah murmured something. I strained to hear. It sounded like "now, now" or "no, no."

"Yes, you are." Marta began to sob.

There was a silence, a long one, then Sarah began to laugh. It was a horrible sound, self-conscious yet impulsive, as if she couldn't help herself. As if she found Marta's distress simply ludicrous.

"Fuck you," Marta said in a quiet voice. She pulled the car back onto the road with a jerk of her right arm and we continued down the highway. The rain hadn't let up, but now Marta drove with abandon. The car accelerated and decelerated in an erratic zigzag as we fishtailed around trucks in the left lane and plowed through standing water on the right.

In the backseat, Ellen stared at the carpet. I huddled against the door, imagining the blissful release of tension if only I could find the courage to fling open the door and hurtle myself out of the car. Out and away from this glimpse into an intimate relationship I could not fathom. It was my first experience with sadomasochism but I didn't even know how to classify it at the time. I just hated both of them. Marta for being the victim of a heartless woman; Sarah because of her obvious lack of caring for a lover she had discarded. For in that moment, I knew positively who had tired of whom.

Sarah's cruel laugh struck me as habitual. As I slumped in the backseat, a speech by Robert in the play raced through my head. After Jerry realizes that Emma has told her husband of their affair, Robert tells him he doesn't give a "shit about any of this. It's true I've hit Emma once or twice. . . . I wasn't inspired to do it from any kind of moral standpoint. I just felt like giving her a good bashing. The old itch . . . you understand."

Ellen turned to me as we sped down the highway. I averted my eyes, aware of a furious flush rising over my chest, neck, and face. Her eyes reflected a manic excitement; her lips curved in a kind of guilty pleasure. Her face—greedy and alive—filled me with an excruciating shame. I'd seen her face like this before, during sex. I recognized that she felt aroused by Sarah's cruel pleasure. Yet her face reflected some part of me as well. The scene in the car was exciting and loathsome in equal parts. I can't be sure, but I knew there was more about violence than sex in the atmosphere that day. Yet I responded to it. My reaction haunted me for a long time.

———

I couldn't feel the same about Ellen, or myself, about any of the four of us after that incident. And one week later, after the opening-night party for *Betrayal*, when Ellen didn't come home, I wasn't surprised. I found out she was with Sarah. It could have easily been Marta, I thought. But of course it couldn't have been. In the car during the rainstorm it was easy to see that Ellen was excited by Sarah's power over Marta, while she dismissed Marta as weak, a victim. Ellen, the personal assistant, had learned to imitate her mentor.

Did that make me, as the one abandoned, the weak one? This thought tormented me for months. Ellen, awash in the excitement of an older lover who possessed glamour and authority, felt only giddiness. I longed to put the episode behind me, envied Ellen her ability to be happy. I felt buried under the weight of emotion and regularly blamed myself for being stuck. I didn't know then that the mere act of expressing feeling, even despair, showed strength, or at least courage.

None of this lessened my anguish at the time. I had trusted Ellen, I told my friend Babs Ford, a sensible person with no taste for the theatrical machinations I craved at twenty. Each time I recalled my body's reluctance to lie with Ellen that first time, a prickling of shame washed over me anew. I'd allowed myself to be pushed into an affair too fast and too soon. I doubted that I knew then that some essential element was wrong or missing. My reluctance was probably just my own fear of being swept away by passion, that most engulfing of emotions.

In the middle of the chaos with Ellen, Adrian dropped in for a visit. I hadn't told him I'd been living with Ellen, so during the two nights he stayed at my apartment, he didn't notice her absence. His lack of perception pained me; how could he not know that something vital to my life was missing? During those college years, I saw Adrian only sporadically; he'd been engrossed in graduate school in Massachusetts. The ripe age of twenty-five hadn't mellowed my brother; he applied every situation only to his greatest interest—the work in progress that was his life. If I'd seen things more clearly, I might have noticed his resemblance to the character of Robert. But seeing clearly wasn't part of my life as a college senior. I wasn't able to see beyond my own obsessions enough to recognize his. And, in spite of everything, I cared for my brother. If I didn't let myself think—or feel—too much, I could still imagine him as a dashing figure, a tarnished knight certainly, but one whose armor and mission captured my attention.

He came to a rehearsal while he was in town, and afterward, I introduced him to Sarah. I expected Adrian to fall for her looks or her charm or her heady mix of intellect and style. Instead, Adrian was cooler than cool. He grasped her hand for the briefest of moments then stepped back. His gray eyes were almost opaque as he looked at her, as unreadable as black ice is treacherous.

Sarah, I remember, looked amused. "You didn't tell me you had such a handsome brother, Amanda." Her voice, musical and yet aloof, cut through the tension like hot caramel melting a mound of ice cream.

Adrian didn't smile. "She takes me for granted," he said. I opened my mouth to protest, but then shut it. Adrian and Sarah weren't paying attention; their eyes flickered a veiled recognition as they looked at each other. I had the strangest sensation that Adrian was measuring something and that he wasn't satisfied how the numbers he'd calculated had added up. My brother was good at math—he wasn't used to numbers misbehaving.

Adrian's mouth twisted to one side as he regarded Sarah, and for a moment he looked indecisive. Then he picked up the leather satchel he'd left on the steps by the stage. "Manda, can you drop me at the train station?"

Sarah nodded slightly, as if giving permission. "We're all finished here," she said. "Go ahead." She still looked amused. But now a little interested too.

Troubled, I took Adrian's arm. "We better hurry if you're heading out tonight."

On the way to the station Adrian was silent. "Strange play," he finally said.

"I think it's the most fascinating one I've ever worked on." Pent-up nerves caused me to gush. "It's so insightful about so many things. Love. And loyalty. The amazing thing is that nothing's explicit. It's all in our minds as we listen for what isn't said."

"Love? Oh, I don't think so. Lust, maybe. I wouldn't confuse the two if I were you," Adrian said, his tone hinting at a repertoire of experience. I stopped the car and he grabbed his satchel from the backseat.

"See you next time," he said. I waited for him to go into the station, but instead he came around the front of the car and leaned over, his face level with my window. His breath left a skim of fog on the glass. "Be careful."

9

During an early rehearsal, Sarah had announced in her melodic voice: "Passion is at the heart of betrayal. *Betrayal* is so compelling as a drama because each of the three people has a deep relationship with the other two. During the course of the play, all three relationships end up compromised: the friendship between the two men, the marriage of Robert and Emma, the love between Emma and Jerry."

A cigarette dangling from one petite hand, she had leveled her eyes at each cast member in turn: "Betrayal doesn't register unless the stakes are very high. Robert feels doubly betrayed because he cares so much, about both Jerry and Emma. At one point he says to Emma that he's always liked Jerry more than he's liked her. He goes on to say, 'Maybe I should have had an affair with him myself.' That's his ultimate attempt to wound. We learn in scene 1 that Robert had affairs of his own that he hid from both Emma and Jerry. But those don't hurt Emma quite as much, because they don't involve the intensity of betraying her with a close friend. The triangle exerts pressure that radiates outward from Emma's betrayal: each duo is in turn pitted against the singleton."

I recounted this speech to my friend Babs, a graduate student whom I'd met two years before, who had studied the play in one of her classes on contemporary drama. We had just received our food late one night at a café on the highway. Babs separated each of the triple decks of her club sandwich. Carefully, she slathered mustard on each section, and then reassembled the parts. She raised one wedge, took a huge bite. "I like that about the high stakes. Betrayal doesn't pack much of a punch if you don't give a damn to begin with."

I nodded, weary of the subject but consumed by it all the same.

Babs's tone was almost dreamy. "Betrayal feeds on lies as well. On the desire to keep things the same on the surface. Think about it: Emma and Jerry keep up their affair for seven years; neither of them wants a divorce. If one of the parties demands change—or tells the truth—it destroys the status quo and the house of cards collapses. The lies are kind of like the bread in this sandwich. They're the glue. They keep everything compartmentalized and in its place."

"Yeah." I picked the sauerkraut out of my Reuben and draped it on the edge of my plate in a gloomy stupor. "Robert thinks he has a great friendship and a solid marriage. Then he finds out the real intimacy is between the other two people sleeping together. He's left in the cold, on the outside. Until Jerry realizes he's the excitement keeping Emma and Robert together. And Emma worries that the friendship between the two men is the most intimate of all."

Babs dropped the bread crusts onto her plate, their edges curled toward each other. "Betrayal just keeps cycling, embracing two of them at a time, isolating the other."

I found out that Ellen and Sarah had been sleeping together for weeks before the day of the rainstorm. In the car that stormy day, Ellen had found Sarah's laugh delicious because of their secret liaison. She couldn't mask her delight that this powerful woman, who rendered the successful, formidable Marta into a whimpering creature, was her clandestine lover.

When I found out about Ellen's affair with Sarah, I packed my few belongings and fled our small, second-floor apartment. I didn't ask Ellen to explain. I didn't want to hear her defense, or lack of one. I just couldn't stay one more day. The truth was I couldn't look at or sleep in the bed we had shared. I'd thought Ellen and I had shared a unique connection, but now I felt that Sarah had been part of our intimacy the whole time. Without even knowing it, I'd been the lone leg of the triangle pitted against the power of two.

Ellen phoned me at Babs's house, knowing it was the first place I'd go. "How could you?" Her voice thrummed with nerves and anger.

"How could I? How could I?" I stammered. "You're kidding, right?"

"No, Amanda, I'm not." I could hear her chewing furiously on her nails. "You weren't thinking! How do you know I even care for Sarah? That I'm not just experimenting?"

"What?" Outrage robbed me of rage. I didn't have enough energy to even slam the phone down.

"Don't you see? It was all for you, for *us*," she said. "I've been studying her for weeks so I could tell you."

"What?" I said again, my voice stupid with shock.

"You've always been so interested in her," Ellen said eagerly. "Now I know more, much more."

"I don't care what you know," I said, fury finally leaking into my voice. "I don't want to hear it. Any of it." I moved the receiver away from my ear.

"Wait. You're pushing me further into her web. Don't you see? Now I have nowhere else to go! Amanda, come back." At this last, her voice pleaded with me.

"I can't," I said. "I can't see you." And, truly, I was completely blinded by betrayal.

"Please." Ellen sounded strangely desperate. "Come back. Keep her away from me."

I was too confused to speak. Ellen sounded as if I had betrayed her by leaving when she was the one who left me. Her words were a jumble in my ear. It was like one of those Dada experiments where words were thrown into a hat, shaken and stirred, and then read aloud as a poem—I recognized discrete sounds but the meaning of the whole did not compute. At the same time, tears ran down my cheeks. I gripped the phone so tightly that the muscles in my hand cramped.

At my silence, Ellen's voice rose. "She's a spider, Amanda, a witch." A silence, and then in a furious whisper: "You just don't get it, do you?"

I hated having her voice in my ear—that voice that I had once longed to hear—but I couldn't release the phone. "Look, Ellen, you're free. You left me because you wanted to. I have nothing to do with this. Has your leaving me pushed me into getting involved with someone else? No, it hasn't. And that's not the same anyway, because you left me! You're not making sense."

"Amanda, you don't understand . . ."

"This has nothing to do with me." I finally dropped the phone.

She was right; I didn't get it. Ellen was playing a game. Perhaps Sarah invented it, but both assumed I played along. Yet I didn't make the right moves because I didn't even know how to stand on the game grid. I may have found Sarah wonderfully glamorous, but I had loved Ellen. That was all.

Ellen's duplicity, and my slowness in realizing it, caused me to doubt myself all over again. I simply hadn't guessed soon enough. Gullibility is also at the heart of betrayal. A simple heart cannot compete with a defended, plotting one, I told myself, awash with self-pity.

The night that Ellen called me, I wept on the sofa next to Babs, who had given me a room in her house, a 1950s frame bungalow on Oak Street she rented from her uncle. Babs-on-Oak was shorthand for security at that time. I increasingly came to depend on this friend who proved to be as stalwart as that mighty tree.

The sofa, its warm brown leather scratched and worn, cushioned me after what I had come to see as my near-fatal collision course with the feckless Ellen. A bottle of Johnnie Walker Red sat on the table. The ice cubes in our glasses had long since melted. Babs never had any money but she always had decent scotch and food, which she generously dispensed.

"How could she say that? That Sarah was a witch and that by leaving I was pushing her toward Sarah, deeper into her 'web'?"

"I don't know." Babs's large, fleshy face creased as she puzzled it all out. She twisted the glass in her hand. "I guess because she felt she had no control over how things went."

"What do you mean?"

Babs brushed a lank strand of brown hair off her forehead. She squinted at me as she thought, hunching her shoulders. "Ellen gave away her power. She called Sarah a witch. That could mean that Ellen felt under a spell and couldn't help but behave the way she did. She wanted you to prevent her because I guess she couldn't stay away from Sarah by herself." Babs's mouth twisted. "It's pretty pathetic. Or else scary as hell. I can't decide which."

I shivered and slugged down the last drops of whiskey in my glass. "Sarah might have a lot of power. But Ellen has a mind, a will. If that's who Ellen wanted, how could I keep Ellen from Sarah?"

Babs took off her square-framed glasses and slid them on top of the book she'd been reading. She poured us both another drink. "Sometimes we just want other people to save us from ourselves."

My own eyes blurred as I looked at Babs. She had a deceptive face. Her blunt features and pale skin appeared bland on first sight, yet her looks quickly gained depth and luminosity as she talked. In conversation, her intelligence and just plain goodness shone.

"Maybe Sarah says the same thing about Ellen. That she's a witch. She certainly bewitched you," Babs said, her voice sympathetic rather than critical. "You didn't seem quite yourself around her."

"What hurts the most is that she's angry," I said. "But she doesn't seem sad. She has no grief for what she and I have lost."

Babs nodded shrewdly. "She'll pay for that someday. If she disregards how you feel, think of how she'll treat herself if she's ever in pain or in need."

I failed to see the wisdom of this. I was too busy being steeped in my own misery. "Oh, Babs, I've been so stupid."

Babs opened her arms. I sidled over and let her enfold me against her generous chest. "Sweetie, you're not stupid. You're just out of your league. Who wouldn't be? If it helps, I don't get it either."

"Babs, you don't know these people." A serious student getting her PhD in American lit, my friend avoided social turmoil in general as a squandering of both time and moral principles.

She smiled her sweet, slow smile. "Thank God," she said. "I just lead my unglamorous life. At the moment, it feels like sheer bliss."

This admission revived my sniffles. Babs replaced her glasses firmly on her nose. "Manda, you need some food." With that pronouncement, my dear and thoughtful friend trundled on short legs into the kitchen to make me dinner.

I saw myself then as a naïf, victimized and plundered. Yet had I not admired the elegant Sarah, the urbane Marta? Their very sophistication, their veneer of cynicism toward plodding, ordinary mortals, had attracted me. I envied their worldliness and sought to emulate it. I was swayed enough to turn my back on my own moral code, one that valued caring and good faith. I played at a game I didn't even believe in. I would spend years trying to rediscover the simplicity of feeling I had renounced in that season of my life.

———

So many years after those events—twenty-three years, a lifetime—I pulled over to the curb, a few doors away from Teresa's house, and rested my head on the steering wheel. The faces of Sarah and Adrian, like bolts of lightning, flared against my closed eyes. Sarah had reawakened the sense of helplessness I'd often experienced with Adrian, my oh-so-intelligent and peerless sibling, whom I had loved and feared so blindly in the early years of my life. Sarah also seemed out of reach, untouchable. Given my limited experience, I had no resources to compete or to retaliate. Ellen, I forgave. She, like me, was too young and too naïve to even understand how she was being used. Sarah discarded her six months later. No, it was Sarah with her aura of invincibility, her cool style and looks, who resonated with my personal history. Her appraising gaze became the stuff of nightmare—and fascination.

10

Teresa answered the door on the first knock. In the hallway by the front door, on a narrow table, stood the yellow roses. "Still in their prime." Her voice expressed her pleasure as she swept her hand toward the full-blown bouquet.

The blooms did look wonderful against the pale green walls of the hall. I followed her into a small, comfortable room where a cordovan leather sofa and an armchair anchored a rug in an L-shape. A low-slung glass coffee table rested between the sofa and a gas fireplace. The night was cool and a small flame burned in the grate. I handed her a bottle of Pinot Grigio.

She took the wine down a short hall into the kitchen. I heard the sounds of the cork popping and the clink of stemware. Teresa returned with two glasses of wine.

"I like your art," I said, admiring a series of landscapes done in oil pastels. "Do you paint?"

"My niece did those." She offered me a glass and drank from hers in front of a scene of olive-green hills dotted with wildflowers. "She spent a year in Umbria, near Orvieto. She captures the light beautifully, I think."

"Have you been there?" I stepped closer to inspect a depiction of a walled city high on a hill.

"Once, while she lived there. Very seductive." She made a wistful face. "The pace of life is much slower. I was afraid I might get used to it."

"Why not get used to it?" I asked, meaning it. "I mean, if you can find a way."

Teresa's soft skin creased deeply around her eyes. "I've never found one. I finally have a position I like here in Austin. After struggling for twenty-five years in the academic world to find a place where my work is supported and my colleagues appear to value my contribution, I don't want to leave this new job. It may not seem like much, but it means a lot to me." She turned away from the paintings and gestured at the sofa. "Come, sit."

She took one end of the sofa, and I settled into the other. I sampled the wine before I said, "I think I understand. Many of my best friends are still academics. I know how hard it is to find a position that's satisfying and not mired in politics." I thought of Babs, who had finally landed a well-deserved endowed professorship at Cornell. "My best friend from college, a brilliant, brilliant woman, was almost destroyed in her last position. Being exceptional is no guarantee . . ." I broke off. "I'm sorry. I just realized you hadn't even mentioned politics and here I am off and running on a tangent."

Teresa tucked a pillow behind her back, slid slender fingers through her fine hair. "I hardly have to mention it. Anyone who's been in an organization knows how contentious it can be. Especially now, when there's so much competition and so few resources. You work for yourself. You're lucky."

"I'm an escapee from academia, not exactly driven out, but close. I went out on my own to get away from bureaucracy. I used to teach. Now I paint a little, work for John. I find the financial world a bit more predictable than my old life in higher education. Finance can be rocky, too, but it doesn't feel as personal."

Teresa's chameleon eyes, today appearing a warm brownish green against the brown of her pullover, looked interested. "Ah, a painter. That makes sense. I wondered how you became a financial advisor. There's something about you that . . ."

"Doesn't quite fit?"

"Not exactly." She waited a moment. "I don't know any financial advisors, except you and John, so I don't really have a type. It's just that you seem to have a lot of interests outside of finance. Art, performance . . ."

"Theater was my subject in college. I have an MFA in directing, actually. I thought the theater would be my life. And it was for a long time." I didn't mention how it had almost swallowed up my life entirely. "I discovered painting much more recently."

"And so you taught, what, college? Conservatory?"

"Several places. The longest time I spent anywhere was at Lake Forest."

She chewed her lip. "Good school. I'm surprised you left—prestigious college, the Chicago area. Good location for a career in the arts."

I put my glass down on the coffee table and leaned back, trying to release the tension I always felt around this issue. "Well, the woman who recruited me was fighting with the department chair. I didn't feel I had the support to stay. So it wasn't much of a call."

Teresa removed her watch and rubbed her wrist as if the band had been too tight, and I found myself wishing that time itself could be managed so easily. "I knew some people there in English," she said.

"Oh?" I glanced around the room. Where was this going? I spoke as lightly as I could manage: "I had no business teaching at a university. I loved my work, the students, but I found out I wasn't cut out for the world of academic programs, fighting over the season, oh so many things." I tried to smile as Teresa stared at me with obvious sympathy.

"So was there a battle over your getting tenure? Is that when you left?"

"I didn't actually put my file forward. The process scared me—the elusive standards, the scrutiny. I couldn't face it. The fall I would've gone up for promotion, I left to take a job at a small college just north of here, in Georgetown. It was nice, but after three years I realized it was time to do something else." My words stirred up an old feeling of exclusion that I'd have to examine later. I raised my glass in a celebratory way that I didn't feel. "So, art and finance. Strange bedfellows. But, for me, compatible."

Teresa raised her glass and nodded in a measured, careful way. A timer went off in the kitchen. "Ah, time for the grill. Here, have some more wine and I'll be right back," she said, levitating with a dancer's grace out of her chair, refilling our glasses, and swinging out of the room.

I felt unaccountably gloomy. How had we gotten on the subject of teaching and tenure? As I'd told Babs many times, the academic world appealed most resoundingly to me when I wasn't a part of it; when within its institutional walls, I'd found it confining. She had grinned and said, "Sound familiar? It's like family." I resolved to turn the conversation somewhere else.

Over a dinner of excellent grilled swordfish, new potatoes, and asparagus, I asked Teresa about her acting career. "I'm like you," she said. "An escapee. Except I escaped into the university system, not out of it." She remained clear-eyed as she continued, "I couldn't take the professional theater. The criticism, the envy, the competition. The sheer uncertainty. That's really it."

I couldn't help but feel an ironic twinge that Teresa had found relief in the academy, the very place where criticism, envy, and competition seemed rampant. "And are you sorry you gave up acting as a career?"

Her smile exuded relief. "No. I honestly love teaching. And I love teaching American drama. The text was always my great love, not the actors and not the tech. Or the squabbling egos." She paused. "I'm not, I hope, being sanctimonious. You honestly can't put yourself on the line the way you have to in the professional theater without your ego getting in the way."

She was quiet a moment. "I'm really much happier now. But, there are times when I do have the occasional regret. The 'what if' kind of thing."

I nodded. "I guess that's the curse of living, isn't it? You want to try new things, but as soon as you leave the old path you wonder what would have happened if you'd stayed on it just a bit longer."

Teresa looked melancholy for a moment. "You're right. Maybe it's only in the courtroom that anyone imagines certainty. I've always thought the phrase 'beyond the shadow of a doubt' impossible. At least for us humans."

Feeling a sense of camaraderie about my own misgivings, I said, "But you like to keep up by accepting a part now and then?" I knew how tenacious the acting bug could be. "Once the theater is in your blood . . ."

Teresa's laugh showed a chipped front tooth. This slight imperfection in her well-shaped mouth charmed me. "Yes, it's true, I've always been smitten with the thea-tuh." She pronounced it with deliberate affectation, with three elongated syllables.

"I do love it when the old greats pronounce it that way—it suggests a world all its own. It reminds me of the brief connection I had with Irene Worth late in her life. She was doing a benefit performance of one of her recitals—something she'd created from Edith Wharton's work. My partner at the time produced the benefit. I was only a hanger-on but I assisted with Miss Worth's many requirements and demands." I laughed. "As you might imagine, there were demands."

"Ohhh, what was she like?" Teresa asked, as wide-eyed as a teenager.

Miss Worth was legendary for both her dramatic flair and her drop-dead charisma: the mere mention of her presence could still a crowded room.

I started to laugh. "Just as you would expect. I was totally smitten, of course. Everything in her life was grand. She'd forget something trivial, to return an unimportant call, say. She was able to pull off an outrageous sense of import, even about something inconsequential—and with a perfectly straight face. She'd say something like, 'Oh, I meant to phone you. Forgive me . . . it's such a stone in my heart.'" I dropped my voice an octave and tried to capture the deep resonance of that famous voice.

Teresa clapped her hands together and broke out in a delighted laugh. "Perfect," she said. She reached over and touched my arm. "I would love to have been there."

I covered her hand with mine, just for a moment, and she looked at me, the warm light still in her eyes. She hesitated, her lips parted slightly. "That must have been wonderful." She squeezed my hand and then withdrew.

"Would you like dessert, or coffee? Cognac? Any of the above?" She stood and picked up the plates.

"Cognac sounds good." I followed her from the dining room into the kitchen, carrying the water glasses and the silverware. The kitchen was roomy, with pine floors and cabinets. "Nice," I said.

"I like this house. A lot of the houses around here were built in the sixties but I got lucky and found this one. It's twenties," she said in answer to my look. "A former owner moved it from a small town in Texas—Lockhart, I think. Some of the infrastructure is shaky, but it has a lot of charm."

She poured the brandy, handed me a snifter. "I want to show you something," she said and led me into a room across from the dining room. It was small, packed with bookshelves, a computer, and a fax machine. "This is my study obviously, but look." She pointed to a diploma for her PhD; the degree was awarded by the University of Illinois in 1980.

"Yes?" I felt curiosity, nothing more.

"Well, I haven't been entirely honest with you," she said. "We actually know two of the same people."

I was baffled, but somewhat uneasy at her "haven't been entirely honest" statement. "Really? I taught in Illinois much later than you were there. And I don't know if I ever even visited Champaign-Urbana . . ."

"I went to school with Sarah Moore in the mid-seventies," she broke in. "She was with Marta Conway then. I think Sarah was once your professor."

"She was. Both of them were." My voice sounded wooden. "Sarah was my undergraduate advisor. But how—?" I took my eyes from the framed degree and looked at Teresa.

"There's something about the way you speak, you remind me of her." Teresa laughed uneasily. "Sarah's and my paths only crossed a year, before she and Marta accepted teaching jobs in Minnesota. Later, Marta came back and we became friends. But Sarah and I stayed in touch. She talked about you."

"About me?" My face felt hot, the room impossibly stuffy.

"Well, I don't mean she said anything personal . . ." Teresa began.

"I haven't talked with anyone who knew Sarah in a long time," I broke in. "But excuse me a moment—the bathroom is back by the living room?"

"Yes, down the hall and to the right," Teresa said.

She looked at me and I wondered if she regretted bringing up the subject of Sarah Moore. I found my way to the bath off the living room and closed and locked the door behind me. I sat on the edge of the bathtub and tried to breathe my way back to steadiness. Even now, the mention of Sarah had the power to take me back. For there had been a further act in our drama together after I left college.

11

After I left St. Cloud, I had no contact with Sarah. Or Ellen, Jamie, or Kirk. I took a job as a reader for a small publishing house in Minneapolis. It wasn't demanding, but occasionally I'd come across an exciting manuscript, and the real accomplishment came if the press published it. I began to go regularly to the theater at the Guthrie, to the occasional performance art show at the Walker. After two years, I applied to and got accepted into the MFA program at the University of Minnesota for the following year. An attraction to scene design would later prompt me to take painting classes, but performance was the art form that captured me first.

I found directing much more satisfying than I'd ever found acting. In time, I recalled some of the techniques that Sarah Moore had stressed in her teaching—the economical use of movement onstage, strategies to show subtext, the arrangement of objects and bodies to parallel the tensions in a text. I sought to put her valuable professional advice to use rather than obsess on her personal foibles. I told myself I would salvage from the wreckage of that time Sarah's mastery of the directing process, which was indeed her gift. She had shared her expertise with me generously in the time I studied with her. I came to accept that Ellen and I couldn't have lasted as partners with or without Sarah as part of the equation. I didn't forget, or forgive, but I moved forward.

My thesis production, a reinterpretation of Ibsen's *Hedda Gabler*, was a modest success. Having grown up in rural North Dakota, I understood Hedda's sense of marginalization in the play, the fears that time and opportunity were passing you by, the isolating realization of having no real place in the world nor the sympathy of people who recognized your potential. Both frustration and loneliness had a visceral reality for me and I infused that understanding into my production.

More than once I was reminded of my brother Adrian in reworking this narrative of Hedda's progressive demise. If Adrian had been a nineteenth-century woman, denied an education and prevented from forging a real occupation, his brilliance would most likely have been overlooked. After all, no one can shine without an audience, or succeed without a champion. He might have been dismissed, as was Ibsen's protagonist, as too difficult, too highly strung, too much. But his maleness and his ability to succeed in the world protected him, even elevated him from an impertinent and troublesome citizen into a useful one. Imagining Adrian's competitive, frustrated spirit trapped inside the body of a woman allowed me to work on revisiting my own sexual evolution as well. I emphasized Hedda's essential androgyny in an earlier era that allowed no such flexibility. She, like so many women before and after her, had missed her time.

As I was completing the third and last year of my program, several students and I started our own small theater company, Footprints. All four of us were interested in playing with narrative and so we began by adapting fiction for the stage. We received permission from a number of authors to transform their work. We began with Barbara Pym, who had just been rediscovered by English and American readers. Our audiences found resonance in her witty explorations of British village life, and before long, we had a small, literate coterie of people willing to partake in a theatrical experience that was long on language and nuance, and lean on technical flourishes. We didn't have a lot of resources, but we did have time, enthusiasm, and a willingness to improvise.

One Thursday evening in late August the summer after graduation, I had just said good-bye to the last well-wisher after a performance of *An Unsuitable Attachment*, an amusing chronicle of both mishap and reward in the life of one of Pym's excellent women. Prior to leaving, I checked that the stage lights were powered down in the small warehouse serving as our theater, and had just picked up my keys when Sarah Moore stepped back through the door and into the working lights in front of the chairs.

I took two steps back, feeling like a character in a gothic tale shrinking from the chilling touch of the supernatural. It had been seven years since I'd seen her, three since I'd heard that she'd moved to Chicago. She hadn't been out of my thoughts that long, but certainly she'd been out of my life.

Sarah's eyes, smile, and liquid voice surrounded me as they always had, making me feel burnished, a prize worth having. I felt myself falling toward her.

"You have a real flair," she said, automatically assuming the encouraging tone of the professor grading her student.

Only I was no longer her student or anyone else's. I'd told myself in May that I was finished with school. "Thank you," I said stiffly. I towered over Sarah by at least six inches, and although I was thin, I felt outsized in comparison to her. I stabbed my fingers through my chin-length hair, rearranged my wayward bangs.

She looked the same; shoulders squared, the dark, shapely head seeming to float on the slender neck, the frank gaze of interest.

Her attention robbed me of speech for a moment. I fell back on the role of director, casting her as just any audience member, which of course she wasn't. "Are you a fan of Pym's fiction? I can't imagine how else you'd have found us."

But of course I could imagine how she could find me, or anyone she wanted to find. She was a person with a large reach, especially in the small world of theater. The question was: Why did she want to find me? Or perhaps it was only my having left her orbit that prompted her to look. As I observed the proud posture, the small figure draped in black slacks and a short leather jacket, I suspected that Sarah Moore preferred to decide herself if and when people she took an interest in were going to disappear from her life. Fleetingly, I wondered whether Marta Conway had been formally released from the tight range of Sarah's custody.

"I was in town interviewing at the Guthrie," she said, following me out the door. "Imagine my surprise when I opened the newspaper and saw an article on you and Footprints."

Imagine. "What a coincidence," I said, turning the key on the deadbolt to the theater.

"Yes," she said simply. Her small, even teeth glinted in the dim light of the shop windows.

"So . . . you're thinking of taking a position at the Guthrie?" I knew the position of artistic director was open. "The directing position?"

"Yes, that's why I came up. But it's not going to happen. I think I'll stay where I am."

We began to walk down the street. I felt like a character in Christopher Durang's short play *The Actor's Nightmare*—wandering onto a stage where I didn't know the script and had missed all my cues. I meant to excuse myself and go home but, unaccountably, when I opened my mouth, I said instead: "Um, there's a nice bar two blocks from here if you'd like a drink."

"All right." She sounded pleased. And satisfied, as if she expected that I would suggest just that.

We landed in a new wooden structure that had the appearance of an old house. Its paint-deprived wood deck added to its comfortable, down-home appeal. The deck, swept by a humid breeze and mosquitoes, gave the café a Southern flavor. The darkness, the already oppressive August air, closed us in. I felt the city recede, and Sarah's presence loom closer. I realized I had nothing to say because there was far too much to say.

"I don't think I know what you're doing now," I began, as a young woman in crop pants and a black T-shirt brought us our drinks, a margarita on the rocks for Sarah and a scotch for me. I watched Sarah lick the salt on her glass and wished I were sitting in this cozy spot with a good-looking woman across from me, just not this one.

"I'm in charge of a new play program at the Art Institute."

"Chicago still suits you?" I had a dim recollection from an alumnae magazine that Sarah was directing in Chicago. Or had Babs passed this on? Babs seemed to have an ongoing mental Rolodex of the whereabouts of people from our past.

Sarah nodded and looked amused at the idea that she would do anything that didn't suit her. I supposed she intended that I should feel flattered. After all, Sarah had chosen to see me rather than a dozen other things she could have done that evening. But I didn't feel flattered, just uncertain. And when I was confused, I froze. Someone else, a person who didn't give people second chances, would have walked away. But, then, that person wouldn't have invited Sarah Moore for a drink.

"So," I said, as the fatigue of a long day caught up with me. "Why are you here?"

"The interview . . ." she began.

"I meant here, with me."

Sarah looked at me with level gray eyes. "It's been a long time, Amanda."

"That's just it. It's been too long." My bluntness startled me. "You know, after Ellen left, I still had to work with you. You were my advisor. I was so afraid of what I might say, I couldn't say anything. It was a terrible time."

Her face went very still. "And I was no help. I was the grown-up, and I didn't do anything. I didn't apologize, didn't ask if you were able to handle things. I was selfish." Her hand went to her drink then fell back on the table. "I've always been sorry about that."

Could that be true? Sarah had had seven years to indicate her regret. I'd never heard a word. "But?"

"But?" she repeated in a puzzled tone.

"You said you've always been sorry," I prompted. "But you didn't get in touch with me, so . . ."

She managed the hint of a blush. "I wanted to tell you that in person," she said. "I am deeply sorry."

My fingers slid on the sweaty glass of my scotch and soda. An old person's drink, I thought, thinking of my father's veined hands clutching his nightly J&B and water. Eva had raised me to be polite and I almost said "thank you." Instead I said, "I see," but all I could think is that some things come too late in life, almost too late to matter at all. I suspected Sarah knew all about that, about the tipping point when something becomes nothing. Neglect, in fact, might be one of her strongest weapons. That and silence can drive most things away. Most. But sometimes neglect only sharpens the appetite.

I sighed and looked at the table across from us where a man and a woman sat close together, laughing.

"You don't want to talk to me." Her face was unreadable, but her eyes showed a hint of interest.

"I wish I didn't want to talk to you." I reached toward my glass for comfort but found it as cool and unyielding as the woman in front of me.

Sarah smiled then, and there was that enveloping glow again. When Sarah Moore smiled at you, other people and objects receded. That smile, along with her resonant voice, created a high-voltage current. Some people were immune to its seductive vibration. For me, the space around Sarah was a force field calibrated to my particular energy. I gravitated toward it as heedlessly as a metal filing leaping to a magnet.

Her body was very still, her cheekbones flushed as her head tipped in my direction. I wanted to keep that smile and those eyes trained on me. What is pleasure but fulfilling the desire of someone you admire?

"Let's walk," she said.

And we did. We drifted down the sidewalk to her hotel, had another drink at the hotel bar, and then went up to her room.

"Have a seat." Sarah indicated a loveseat in a combination living room and bar area that adjoined the bedroom.

As I watched her pull two miniature bottles of Cutty Sark out of the small refrigerator, I suddenly felt an acute attack of stage fright. The room felt claustrophobic—there wasn't enough air for my outsize emotions, Sarah's expectations, and two human beings in that space. We'd said everything that needed to be said and nothing about what either of us wanted to know, nothing about the confusing welter of emotion and longing and anger swirling between us since the days of Ellen and Marta.

We both sipped our scotch over ice. I strained to hear or to talk but no words came. My lips felt rubbery against the cooling glass as I tried to find strength to leave or speak. I longed to dissipate the tension but I felt enclosed by it and frozen in place. I sensed that neither of us was sure of what the other wanted enough to risk a touch or a misplaced word. We were trapped, I thought, silenced by all the years of silence.

The long moment stretched on, as if we were destined to turn to stone rather than risk a word or a touch. Even the act of breathing might destabilize the delicate balance of our two tense souls suspended in midair.

Finally, Sarah took my hand. She turned it over as if to read the palm. "I never thought I would be with you like this," she said, her head down, her voice a whisper drifting toward me.

Released by this small sign of connection, I turned to look at her, the turn so slow it was more a series of stop frames than slow motion. And just as slowly, it seemed, she turned and raised her head toward mine. The distance between us seemed measured in miles, not inches, and I imagined an entire minute went by as I leaned in and pressed my lips to hers.

The kiss was stiff and awkward, but any meeting of flesh was better than the strained awareness that had paralyzed us both. Our lips lingered and softened.

"Oh," I thought I heard her say, or was it just a release of breath? Her breath or mine? Our bodies came together then as, finally, the constant press of thinking ceased.

———

I wish I could say that seven years of separation, of emotional turmoil, had destroyed the once-intense interest I had in Sarah. But in her presence I fell again into my old role of the student fascinated by her elegant mentor, the younger self eager to be filled by the experience of the older and more worldly other. The pain and longing of the past glazed the present with a golden brush. For a few hours I was very young again, open and uncritical. I felt bathed in the adoration I had always craved from Sarah. Whether that feeling was generated by her or my own fantasies I have no way of knowing. I can only guess. For when you step through the looking glass of your desire, you touch your dreams made flesh.

We spent three days and nights together. Then, Sarah returned to Chicago, to a life I knew little about. I tinkered with an essay based on my thesis, went back to reading for the publishing company, and began teaching a class at Carleton College. Three weeks went by, punctuated by the occasional card from Sarah. That time had the kind of charged energy the atmosphere has when clouds gather every day for weeks without bringing any rain. I was waiting. For Sarah to call and tell me to join her in Chicago or that she was coming to Minneapolis; that she needed me and couldn't live without me.

That call came but it wasn't quite the one I'd imagined. Late one night I came in from a rehearsal of *The Berlin Stories* at Footprints to a message from her.

"Amanda . . ." Her voice was low and flat. "Call me tonight. No matter how late."

When I did call, and she answered, she sounded hoarse and winded. "I need you to come here. Before he does."

"Who?" I felt a clutch of fear. Was she divorced from an angry spouse? Married? Being stalked?

I heard the clatter of ice cubes in a glass. "I can't talk about it. Can you come?"

"I'll be there tomorrow," I responded, a voice inside me aghast at my rashness. I had work, commitments. But I also had a car and could be in Chicago in little more than six hours. I'd leave after lunch.

The few hours before my departure passed in a fever. The drive down I-94 was a blur of wet pavement and glaring lights.

Sarah lived in a town house in Lincoln Park, an area filled with tasteful brick two flats and blooming balconies close in to the city's bustling North Side. It was the mid-eighties, and Chicago was experiencing something of a renaissance, yet another of many growth spurts since the city's manufacturing muscle had lost dominance to newer industries like technology, education, and entertainment. After New York, Los Angeles may have had more people, but Chicago remained the Second City.

Miraculously, I found a parking place on a jammed street two blocks from her place. August had given way to September and less sunlight; by the time I knocked on Sarah's door it was seven thirty and dusk was darkening the shadows made denser by the closely packed buildings. A few drops of rain spattered the bricks as I stood on the narrow stoop at the top of the stairs.

I waited at least a minute and then I knocked, louder. After another minute, Sarah came to the door, her face flushed, her hair flattened close to her head. I wondered if she'd been asleep, but her eyes were edgy, darting. When she looked at me I thought I saw relief in her face. But in the space of a shutter click, the relief was wiped away. I saw only wariness. "Amanda," Sarah said, her tone lifted in surprise. "I didn't expect you."

I stiffened, wrapped in a peculiar time warp. It was as if we hadn't talked the night before, as if Sarah's panic the prior evening had spontaneously combusted out of my overheated longing for a summons.

"You . . . what?" My mouth felt cottony. "When we talked, last night . . ." I began.

Sarah kept the door half-open. She stepped outside and lowered her voice. "Yes. I'm so sorry I upset you." I watched her teeth bite into her lower lip. She shivered. "I overreacted, I'm afraid. You haven't come all this way just to see me, I hope."

Flat-footed, I blurted, "Yes, I have." But all the while I was remembering the lit cigarette sliding between Marta's lips those years ago, her outrage and pain at Sarah's merciless laugh. My mind flipped like a double-sided painting between two images—the face of Sarah coming toward me and the back of her head in the distance as she retreated—as I wondered whose reality I had entered, Sarah's or my own. I saw again the rictal masks of comedy and tragedy mounted on the wall of her college office in St. Cloud. I felt like a fool, a sad, lost clown. I wanted to vanish.

But I remained on the stoop, staring past the open door. Sarah's face went blank as behind her came a voice; then, in the same fractured moment, a tall, blond man abruptly filled the space behind her.

"Hello, Manda," Adrian said.

12

Inside Teresa's bathroom, I ran cold water over my hands and combed my fingers through my hair. In the mirror I saw that my eyes looked sleepy and unfocused, but otherwise my face looked okay. I opened the door and stepped into the hall.

At the sound of my footsteps, Teresa called from the kitchen, "I've turned off the fireplace and turned down the air. It's gotten really warm in here. And I'm bringing us some water. Be right there."

"Okay," I said, glad to have a few more moments to recover.

———

On the rainy day of my abortive rescue mission at Sarah's town house in Chicago, when I came face-to-face with Adrian rather than my grateful lover, I didn't go inside, even though Adrian greeted me with a calm "Hello, Manda. This is a surprise," as he opened the door wider and motioned for me to come in.

"I'm sorry," I'd blurted and rushed down the street. I've thought often what I could have been sorry about—perhaps, for the final time, the death of my illusions about Sarah Moore. Arms out in front of me like a person fleeing a burning building, I bumped into a light post before I reached my car. I remember my shock when I turned to look back and saw that Sarah's house was still in view. I pushed on, my legs leaden. Was it a thin cry I heard behind me, or just the whine of the engine when a vintage MGB rushed by?

I called Babs from a café on the interstate. She'd just taken her first teaching position in upstate New York. "I won't be surprised to find one day that your good friend Sarah Moore has been murdered," she said bluntly.

"Good God. You don't mean it!"

"Amanda," Babs said in her sensible voice, "you can't go around turning people's lives upside down forever without consequences. I think your friend has used up at least ten of her nine lives by now."

"My friend?" I stared at the phone for a moment then put it back to my ear. "She's not really my friend."

This time Babs sounded sharp, stretched thin on patience. "Then what on earth are you doing with her? You're twenty-eight years old. Cut your losses and stop carrying a torch for that woman. She's definitely not worth it."

"Worth it?" I wanted to laugh. What was anything worth? Sarah was beyond a question of value.

"We're talking obsession here." Babs's voice was dogged. "Get a shrink, dear. You need help."

Stung, I said, "You won't talk to me?"

A huge sigh rumbled into my ear. "My sweet Amanda, I will talk to you until you are deaf, dumb, and blind if you want me to. I love you. But my talking to you doesn't seem to shed light on anything, does it?"

"Of course it does! You're my best friend. You're the most sensible person I know."

Babs coughed and I heard a sharp inhale. When had Babs started smoking? "Sensible," she muttered. "No wonder you don't listen to me. Listen, you're in love. Sense has nothing to do with it. You know me—I think anything you do is just terrific. Unless you're hurting yourself. And I just don't see anything good coming out of this one."

"Why?" I had an inkling, but I didn't want Babs to stop talking. Or, worse, get fed up with repeating herself.

"Sweetie, I've met your brother." Babs inhaled again. "Crap! Oh, sorry, a friend of mine left a pack of Marlboros here. I've been trying to stay up and finish this godforsaken essay, and I hoped these cigarettes would keep me awake, but they're just making my cat furious. He just stuck a paw in my drink."

"Babs, smoking is terrible for you."

My friend began to laugh, a sound halfway between a gasp and a giggle. "Terrible for me? Physician, heal thyself. Let's look at the facts: you had an affair with Sarah, who has been your heart's desire for God knows how long." She snickered. "Maybe your 'heart' isn't really where it's at. That's debatable. But—" she cleared her throat—"this woman slept with your lover some years ago. And destroyed your relationship with the same. Not to mention how she treated Marta Conway. Is she still alive, by the way?"

I had no answer for that. Marta Conway had disappeared, leaving no trace. At that moment, I envied her.

Babs paused. "Read my lips," she continued. "Sarah Moore is not a good person. At least not for you. So when you say smoking isn't good for me, I say, well, at least it won't kill me right away."

She coughed. I heard the tinkle of ice cubes and the sound of swallowing. "Let's continue with our facts: she calls you after basically ignoring you for three weeks, begging you to come down to be with her. She suggests she's in danger. You charge right into the cause. And what do you find?"

"I know," I said.

"Do you know? You found Adrian, Amanda. Isn't that more than a little strange? And given your history with your brother . . ."

"You're right." I didn't want to think about my history with Adrian. "She didn't seem happy to see me. But, Babs, she seemed frightened. What if . . ."

"What if she's involved with your brother and he's not overjoyed at her history with you?"

"I wonder if she'd tell him." Wasn't Sarah even more secretive than Adrian? Yet I no longer trusted my perceptions about either of them. I felt both disturbed and deflated. "I don't know. Adrian is—ruthless, when he wants something."

"Oh, for heaven's sake." I heard a scraping sound. "Damn. The last coffee I have in this blasted place is stuck to the paper sack in the freezer."

"Babs . . . can I come up to Albany to see you?"

"Good idea. Take the afternoon flight. Tomorrow, if you can. I'll pick you up."

The last-minute ticket to Albany was ridiculously expensive. I charged it to my American Express, the only credit card I had that wasn't maxed out, and tried not to think about it. I felt like someone dying from an incurable disease. Babs was my medicine. I had to have it, and damn the expense.

The Albany airport suited my mood. In those days it was a humble backwater, which, at four in the afternoon, had no queues of people and no shops. A stray legislator or two drifted through in search of a rental car while I waited for my luggage.

The September air hinted at an early winter as I parked myself at the curb. I was glad of the fleece pullover I'd brought to ward off the airplane chill. Babs arrived a few minutes later in a tan Toyota hatchback.

"New car?" I asked as I ducked inside. My bag and carry-on filled the entire backseat.

"Only five years old," Babs said with satisfaction. My least acquisitive friend, Babs hated spending money, except on books, food, and alcohol. Everything else was discretionary.

She did have, of course, an apartment. It covered the entire second floor of a Queen Anne house a couple of miles from the university. The place, like Babs's mind, had a roomy yet cluttered air, comfort radiating from the shabby furniture and the piles of books marking the scuffed hardwood floors at regular intervals. I breathed in the slightly musty air, tinged with the odors of moldy dust jackets and mimeographed papers as well as the earthy smell of plants. Babs's tabby cat peered down at me from a tall bookcase. Everything looked so utterly normal that I threw my arms around Babs's neck and burst into tears.

"I'm glad to see you too, honey," she said, giving me a mighty squeeze. "Come. Believe it or not, you have your own room, if you don't mind sharing it with Mister." She indicated the gray-and-silver-striped cat who now rubbed a paw over one ear in preparation for leaping onto a shorter bookcase and then landing in a puff of dust on a pile of books.

Babs beamed at her surroundings. She still wore thick glasses but her light-brown hair had been cut in a short bob that suited her. Joan of Arc, I thought, if Joan had been a round-bodied woman garbed in jeans and a long-sleeved turtleneck with a hint of an academic stoop to her shoulders. Solid, tough, utterly dependable. "I'd follow you anywhere," I said.

"Hmm?" Babs looked at me absently and then led me down a long hallway and opened a door. "This bed isn't bad. You look like you haven't slept in a week." She removed her glasses and polished them on the hem of her turtleneck, then frowned at the smudged result, but shoved the glasses back on her face anyway.

"I don't even know." I rubbed my eyes, which were beginning to burn. Tension and sleep deprivation had conspired to give me a throbbing head. My chest felt hollow from exhaustion. "The bed looks awfully good. Maybe I could have a short nap before we think about dinner?"

"Nap away. I have a little grading to finish and then I'm all yours for the evening. I bought food, by the way. So that you can cook." She lightly patted her hands together as if everything important had been settled. "Let me know if you need anything."

She padded away—I realized that she'd worn her scuffed fleece-lined slippers to the airport—just as Mister tiptoed into the room. He brushed against my legs as I slid my suitcase into the single narrow closet. I'd unpack later. I touched the cat's round head and fell on the bed. Before I lost consciousness, Mister crept onto the bed and, with a rumbling purr that reminded me of my granddad's old Buick Roadmaster, wedged himself into the crook of my knees.

A couple of hours later, Babs and I sat at her dining table finishing bowls of spaghetti with pork sausage. I refilled my glass with Cabernet. "This isn't plonk. Your fortunes—or is it your taste—have improved."

Babs ignored this remark. "So, you've had a little sleep, a little food. How do things look to you now?"

My shoulders sank forward. "I have no idea. When I saw Adrian with Sarah, I just froze. I don't know what to think."

"Look, your brother lives in Chicago now. Isn't that what you told me? He's at the University of Chicago?"

I nodded.

"Well, then, anytime you go to that city you could possibly see him. It's possible, yes?"

"*Possible.* Of course. But what are the odds?"

"You mean if you didn't let him know you were coming?"

"Oh, none of this makes any sense!" I looked wildly around Babs's dining room. What was I doing here? What was I doing anywhere?

"Amanda. Listen to me. The fact is, Sarah Moore showed up in your life out of the blue. Why? How do you know she hasn't been with Adrian for some time? How do you know she's not messing with you, drawing you back into her orbit, precisely because of Adrian?"

I stared stupidly at Babs. That thought had never crossed my mind. "But what would be the point of that?"

"Maybe because Adrian wanted to see you. Or let you know he had the power to find you anytime he wants." Babs lifted her stout shoulders. "Some people like intrigue. Others like to make their lovers jealous." Babs pushed back in her chair and grumbled, "How the hell should I know? I'm just a simple country professor."

"I am so out of my league here, Babs. I don't even have a clue what any of this means."

"Yes, you *are* out of your league. Take my advice and stay out. Leave Sarah Moore alone."

Adrian and Sarah. Well, why not? My brother had always been secretive. Why wouldn't he be involved with Sarah, an attractive woman, as brilliant in her way as he was in his? Sarah wasn't only interested in women. I remembered a rumor that she was involved with a male professor at St. Cloud when I was there. I rested my cheek on my hands and watched the light play on my wineglass, noted the intense ruby of the wine against the light maple table.

"Amanda," Babs said softly. "You know Sarah likes games."

I raised my head. "Yes, she does. She's very good at them."

"Maybe," Babs frowned. "She's either very good or very careless. I'm not sure what she seeks to gain from this one."

"I'm not good at games," I said.

"No." Babs's lips were tightly compressed, as if to keep herself from saying any more.

———

The next morning, I woke to a bright autumn sun playing against the lace curtains. Mister was nowhere to be found. I fished my clothes from the day before off the floor. My suitcase still awaited me but I couldn't imagine unpacking its contents before consuming at least three cups of coffee.

In the kitchen, Babs had left a note. "Meet me for lunch at The Fender," it said. She'd included directions and a time, twelve thirty. The clock above the stove read 10:45. She'd also left coffee on, but it smelled hopelessly stewed. I threw it out and went to the freezer for fresh makings.

At the sound of the fridge, Mister appeared looking hopeful. "Hi, guy," I said, reaching down to pat his head. He allowed one stroke of my hand before he slid out of reach. I found a dollop of wet food for him then measured out three scoops from the bag of French Roast I'd found—resting on top of the ice cream—into the coffeemaker.

Cup in hand a few minutes later, I parked myself at the table in front of a bay window. The table, the whole room, shimmered in the morning sun. Outside, the broad leaves of a maple tree fluttered against the glass. The green of the leaves was beginning to be mottled with red. I sipped my coffee, too strong but exactly the strength required to keep me upright, and felt happy to be sitting there in Babs's kitchen, on the second floor of a house on a street I'd never seen before.

Babs had left me several newspapers: *The New York Times*, the *Albany Times Union*, and the *Chicago Tribune*. I'd forgotten what a news junkie Babs was. Her habit was to wake early, go out for a bagel or croissant, and stop at a newsstand on the way back to her place. She always read the *Times* plus the local, so I assumed the *Trib* was in my honor because of my recent trip.

The *Trib* was still neatly folded in thirds; Babs hadn't read it. The *Times*, reassembled but rumpled from use, beckoned. I glanced at the headlines and read through the first few pages as I finished my first cup of coffee. Returning to the table with my second cup, I reached for the Chicago paper. I glanced at the listings of the day's coverage. After a notice of an interview with film director Robert Altman was a mention of an unexpected death in Chicago's art world. The word *tragedy* linked to the story launched my stimulated senses into foreboding. My fingers tumbled through the pages to the local news. Once there, my eyes sought to make sense of a jumble of words: *Artistic Director . . . Sarah Moore . . . death . . . yesterday evening . . . history of depression . . .*

The cup slid from my hand and rocked on its edge; coffee sloshed on the table before I righted it. My fingers tingled, half-scalded, but the burn barely registered. I heard Babs's voice in my ear: *I won't be surprised to find one day that your good friend Sarah Moore has been murdered.* I spun around to look behind me. Mister regarded me quizzically from the windowsill across the room. I desperately wished Babs were here with me.

My mind made desperate calculations: I'd gone to Chicago on Wednesday, seen Adrian with Sarah, and fled the city immediately after. As soon as I called Babs from I-94, I headed back toward Chicago to the nearest Comfort Inn off the highway. I flew out of Chicago yesterday morning. Today was Friday; the paper said Sarah's body was found last evening. Was Adrian still with her a full day after I saw him? For all I knew, Adrian lived with Sarah much of the time, although his own apartment was near the University of Chicago, quite a distance from Sarah's neighborhood.

I read the full article again, carefully this time. A friend had arrived to pick Sarah up for a dress rehearsal. When there was no answer at the door, no response to repeated phone calls, she'd used her key and found Sarah in her town house, in bed. A bottle of sleeping pills lay on its side in the bed, the remaining pills littering the pillow. Suspected cause of death was heart failure. The friend, the managing director of the theater, mentioned that Sarah regularly used the sleep aid, and disputed the possibility of a drug overdose. However, it was possible that in sufficient quantity the drug may have compromised her heart function. Dr. Moore had suffered from chronic fatigue, she said. A medical investigation was in progress.

I recalled Sarah telling me that her mother had died in her forties from a heart attack; she herself was scrupulous about her diet. I realized that much of Sarah's history was a blank to me. She'd never, for example, mentioned chronic fatigue. I only knew that the disease often produced depression.

The last image I had of Sarah—tense, removed, a picture of fear and withdrawal—plagued me. Her gray eyes, usually calm and steady, had skittered over my shoulder, scanning the sidewalk. She'd been unwilling to let me in to whatever private hell she'd found herself in that day. What was the connection between a failure of nerve and heart failure? I wondered.

Unbidden, a phrase came into my head, one Eva had uttered about Duncan: "His heart stopped." Duncan and now Sarah had suffered the same fate. Two people I loved had died immediately after exposure to Adrian. If my mother still had her mind, she'd have dismissed the two events as terribly unfortunate coincidences. *Heartbreaking*, she might have said, oblivious to the irony.

Babs had said that Sarah liked games. If only Sarah had asked me, I would have told her it was unwise to play games with Adrian. He took them seriously and he never lost.

It never occurred to me to pick up the phone and try to reach my brother. To find out if he was even still in Chicago or to ask him if he knew anything about what had happened to Sarah. Instead, I wondered in my mental fever if there could be another Sarah Moore who directed at the Goodman. Forty was the age given of the deceased. I calculated: I was turning twenty-nine in November. Sarah was eleven years older than I and her birthday was this month, two weeks ago in fact. It occurred to me that I hadn't even sent a card. I hadn't had the energy; I'd been holding my breath waiting for her to call.

A moment later, I found myself holding the table tightly, sweating and shaking. Sarah was gone. And Adrian had been with her. I turned fearfully toward the phone, terrified it might ring, and then my eyes locked on the front door, at the deadbolt that I could only hope was fully engaged. I felt as if I was in a slow-moving train wreck and that the shock waves and destruction were just starting to hit the car I was riding in. The track in front of me had collapsed, a torture of twisted metal. There was no way forward and no way back. What if Adrian was looking for me? What if he found me? What if I was next?

After a while, I released my grip on the table and turned toward the bay window. Outside, the maple tree bent almost forty-five degrees in a burst of wind. I watched the clock hand move to twelve fifteen. I'd been sitting staring at the same page of the newspaper for at least an hour. My eyes were dry, my throat parched, my heart a quick treble beat in my ears. Terror encroached through my state of shock like the chill that creeps over your body in an early-morning mist. If I had stayed in Chicago . . . But I couldn't have stayed in Chicago.

I rose unsteadily, slid the paper under my arm, and made for the door. I'd go meet Babs. She'd figure out what to do. What to think. I couldn't feel much of anything. I couldn't afford to. Not yet.

13

Those events of fourteen years ago flashed forward in all their cataclysmic intensity as I returned to Teresa's study, the clock now inching toward midnight.

"Everything all right?" Teresa asked as I dropped into the chair adjacent to the sofa. I feared that I'd been absent for too long, but Teresa's face showed no sign of impatience. A glass of ice water stood on the blotter and I raised it to my lips and drank half of it. The cold clink of an ice cube against my lips was bracing.

When I didn't answer, she said pointedly, "Amanda, I'm sorry if I've upset you."

Teresa's voice startled me. My eyes were calibrated to the past; as I struggled to focus them in the present I felt like I was looking into the future. "I saw Sarah right before she died. The day before."

"Did you? How terrible. What I mean is that her death was terrible. She was so young." Teresa was now sitting on the sofa under the window. The cream-colored sofa sagged beneath her weight. She put her water glass on a small side table. The glass wobbled as she set it down, and I noticed her fingers were trembling. Her hands, now huddled in her lap, looked defenseless.

"Do you know anything about what happened to her?" I looked up and noticed again the diploma Teresa had pointed out to me on the wall. Next to the glass of water, the snifter of brandy I'd been drinking wasn't quite empty. I drained the last half-inch of liquid in the glass.

Teresa's hazel eyes looked almost amber in the soft light, reflecting the camel-colored sweater she wore; they also looked wary. "No," she said. "I hadn't seen her for at least a year."

"I never understood it." The muscles in my neck throbbed; I tried to relax into the high-backed desk chair. "Her illness—chronic fatigue. It seemed so odd when I found that out. I'd spent time with her so recently, and she seemed vital. You know, she had a lot of energy."

A ghost of a smile played on Teresa's lips. She nodded. "I couldn't keep up with her," she said. "But, then, I've known other people who say they're exhausted all the time, yet they seem to have energy to burn. Maybe we mistook anxiety or mania for vitality."

I kneaded the left side of my neck with my right hand. I was having trouble focusing on this almost academic parsing of Sarah's condition. In spite of the air-conditioning, the atmosphere in the room felt stuffy and yet charged, like the suffocating blanket of an Austin evening under heavy skies. "I have to ask you something." My hands felt damp and cramped. I crossed my arms tightly over my chest.

Teresa looked alarmed. "Yes?"

"If we're going to be friends . . . and I really hope we are . . . Well, I have to know something about you and Sarah."

She picked up her brandy glass, which, like mine, was empty. She tipped it on its side and watched a drop disperse slowly into a tawny streak from the bottom to the lip of the glass. "Were we involved, you mean?"

She looked at me frankly. The room was very small, and by leaning forward, she could touch my knee. Her hand rested there, just a moment, and then she leaned back. "No, I was never romantically involved with Sarah. I admired her, of course." Her mouth took on a sad twist. "Like everyone else. But you see, I was very close to Marta Conway."

"Oh." I felt almost afraid to breathe. "I always wondered what happened to her."

"After Sarah dumped her, you mean?" Teresa stood up. "Let me just get us a refill." She left the room and I heard water running in another part of the house. When she returned, Courvoisier bottle in hand, her face had a fresh-scrubbed look, and the strands of hair around her forehead were damp. She poured us each another drink.

"I saw a lot of Marta after their breakup." She resumed her seat, one hand holding the arm of the sofa tightly. The other hand picked at a loose thread of fabric on the seat. "I think I told you I met Sarah in class at Illinois as she was finishing her program. That was in the mid-seventies. She was with Marta then, but I didn't see them socially so I barely knew Marta. But, years later, after Marta and Sarah broke up—after you knew them in St. Cloud—Marta came back to Illinois to finish her PhD.

"All she had left was to finish writing—you know, she already had the dreaded ABD, 'all but dissertation,' so her coursework and exams were done. When Sarah had completed her program years earlier, they were both offered teaching jobs in St. Cloud, so Marta decided to take a break after she finished her qualifying exams. It seemed too good to be true, two jobs in the theater department, one in directing and the other in acting, so they jumped at it."

Listening, I wondered if the fact that Marta had left school without her degree added to the insecurity she appeared to feel around Sarah when I'd been around the them. Ellen had pointed that out to me once but Marta's poise had made me dismiss the idea.

Teresa had resumed: ". . . but, the job market in higher education was changing. Marta wanted to go into administration and knew she had to have the doctorate. So after her relationship with Sarah ended, she came back to Illinois to finish. I was still there and we met again. Marta was doing research in the fine arts library where I had a study carrel. It was just a postage stamp of a place, really. I felt claustrophobic in the space, so I hung out in the reading room and so did she." She stopped and took a deep breath.

"That can't be all." My voice sounded accusatory. "I didn't mean that the way it sounded," I said hastily. "But I know Marta was in awful shape. She was hospitalized for a while in St. Cloud. It's hard to imagine her calmly doing research in the library." I rushed on: "I felt very bad about it all. Their relationship blew up during, of all things, a production of *Betrayal*."

Teresa looked startled. "I see," she said. "The play is every bit as cursed as *Macbeth*, isn't it? For some of us," she added ambiguously.

"I felt almost responsible," I said. "It's ridiculous, I know. My own life was in shambles. My lover, Ellen, left me to be with Sarah. That's why Sarah and Marta broke up."

"And you and Ellen, too, I imagine?" Teresa sighed. "But I doubt Ellen was the reason they broke up, Amanda."

"Why not?" I asked. "It couldn't have helped."

Teresa removed her shoes, soft brown leather slip-ons, and tucked her feet under her on the couch. "I talked to Marta many times. As I said, we were close friends. Sarah had a pattern of getting involved with students, among others. Ellen wasn't the first. But, perhaps, that affair was the most devious."

"It was that play," I said emphatically. "Somehow, when you're spending every spare hour talking about betrayal, it affects you like a poison." I pushed the liqueur glass away from me. I wished I felt more clear-headed.

"Yes. I imagine it was very painful for you. You were, what, a senior? Twenty or twenty-one years old?"

"Twenty." Tension pooled into the base of my neck and spread upward. "It was painful. You see, I adored Sarah. She was my mentor. I know now that I was naïve, and very young. I didn't know very much about relationships then, and nothing about long-term ones." I bit my lips. "It's embarrassing to say it now, but Sarah was everything I wanted to be—I thought. She seemed so sophisticated and intelligent, so charming and charmed."

Teresa just nodded.

"Until Ellen left me for Sarah, that is. Until I felt contaminated by all the intrigue that once seemed so enticing. And I saw how devastated Marta was. And I felt as though I was falling apart myself."

"And then?"

I looked away, at the wall just behind Teresa's head. "Then I thought she was the most manipulative person I'd ever known."

———

Sarah's funeral had been closed to all but immediate family. I didn't know anything about her family beyond her parents; her father and stepmother, I thought, were both still living. I knew she was an only child. I remembered something about cousins back in South Carolina where she was from. I scoured newspapers and called old friends from St. Cloud, but no one knew anything about it.

The next two months passed in a numb swirl, a haze of forgetting. I couldn't put what happened to Sarah out of my mind, but I noticed that nothing else registered. The days came and went, and as soon as one faded into another, the specific markers that are essential to memory seemed to have evaporated. Death takes someone away from you. It also takes you away from yourself.

In November, on my twenty-eighth birthday, Adrian called. His peculiar scratchy voice assaulted my ear and yet I couldn't hang up. Ironically, he seemed a lifeline to Sarah; that final tableau on the stairs of her town house had assumed in my consciousness the precise detail revealed by an old-fashioned camera flashbulb exploding over and over. The moment had only grown sharper in the two months since Sarah's death.

"I thought I'd see you at Sarah's memorial," he said. He sounded almost annoyed, as if, by my absence, I had let him down.

"You were there?"

"Of course. Her parents wanted me there."

Adrian had met Sarah's parents? Doubt and envy assailed me equally. "So you knew them well?"

Adrian sighed, a harsh rush of sound in my ear. "Manda. Sarah and I had been seeing each other for some time."

I shut my eyes, remembering the veiled way they had looked at each other when Adrian had come to rehearsal all those years ago. His casual use of "seeing each other" sounded a wrong note. Because, if he and Sarah were so close, why was he calling me after her death? There were gaps in his knowledge and he wanted me to fill them.

"What does 'some time' mean? How long?"

"I'm not sure that's something you need to know right now."

"Fine. Look, there is something I need to know: Were you with Sarah when she died?"

"Jesus. Of course not." Adrian's voice rose higher with tension. "Do you think I would have just stood by if I'd been there? I was very fond of Sarah."

"*Fond.* What a funny word that is." I felt fury rise in my throat like bile. "Does that have anything to do with love? Because I did love her. I wasn't just 'fond' of her. I may not have known her parents but I was in her life."

"I know you thought she was a model of perfection when you were in college. A saint perhaps." His voice had a sarcastic edge.

When I didn't say anything, he said, "Take it easy. I don't know anything about your relationship to Sarah. She didn't talk about you."

Stung, I said nothing. I'd suspected that Sarah hadn't been as consumed with me as I had been with her that last month of her life, yet she appeared to have been having regular contact with Adrian, of all people, living some sort of double life. Had she really been "dating" my brother, taking him to meet her family, posing as a heterosexual woman? It all seemed an impossible muddle. "Tell me how you knew Sarah."

"We met, as you know, when you were an undergraduate in Minnesota. Rehearsing that show you were part of. Then, when I moved to Chicago, we bumped into each other a few times at museums. We weren't really friends until last year. Christ, I don't know why I'm telling you any of this."

Because you feel guilty, I thought. "I suppose to convince me that you knew Sarah better than I did."

"Don't be contrary," he said, reciting a phrase of our mother's I detested. "I have no idea how well you knew her. Look, we were having an affair for a few months. That's all."

"If that's all, why did you know her parents?"

I heard a thumping noise in the earpiece, as if Adrian were hitting the tabletop. I imagined him with a hammer in his hand, tapping it compulsively, its rhythm an accompaniment for his hyperactive mind. Or as punctuation for the subtext of his call, his peculiar cat-and-mouse method for gathering information. Then, the line cleared. Adrian resumed: "Her father, Paul Moore, is in the American Studies Department at Chicago. I've served on thesis committees with him. That's actually how I got to be friends with Sarah—he invited me to dinner at their house with him and his wife—Sarah's stepmother—and Sarah was there."

"I thought you said you bumped into her at museums?"

"Once or twice. Before the dinner."

Jealous, I imagined Sarah's parents thinking Adrian quite a catch for their daughter. But didn't they know Sarah liked women? As soon as that thought hit me, I wondered if it was really true. Maybe she was equally attracted to men and women. Or, maybe she didn't really like men or women sexually. Maybe she just liked attracting people, feeling the power of seeing someone fall under the spell of her voice, her manner, her sculpted profile. I pictured the knowing half smile of the priestess gracing a Tarot card, the cool untouchable face of Isis. "So what happened to her?"

Adrian's voice dropped to a whisper. "I don't know. She seemed disturbed during those last few weeks. She wouldn't talk to me about it. Do you know?" he asked warily, but hopefully.

Anger made my voice brittle. "You said she didn't mention me."

"She didn't."

I debated whether or not to tell Adrian about my own involvement with Sarah. A sudden strong sense of caution guided me. Something was eating at Adrian; he was fishing. Then an old memory struck me, of coming home from the movies with Adrian in my parents' car on a cold winter night. The snow crunched under the tires. I wasn't old enough to drive so I was probably twelve, Adrian seventeen. When he parked the car, I'd thanked him for taking me. "This isn't a date, you know." His voice was sarcastic and angry. I'd rushed from the car, away from my embarrassment and confusion.

Had Adrian and I ever discussed sexual details about anyone we were dating? I didn't think so. I waited a moment, carefully putting thoughts of Sarah and Adrian together aside. "Well, then how would I know anything?"

Adrian sounded unexpectedly eager. "You knew her good friend. Marta was her name, Marta Conway. I thought you might know how to get in touch with her."

My sense of suspicion grew. What was Adrian getting at? "I thought Sarah hadn't seen Marta for years."

Adrian laughed. "Oh, I don't think that's true. Sarah talked about her a lot."

I could hear Adrian's unspoken thought: *as opposed to how little she talked about you.* I felt like I'd wandered into a labyrinth and every path led to the same obscuring, impenetrable hedge. "I see. Well, then I assume you saw her at the memorial?"

Adrian's voice was tight with frustration. "No, she wasn't there. We didn't know how to contact her. That's why I'm calling."

We. "Oh. And I thought you were calling to wish me a happy birthday."

His rapid breathing pulsed in my ear. "I was getting to that. I never forget your birthday." He paused. "Yours and Duncan's."

I felt a slow, creeping sensation between my shoulder blades, as if someone was staring at my back so steadily that the pressure of their eyes made my skin crawl. I wanted to hang up. "Look, I don't know where Marta Conway is," I said. I could feel Adrian suppressing a sigh on the other end, or an explosive comment.

Finally, very softly, he said, "Christ."

"I doubt she could help you if you found her," I said, aware that Marta's unavailability made her even more tantalizing to Adrian. His desire to locate her was like a deep thirst that only a rare fluid could quench. And Marta had the only vial of the liquid.

When Adrian said nothing, I asked, "How old would Duncan be if he were still alive?"

Adrian hesitated and then stammered. That's when I hung up.

A thin film of sweat shimmered on the cradle of the phone I'd been clutching. I watched the plastic dry almost instantly. The fingers of my left hand ached. I feared for Marta Conway. Why did Adrian want to see her? I wished I knew her address so I could warn her. Adrian could be under suspicion by the police for all I knew. Maybe if Adrian knew where Marta was, he could divert official attention toward her and away from him, painting a picture of Marta as a scorned lover, a mentally unstable personality with a grudge against Sarah.

Adrian could be so logical, so reasonable, on the surface. If it suited him, he could implicate Marta with facility. My nerves hummed from the phone call. Just as easily, I supposed, he could implicate me. I could hear his dispassionate voice discussing his neurotic sister who suffered, in his view, from unrequited love for her former professor, imagined him reciting a litany of situations that cast doubt on my stability. I resolved to tell Adrian nothing. I hoped that Sarah had destroyed the letters I'd sent her.

My watch registered a quarter to five. I quickly called information and then dialed the number to the University of Chicago switchboard. There was a Dr. Paul Moore on the faculty in American Studies. It was plausible that Adrian knew Sarah's father and had met him as he said he had.

I shut my eyes. Images of Sarah's nervy face that last day, Adrian's bulk looming behind her, fluttered behind my lids. I wrapped my arms tightly around myself, shivering in the small, drafty house I rented. Its ancient heater struggled against poor insulation and the damp Minnesota cold. Instinct told me Adrian felt threatened. The victim's companion is always the main suspect, and, according to him, he was the companion of record.

I had been a mere shadow on the periphery of Sarah's life. Perhaps, in this case, that was fortunate.

The conversation left me feeling low. I couldn't get my brother's voice out of my head. Adrian had been so rattled he'd stumbled over which birthday Duncan would have had. Of course, my twin would be the same age I was now. Had Adrian forgotten when we were born? Or maybe he was too distracted to even remember that Duncan and I shared a birthdate. I assumed he had forgotten my birthday, although some vestigial memory had urged him to call me today.

I opened my appointment book and made a note that Adrian had called me on November 21, 1986. I wondered when I'd hear from him again.

———

After Adrian's phone call, I searched for Marta Conway. Not in any systematic way, but merely by contacting old friends and friends of friends. As I traced her movements since leaving St. Cloud, I began to feel that the two of us shared several defining features. We both loved the theater and yet were shy of the limelight. We were susceptible to outsize personalities, attracted to those with the kind of charm that veiled a ferocious self-focus. And we had both been betrayed, and discarded, by Sarah Moore. I had allowed myself to be vulnerable to Sarah twice, once when I was her student when she came between me and Ellen, and then seven years later near the time of her death.

Marta, I knew, had spent seven years with Sarah. Seven, the number of chakras in the body, the number of deadly sins, the number of Job's sons, and the number, according to some, of spiritual perfection. Surely seven years had been enough time for several cycles of crisis and redemption between those two strangely alike but separate people. Once again, I thought of the masks of tragedy and comedy in Sarah's office. Like all oppositions, each reflected the other.

The odd thing was that Marta's colleagues in the Theater Department back at St. Cloud had no current information about her. One told me that Marta had finally finished her PhD and gone on to teach at a small college in Vermont. Another that she'd become department chair at a community college in Florida and then left to go back into regional theater in Sarasota. But all the leads ended up dead ends. She seemed to have vanished.

My romantic version of Marta was that she had left the country, perhaps to a place in the same stage of transformation she was in herself, somewhere in Central Europe perhaps, or Northern Africa. I imagined her traveling country to country, carrying little with her, buying what she needed in any city or village where she happened to land. Marta had always had about her an air of affluence and of perfection: carefully coordinated clothes, always set off with a touch of flamboyance (I remembered her experimenting with single colors one year, dazzling us week after week with an array of oranges, blues, and greens in rolling profusion); a voice perfectly pitched and articulated. She used a cigarette like no one else, pointing the slim cylinder at an accusing angle at any student or colleague who displeased her. One rarely saw Marta without a Pall Mall, held between thumb and forefinger, often unlit. She appeared perfect and perfectly composed. That, at least, was the impression she gave until she shattered during the season of *Betrayal*.

I even put Babs, my historian, on the case—Babs with the focused mind, the clear head for other people's motives. It was the era before Internet searches and cell phones; people could evade the networks of attachment much more easily then. Babs came close in the fall of 1988, one year after Sarah's death. She found a notice in the alumnae magazine of Bowdoin College that Marta had published an article about language and silence in Harold Pinter's work. Apparently, Marta had gone to the small liberal arts college near Portland, Maine, as an undergraduate and so had Babs, not at the same time of course. It was a detail that had escaped me and, surely, an amazing coincidence.

"Not really," Babs had replied. "Maine is a tiny state. If you're from there, chances are you know someone who knows someone who knows someone."

"But isn't it odd, after all this time, that she wrote about Pinter? And *language and silence*—it seems like a sign, a clue deliberately broadcast."

Babs had rewarded me with one of her rare belly laughs. "And broadcast straight to you? Oh, Amanda, there are some people who see coincidences everywhere. Who manufacture them even if they don't exist. You're one of those people." Her voice deepened a note. "You positively dine out on incongruent moments. Or maybe you attract them—wherever you are, strange things collide. You're amazing. I applaud you for your consistency, but I think you're making a mistake this time."

I suspected Babs had been reading too much of some late nineteenth- or early twentieth-century writer or another. Dining out on strange occurrences or on gossip sounded suspiciously like something characters would do in a story by Henry James. Babs tended to serially OD on one favorite author after another, over the course of her infatuation traveling to places they wrote about, eating foods they mentioned in their diaries, eventually beginning to sound like them.

"I don't think that's true," I said stiffly. "The language of *Betrayal*—so deceptively simple—seems like a kind of code. The short and long pauses, the silences, are part of it."

"You mean punching up the import of what isn't said?" Babs good-naturedly abandoned any pretense at being above the lure of intrigue. "I like to think of myself as a student of subtext. So you think Marta Conway is trying to tell us something with her silence?"

"Well, not us. But someone."

"Hmm. Too bad we don't know who that someone is."

"I'd settle for just knowing where she is."

"But what would you really say to her if you found her?" Babs's voice rose in genuine interest. "She always seemed very private. A bit formidable, if you want to know the truth."

"Formidable? You think so?" The idea of Babs being intimidated by Marta amused me. "I'd just be happy to know she was somewhere in the universe."

Babs snorted. "That wouldn't be enough. Not for you."

———

That conversation was thirteen years ago. In another life. Since then I'd left Minnesota, wandered around the West Coast for a couple of years, taught in Illinois, and then settled in Austin, Texas. Really, everything had changed, and everyone. The exceptions were Babs who, once committed to a friend, was impossible to shake off—I was grateful for that—and my brother Adrian. They were the same age, as coincidence would have it, five years older than I was. That detail was all they had in common. Except that they were both far smarter than anybody else. Babs tended to de-emphasize that fact until you knew her well while Adrian wore it like a shield on first meeting—and forever after. Another way of putting it was that Adrian led with his intellect, while Babs finished with hers.

If I had to assign mythic totems to these key people in my life, I would give Adrian the helmet of Mars and Babs the scales of Justice. Justice may have balanced scales in one hand, but she has a sword in the other. And, like Justice, Babs could be fierce as well as fair. I was always glad to have her—my usually gentle, but sometimes ferocious, warrior—on my side.

14

Fractured images break into my consciousness at times before waking, or at others when I pause, my hand hovering over the phone, as I entertain the impulse to call my brother. The sequence resembles a defective loop of film that stops in the same place every time. The end of the story shimmers outside the edge of the frame.

Linked to winter and ice, the images are cast in the harsh light of the northern prairie. Tantalizing moments of this memory had always been with me, but now the pieces reassembled and became insistent. When I first moved to Texas, these fragments knocked on the door of my wakeful state less often. Bound up with a frozen landscape, they seemed incongruous in Austin, a place where freezing temperatures are rare, where the presence of the slick of ice is so freakish people cancel all activities at the sight of it. The memory hadn't faded in a warm climate, but for a long time it was displaced into an uneasy space between fantasy and nightmare. My work with Helen dislodged this fragile equilibrium and propelled the past forward.

When I was thirteen our family left our farm and moved into a second-story apartment in the nearby town of Jamestown, North Dakota, for two months during a winter that broke records for the number of days temperatures remained below zero. Duncan had died the year before, and it was as if his loss heightened my father's intolerance for harsh weather. Heavy snows banked the house and drifted blindingly across the road that year, making Adrian's and my commute to school, and my parents' journey to shop or work, arduous. All my friends lived in town; I'd always wanted to leave the farm and join them. But our farmhouse, shabby and in need of updating, had two stories and a root cellar with several small rooms where a young girl could hide. I hated the confining apartment. Small and inconvenient, it had only two bedrooms and as the youngest in the family, I had to sleep on the hide-a-bed in the living room.

But worse than sacrificing my room was surrendering the freedom to roam the acres of land and woods of the farm. In the apartment in town, there wasn't a cellar door leading out into the woods as there was at home when I needed to escape. In the farm's musty basement, a doorway led to a set of old stone steps and then an overhead wood door. When I pushed on the panel, it separated and flopped open like two large shutters; in moments I could sprint up the five concrete steps and disappear into the garden in the backyard. I imagined that the trapdoor in the dank basement that led to the garden and to the grove of elms beyond was my private passage to adventure.

When I was younger, maybe six or seven, I'd pretended the door was my private elevator into new dimensions of time and space. As soon as I stepped into its frame, I made a wish, and the doorway whisked me away to anywhere I desired to go. I'd whisper the names of places I knew nothing about, names I'd seen in books or on maps—Uzbekistan, Istanbul, Irkutsk—and by conjuring up a landscape and the creatures that inhabited it, I lived an afternoon or a whole day in each one. The cadence of the syllables in the name itself might suggest mountains rather than rivers, green hills instead of desert. It didn't matter, because in my own International Elevator I could change floors—and worlds—at any time. When I opened my eyes and stepped out, I never knew if I would find my feet touching land, sea, or the silver lunar surface.

When we were growing up, our parents were in the habit of spending many nights away from home during the winter. The farm rooted them in place in summer with the cycles of planting, tending, and harvesting. But as the temperatures dropped, the wind blasted down from the north, the snows deposited a blazing carpet of white, and the farmland lay dormant. In deep winter, the fields made no demands. Our father, Harry, a saxophonist in a jazz band, played most weekends at clubs in small neighboring towns; it was nothing for him to drive fifty or a hundred miles for a gig and return early the next morning. Eva, restless from the

confinement of her daily chores of cleaning and cooking, much antici-
pated these outings and accompanied him, leaving me home alone with
Adrian. Adrian seemed increasingly remote, but I missed Duncan so
intensely that I didn't trust my perceptions.

My brother turned eighteen that winter. He played clarinet in the high
school band but, otherwise, his hobbies were solitary. He roamed the
farm, and after fall hunting had ended, kept up his monitoring of the
terrain. It was his territory. His prowling was a way to interact sensuously
with the land, like a canine predator. Mainly, he kept a rigid schedule of
studying that included no sports and few friends. He might have wanted
to play football or basketball. I didn't know. But Adrian was conscripted by
my father to help on the farm, like every son in a farm family, and farm
work conflicted with practice times in spring and fall.

Adrian, with his pale-blond hair, chiseled face, and cloudy gray eyes,
was fiercely handsome. Gifted in the abstract language of mathematics
and science, observant about nature, he was impatient with conversation
and with most people. Physical phenomena absorbed him, kept his restless intelligence focused away from the turbulence of emotions he
couldn't understand or control.

About this time, I discovered Sherlock Holmes. I thrilled to the detec-
tive's microscopic examination of human motive and behavior, and
delighted in the chase itself. Sometimes I trailed surreptitiously after
Adrian, tracking his movements and his activities. I'd learned from my
reading that if you observed what people paid attention to, you could discover the secret of who they were. I practiced Holmes's close observation
and deductive strategies. And so I honed my knowledge of my brother. An
investigator of the natural world, he studied the stratifications of soil and
rock the way a sculptor observed the nuances of the human face. And I in
turn became an artist of the particular. I gravitated to the vagaries of one
human face; I knew its every twitch and the multiple meanings that might
lie behind each quiver.

One Saturday night, the weekend after New Year's, I'd gone to the movies with my friends and come home to an empty apartment. Our flat had
a private entrance on the street that led to the second floor. We always
locked that door at night and we each had our own key. I made sure to lock
the door when I came in that night.

Adrian was due to arrive from a band trip that night and for an hour or so I waited for him, but around midnight I went to sleep. In those days, I didn't usually want to go to bed. But when I did sleep I was like the child who looks in the mirror and passes through to the other side, entering a parallel life and losing the way back. Nothing could rouse me until I had wandered out in my own time. These dead sleeps, as I came to call them, with their sensation of time lost, functioned as a kind of narcotic. Not a drug I voluntarily took, as I could not predict when I'd sink into one of these black-hole spells. Years earlier, my sleepwalking had unnerved the household. Even though that period was past, my dreams wrapped me in a tight, soundproof cocoon.

That night, I remember dreaming that a stranger was trying to force his way into the apartment. The sound of his fists hitting the door rolled up the stairs, and then crescendoed into the rapid-fire drill of boots battering the wood doorframe. I heard the sound as I wavered in and out of the dream, wandering in a deep, labyrinthine cave, dropping down into a narrow passage and then climbing toward sunlight.

The hammering on the door roused me enough that I'd struggle to the surface and then fall back again, as if currents in deep water sucked me down. Confused, frightened by the drowning sensation and the loud assault on the door, I fought awakening. Conflicting voices sounded in my ears. *Don't get up! Wake up!* In the dream the blows against the door grew louder and louder. I heard the sound of wood splintering, one board at a time.

The air closed in around me, as if there were layers of cotton wadding packed around my nose and eyes. I twisted on the sofa bed, my head blurry with the sound of wood separating, the light from the street filtering across the living room. I thought I heard the living room clock strike three.

Or maybe three boards shattered onto the floor. The stairway echoed with crashing footsteps and Adrian stood in the doorway to the living room, his face red and chafed with cold, panting, liquid streaming from his eyes and nose. "What are you doing?" his voice rang out, eerie and high. He advanced on me, as I still struggled to rise to the surface from the depths of the dream.

"I'm asleep, I'm asleep," I chanted in alarm and confusion.

"You're asleep? Asleep!" His voice cracked. Tinny, it ground on my skull with the insistence of metal on metal. "Are you crazy? Do you know how goddamned cold it is outside, Manda? This is North Dakota. In January. Do you understand? Listen to me: it's thirty below. I almost froze to death."

I tried to listen, to focus on Adrian, but my eyes, sluggish and encrusted with sleep, registered only a blurry form. Who was it? The man in my dream, the man trying to break in? I saw the familiar outlines of my brother, bulked up by his parka.

"Ohhhh," I groaned, wishing to go back down to the depths again. This fuming person couldn't be Adrian. Why would Adrian pound on the door when he lived here? I knew he had his own key. I let my eyes close and wondered if this was how death was, a heaviness dragging at you, not letting you move your arms or legs or open up your eyes.

"I couldn't find my key!" he panted. "You were supposed to let me in!" Before I could protest, Adrian's face, purple with rage and cold, came closer. He screamed my name in an explosion of sound, "Manda!" And then I felt the air rush over me as he came toward me.

And that's when the film breaks, every time. With Adrian on the move and me staring from the sofa bed, my eyes open wide and yet struggling to see. Did I think of my International Elevator, of stepping in and being whisked away? I don't think so. I think terror froze me solid.

———

My therapist tells me that just because a memory surfaces with the sharp detail of reality, the bone-deep feel of truth, doesn't mean it has any basis in fact. I don't find this comforting. Imagine that you're diving under the sea and your air supply is cut off. You panic. The sea encases you in its watery embrace, a slow, cruel stranglehold. You sense your life ebbing away. Every cell in your body screams for air—your craving erupts along your nerves like the shrieking of starving young birds, high-pitched and incessant. You go limp as you give up and let go. But just before you lose consciousness, your throat convulsing, your face breaks the surface of the water. Miraculously. That first gasp of air sears your throat and lungs, your very core. You shudder and cramp with the shock of it. It's a release, one that hurts like hell. You disregard the pain in your gratitude at being alive. Yet the fear of drowning stays with you; you can't forget the press of water, the crush of heart and lungs. You alternate between terror and relief, despair and hope. You wish your life could be the same as before. You know your life will never be the same.

That's what recovering a fraught fragment of your history is like. First, an unstable piece of your experience is lost to you; it abruptly cracks off like a stress fracture on an ice floe and falls into the deep. Soon, the unspeakable is burrowed so securely in your unconscious that layers of personality are built around its absence. You pay a price for this instinctual burial: the layers insulate you but they deaden you, too. Deep inside there's a small space as inaccessible as a locked and barricaded room. Behind the door to this room a secret hibernates. Of an event that reshaped your sense of who you were so completely you couldn't absorb it. It's as if, amid the solid outline of your body drawn on a wall, the line is broken in one place. You try to fill in the blanks, but there's an empty place, a yawning gap. It's like an extra gut and it's very hungry. It demands constant food in the form of attention and distraction. You pretend the hunger isn't there, you smile, you stay busy, you soldier on.

But no matter how well you perform your life, part of you is simply lost. You're diminished every bit as much as if you tipped Alice's shrinking potion marked "Drink me" down your throat. You're not all there. But if you're very lucky or very unlucky—take your pick—this secret from your past revisits you. The key to the secret place appears; it opens your psychic strongbox and the missing event claws its way out. Materialized through a catalytic event, a dream, or déjà vu, the key itself appears from nowhere. And then, well, you have to find the door that the key opens, don't you? You respond as best you can, just like the swimmer who's blessed with life-saving oxygen at her last gasp: she doesn't think, she just breathes in.

I connected a recurring pain in my shoulder to the night Adrian broke down the door. After the car accident, the sensation recurred during my regular massage appointment. I experienced a sharp pain in my rib cage that flamed across the left side of my body like the scrape of a claw. As my therapist, Malcolm, worked the muscles around my shoulder blade, applying the usual pressure, a rising panic flooded my neck and throat. I couldn't breathe properly.

"Less pressure," I said once and then again, yet still a raw burn swept up through my torso and into my neck, as if the nerves had been ignited and left to blaze. The sensation pinned my body to the table. My insides seeped pain, but the force bore upon me from outside. It was as if someone weighed upon me, willing me to succumb. My spirit, a small voice crying out to be heard, felt pushed deep inside.

Shaken, I rose from the table after the session, dressed, and went into the lobby. Malcolm raised his shaved head from his appointment book. "Are you all right?"

"I think so." I raised my arm cautiously. "My whole left side aches."

Malcolm's eyes registered the pattern of the movement. "Your left shoulder didn't seem particularly congested." He ran his hand lightly along my back. "But, here," he traced an area leading from my neck to mid-back. "This whole area moves as a block. When it moves at all."

"It's very sensitive. And painful."

Malcolm rolled his shoulders in slow motion. The muscles bunched and then lengthened under his polo shirt. I found it hard to imagine that his loose limbs harbored the resistant tissue so common to his clients. "We'll keep working on it."

I nodded, but a part of me didn't want to be touched, not now, not ever. I reluctantly made another appointment and left.

———

My father died twelve years ago in a car accident, driving home after a gig with his band one Saturday night. Five years later, Eva moved into a graduated living facility in Moorhead, Minnesota, where her favorite aunt lived, a pretty white house with a porch and lots of trees. The place was small, with gardens that the residents puttered in; they planted and tore out vegetation in an endlessly satisfying cycle of renewal. It didn't matter if the plants were nurtured or destroyed—for the patients, the ritual served as therapy. Eva suffered from mild dementia that could only worsen with time.

On the subject of Adrian, Eva had lost her memory a long time before. Or maybe the word *lost* failed to capture what happened to her accounting of that period of our lives. Her memory was, like all of ours, selective. Some events were carefully catalogued, others misplaced, and still others passed through the filter of her mind's eye—the gauze of nostalgia perhaps, or the glaze of self-justification, or something in between. In this, Eva was no different from you or me. I mourned the condition of my once ultra-competent mother.

But the state of her deterioration preoccupied me in a very selfish way as well. For Eva was precious to me. Besides Adrian, she was the only witness to the hidden episodes of my childhood. Duncan had been gone for so long Eva's mind denied he was once here. I didn't forget him, ever, but he was a witness only in my memory of him.

I doubted much time remained to find out what I needed to know. And sometimes the pressure to know, really know, made me panic. What if I remained forever lost, even to myself? As a young girl, I'd studied Adrian's face: thin-lipped, angular, the blond cap of hair shiny and immaculately combed, parted on the right. I admired my brother's glacial beauty. But it frightened me, too. A favorite saying of Mother's was that he had the face of an angel. When Eva said that, I recoiled at the thought that anything called heavenly could be as removed, as untouchable, as Adrian appeared to me. Flawless, expressionless, dispassionate, his was the face of dread. But now the constitution of dread had changed. It was the *not* knowing Adrian that scared me the most.

I harbored a desire to occupy the landscape of Eva's brain, which, once I'd been denied it, had transformed into a territory of endless fascination. In a particularly brooding state of mind once, aided by several glasses of scotch, I imagined my mother's mind occupying a position somewhere between a fun-house mirror and a crammed attic, awash with images of Adrian at every age. Some hung from the ceiling on mobiles; others ballooned up from the floor like inflatable dolls. In one corner stood a bright, shiny chest, a repository of the past. As I concentrated on the chest in my mind's eye, it expanded and glowed. Eva lifted its enameled lid and exclaimed at its contents, her trove of loose black-and-white snapshots stacked willy-nilly, all with curled edges. Bent over this chest, hands palsied with eagerness, she carefully gathered up the most striking pictures, the ones that attracted her most. Like a greedy child she grasped them by the fistful and pressed them to her chest. But there were too many to hold and some spilled; they slipped away like piles of glitter. They scattered at her feet, winking up at her.

"Yes," she crooned, rocking her treasures, precious fragments of a more vital, more triumphant time, against her soft breasts. "These feel the best. This one and this . . ."

She lifted out one picture and another and passed her hands across them as if they were made of the rarest, most perfect silk. A winsome smile, a tear, a rapturous glow stole across her face. "That's him. That's my Adrian."

When I described the scene I've conjured to Babs, it was clear that she recoiled from this macabre portrait of Eva. But my imaginings weren't all that far from the realm of possibility. In fables, children sometimes have a physical mark that allows their mothers to pick them out no matter their disguise. Eva and Adrian shared such a bond; a connection I'd come to discover that had mystical, physical, even alchemical dimensions.

But Mother offered little help on my history with Adrian even before her health declined. Over the years I prodded her for details of my childhood growing up with my older brother. Once, after months of building up my courage, I confronted her when she still lived on the farm. We were harvesting green beans and in the bending and snapping motion my face was continually hidden from her; it seemed a safe time to ask. I feared if she could see my expression as we talked she might see my hunger for answers, for any crumb of explanation. I still yearned for reconciliation with Adrian. Deep inside me the younger sister lived who wished that someday her older brother might discover her true self.

Eva, in a soft blue pullover and matching sweatpants, her sure fingers lightly but critically assessing the plants, crouched down in the row ahead of me. She hummed an old tune my father liked to play, "Fly Me to the Moon." I liked seeing her large-boned body bent in the daily round of weeding, tending, and plucking the fruits of her green thumb. When she gardened, Eva's restless energy dissipated; instinctive body knowledge about plant life replaced her mental churning.

I felt almost guilty breaking into her easy rhythm, but I steeled myself. If not now, when we shared this simple caretaking activity, then when? I hesitated, searching for a graceful way into the discussion; finally, I just blurted a rush of words: "Mother, I've been wanting to ask you something . . ." I hurried on at her nod. "Do you remember that winter when I was in junior high—something happened one night when I was alone with

Adrian? You remember when the door broke? I think something happened that night. I was injured. I don't—"

Eva's back stiffened. But then her spine uncoiled and she turned toward me, a fringe of curly gray hair escaping from under her straw hat. Her face took on a lean and hungry cast for a moment.

"Adrian?" Eva repeated the name as if it were a special flavor that gave her mouth pleasure. Her glow of delight passed as quickly as it had appeared; she turned away, focusing on the tall columns of the elm grove in the mid-distance. She shaded her eyes with one hand and frowned as if seeing something unexpected among the branches. "Don't be silly. Adrian would never hurt you. You're his sister."

She bent and hefted the pan at her feet that contained the jagged mound of picked beans, pursed her lips, and then set it back down into the black earth. She began to walk toward the house, saying over her shoulder, "Why don't you keep at it for another ten minutes and then we'll have plenty."

15

I had an appointment with Helen three days after the evening at Teresa's house when we'd talked about Sarah's death. I hoped to find a way to keep my new friendship with Teresa free of the painful past with Sarah and Marta.

Helen brought me a glass of water and then sat across from me. Helen wore dark red loafers. Her feet rested on a round rug woven with green and gold threads. The low table between us typically had a few books, coasters, sometimes plants from Helen's yard. Today a single blue iris stood in a vase next to a stone fetish of a bear. I reached for the bear, its smooth surface cool against my hand. I hadn't slept much the night before, and I felt irritable and close to tears.

"I'm such an idiot," I said, before she could ask me how I was feeling.

"Why do you say that?" Helen sipped from a huge mug of tea. I imagined it to be bottomless, as no matter how much she drank, she never got up to refill it, nor did it ever seem to be empty.

"Oh, it's Teresa. I feel so drawn to her. She seems so nice, so kind—so *normal.* But she knew Sarah and Marta. I suspect it's possible that she had an affair with Marta. They were 'close,' she said. Oh, I don't know." Nerves kept me talking. "And I haven't even asked her about Adrian yet."

Helen glanced to the side of her chair, where her notebook lay open next to a table lamp. "Remind me how Adrian fits in with Teresa."

"I don't think I told you this, but more than twenty years ago, when I was visiting Adrian at Amherst, I saw him look at a woman while we were sitting on the lawn—another faculty member, I think. He ran after her and spoke to her. When I met Teresa I recalled that time, because she was so like the woman who'd attracted Adrian's attention. It seems so unlikely, I know, but now I'm sure Teresa *was* that woman talking with Adrian that day."

Helen simply nodded, so I continued. "She was younger, of course, but I'm sure she was the person we saw. Adrian seemed so struck by her, in that way of his. Oh, I can't explain what comes over him when he's attracted to someone." I thought of the peculiar quality of stillness that came over Adrian's face at such times—a single-minded, dogged expression of pure focus. "It makes me think there's certainly a possibility she knows him. After what happened to Sarah, there's a part of me that doesn't even dare to ask. I can't bear the thought of Adrian contaminating anything in my present life." I lowered my voice. "I sometimes imagine him reaching across time, as if there isn't enough distance to put between the past and my life now."

Helen set down the bottomless mug and pushed up the sleeves of her cotton sweater, blue, like her eyes. The sweater, just rumpled enough to look comfortable, draped her torso loosely. "It would be fairly easy to find out whether she taught at the same college as Adrian then."

I laughed. "I love this about you, Helen. You don't say that I'm being paranoid or obsessive, you just regard my ravings as if they're perfectly reasonable."

Helen's thin lips curved into a smile. "You don't need me to put you into categories you label as dysfunctional. You tell yourself those things all the time. I've heard you." She cleared her throat. "Not that I would call you paranoid or obsessive. Frankly, I don't blame you for being cautious with Teresa. Sarah Moore was a devastating person in your life. As your older brother was, and still is. Teresa certainly knew one and perhaps both of these people. It doesn't seem paranoid to wonder about her relationships with either of them. And how can you not wonder why she's interested in you now. After all, she sought you out, at your office."

"Yes, yes, exactly!" I pounced on that detail, one that had been worming its way into my suspicions for some time. "She found me. Why? And why did she tell me recently I reminded her of someone. Sarah Moore to be exact. That doesn't sound disingenuous to me."

"Let's take a step back," Helen's calm voice broke through my rising agitation. "How do you feel about Teresa?"

"I'm very attracted to her."

"When you're with her, do you feel she's accessible to you?"

I considered this. "If you mean open, well, she's not always forthcoming," I said slowly. "But that might just be her style—she seems to have a natural reserve. I do feel good around her in the main."

"In the main?"

"Well, when we spoke of Sarah the other night, I didn't feel comfortable. I'll never be absolutely comfortable talking about Sarah. But, even then, I felt relieved. I didn't feel like I was taking a risk telling her about it."

"Does she remind you of anyone else in your life?" Helen asked.

Aware that I still held the stone bear, I replaced it on the table, taking a moment to turn its face toward the flower. "Why do you ask that?"

"She's older than you, as Sarah was. She's successful and attractive. She's an academic. I'm curious if that makes her feel familiar."

"She's not like Sarah," I said flatly. "She listens. She's not 'onstage' the way Sarah was."

"'Onstage,'" Helen repeated. "Tell me about that."

"Oh, I wish I could show you," I said impulsively, but then Sarah's profile, the lips turned slightly down, rose before me.

"Why don't you try?" Helen took off her glasses and waited.

From classes with Marta, I knew how much actions were animated by the essence of a person. Sarah's essence felt far out of reach. Empty of ideas, I heard Marta's voice: *Try technique, Amanda. Think of it as a job, forget divine inspiration.*

I rose to move around the room but changed my mind—Sarah's stillness was her great gift. "I don't know how to show you." Seated again, I tried to conjure the stage that so often framed Sarah. "When Sarah directed, she perched at the edge of her chair in the theater, or paced slowly up and down the back row. She *prowled*, yet at the same time her face was very still and alert. If someone called to her when she was absorbed like this, she wouldn't move for several seconds, then very slowly she'd turn to look at the person who spoke. It was as if she knew everyone was watching her every movement. And everyone *was* watching. Because if you're graceful and lovely, as Sarah was, and you expect an audience and you play to your audience, then you have one. It's just that simple. She was *studied*."

"And Teresa's not like that?"

"No. She has a kind of modesty about her. She's unassuming in some ways. I get the feeling she doesn't care if you're watching. It's fine if you are, but . . ."

It was late in the day, and the room was darkening; the star-shaped leaves of the sycamore trees outside the window blocked the sunlight. Helen's blue eyes looked almost opaque. "You have that quality too," she said.

"What?"

"The quality you attribute to Sarah. But I wouldn't have described it that way. I might have said you were a naturally dramatic person."

"Oh." I sat very still. Did Helen find me insincere? A fake?

Helen smiled, her face soft. "Don't worry. I just mean you're very compelling when you speak. I imagine that people notice you when you're in a room, that's all."

My face flushed. Her words startled me just as Teresa had on that evening when she remarked that my voice reminded her of Sarah's. "That's funny."

"Is it?"

"I sometimes feel utterly invisible, that's all." I pulled a Kleenex out of the box at my feet and dabbed at my face. My cat, Holloway, often hid behind blades of grass; it occurred to me that the grass provided about as much cover for her as this tissue did when I pressed it to my eyes.

"Sweetie," Helen said, her voice tugging at me. "At one time in your life maybe someone treated you as if you were invisible. But you're not now."

In the face of her sympathy I felt even more exposed. She didn't seem to understand that this issue was very important, but not in the way she thought. I wasn't talking about the pain of not being seen when I was a child. "But I don't want to be an actor like Sarah was. Looking back, I don't know if anything she ever said was true. She was a performer. She didn't just talk—she held court. I realize now that when I thought she was just speaking to me, only to me, that I could have been any one of a number of people. I was just . . . the audience."

"Ah," Helen said. "That's different, then. I don't experience you that way. I believe you when you talk about your feelings. I don't think you're performing."

"Sarah didn't talk about her feelings. Not really." My throat felt tight. "I'd sometimes wonder if she had any."

Helen looked at me seriously. "If Sarah was as narcissistic as you say, she felt a lot of pain. She needed a lot from people, and from her point of view she probably never received enough. There was a dark, empty place inside her." Helen stopped abruptly; perhaps she thought she was lecturing.

"No, go on," I said. "She was very demanding. That's true. And sometimes when I was with her I found myself thinking, *She wants intimacy. But not necessarily from me.*"

Helen nodded. "She may not have been able to relate to other people's unhappiness, but she would have felt her own acutely. Unfortunately, that doesn't make her sensitive to others. Quite the contrary—her own pain obliterated everything else."

"Her pain made her want to obliterate everyone else," I said absently. "Yes, that makes sense."

But I couldn't get past Helen's comment about my being dramatic. My hair, wispy and fine, needing a cut, drifted across my forehead. I swiped it away with both hands. "Something you said disturbs me. When I was in college, I did study Sarah. I wanted to talk like her, be confident like her. But then, later, I realized how *empty* pure style could be without anything behind it."

I stopped talking, remembering how I'd envied Sarah's manner because it was such an effective mask—I'd wanted one to hide behind myself. I confessed to Helen: "I know what it's like to feel empty. How lonely it can be."

"Of course you know. That's partly why you're here. You want to change, to grow. But back to how you wanted to emulate Sarah at one time. I understand that. I also see that you're uneasy about Teresa. You say she doesn't fit the pattern—an older woman, accomplished, who finds you of great interest and so pulls you in—and yet there are similarities."

I still had the Kleenex clutched in my hand and I stuffed it into a pocket of my jeans. "I don't know now. I guess I've been susceptible to that pattern, as you call it. Sometimes." I thought of Babs, five years older and accomplished, my dear friend who would do anything for me. Sexuality did not seem a part of our relationship. I shook my head. "I do like older women, as friends. I like learning from their experience, their wisdom. I've told you about my best friend Babs, for instance. But I also feel a kinship with them. I feel older sometimes myself."

"An old soul?" Helen smiled.

"I can relate to that. Although around you, I feel I have much to learn."

Helen nodded and thought a moment. "I meant to ask you earlier, when you mentioned your visit with Adrian at Amherst when you were in your early twenties. You've said how you hated him after Duncan died. And yet you visited him when he moved away from home. You cared about his opinion of you. Why?"

I felt a moment's panic. "He's all I had left. You're right. I did hate Adrian. I blamed him for everything. For Eva's coldness to me. And for Duncan's death. But don't you see, I still needed Adrian. I hated him but I loved him too. He was a fixture in my life. A touchstone that I needed."

Helen waited, vigilant in her overstuffed chair. Her posture reminded me of the stone figures in the courtyard of a museum I often visited in San Antonio—erect, poised, still as an unruffled pond. Unbidden, a thought came into my mind: *Still as a serpent.* Aloud, I said: "Adrian was like a snake. Coiled and watchful. Other times he was like any other older brother—annoying at times, unexpectedly sweet at others. He tried to get me to trust him. He tried really hard. He drove me to band practice and to drama club rehearsals when I couldn't drive yet. He waited for me after school. Sometimes he cooked breakfast for me, just the way I liked it, when Mom and Dad were off somewhere."

"Was that enough? To win your trust?" Helen replaced her glasses and looked at me with concern.

"Of course not. But I was terribly lonely." I felt tears gathering in my left eye. My right eye felt hot and dry. "Sometimes when I'd be working in the garden with Adrian and he didn't know I was watching him, he looked sad and far away. There was something in the curve of his cheek, the way he held his head—he looked like Duncan, only older."

Gently, Helen said, "Maybe both of you felt sad and far away after Duncan died."

I nodded. The tears spilled out of my left eye and coursed down my cheek. "In time, we talked about Duncan. Or maybe I just talked about him. How much I missed him. And Adrian sometimes listened."

"And other times?"

"Other times he would get very angry. *Stop it*, he'd say. *I can't hear any more about Duncan.* Once, he said to me, *Look, when will you get it through your head that I'm here and your precious Duncan isn't?* That really upset me. I think I've said this before; there have always been two Adrians. The good Adrian and the bad Adrian." My voice sounded small to me when I added, "I always wanted the good Adrian to like me." Desolation descended on me and I squeezed my chest. "Don't you see how it's possible to love someone and dislike them at the same time?"

"Of course I do," Helen said quickly. "I know very well. We see so many paradoxes in the people in our family of origin." She added, "Or in the people we're married to. People can be very complicated. And upsetting. And there you are, living with them, without anywhere else to go."

Helen turned to look out the window. I was about to ask her a question about her family when she turned back to me with renewed energy. "Your feelings for Sarah were polarized like that too. Even now I think you can see why you loved her. And perhaps still do."

"Yes." As if the walls had skin, grief seemed to seep from the very pores of the room.

Helen's voice was quiet. "Amanda, I have to ask you if Adrian was sexually abusive to you. You talk about his breaking down the door, frightening you . . ."

An old knot of dread stirred in my abdomen. "I don't know. He bullied me and hit me but that's all I know. I just can't remember."

Our hour was almost over. I felt unsettled and incomplete.

Helen glanced at the clock. "This isn't a good place to end, but maybe you can draw or paint what you're feeling," she suggested. "About Adrian and about Teresa. And we can talk about it next time." I had brought sketches in to her before, and sometimes made collages of dreams I'd had that we then discussed in my next session.

I stared at my watch and checked it against the black-encased clock on the wall, its ticking more muted today. "I want to know how Sarah died," I said.

Helen rubbed the side of her forehead; she looked troubled. "How, or why?"

"Those are two sides of the same thing."

Home from my session with Helen, I headed for my office and the photograph albums in the small bookcase but I couldn't find the photo I was looking for. Then I recalled a cardboard box full of loose photos I'd stored in one of the bedroom closets. I rummaged through the back of the closet in my bedroom first and located the photos behind a stack of shoeboxes.

The daylight was fading and Holloway was clamoring at the back door as I brought the box into the hallway. I let her in and turned on lights inside before continuing into my study; while there I found three black folders beneath the loose photographs that contained the formal studio portraits that had been so popular in the early seventies. An eight by ten had been taken on Duncan's and my twelfth birthday at the photographer's office near the old library. The background was sky blue. Adrian and Eva were standing at the rear. My dad was sitting in front, in the middle, one arm around me and one around Duncan. Adrian looked blond and stern, like an Aryan prince. Eva's head was bent slightly toward him. The three of us in front were smiling, Duncan and I happily squished in Dad's embrace.

That picture was taken almost two years before Adrian graduated from high school and went away to school. I reached for a snapshot taken the day Adrian packed his car to drive off to college in Minneapolis. Duncan wasn't present in this photo, of course. Dad stood on the passenger side with me, his ash-blond hair threaded with silver on the crown, the color of my hair now. His face had sprouted new lines of tension that weren't there in the studio picture taken the autumn before. But in this photo he wasn't smiling; he stared straight at the camera with a vacant expression. My head grazed Dad's shoulder; my willowy body leaned into his comforting solidity. Adrian stood by the open driver's door, his right arm lifted in a half wave. He was looking at Eva, who was taking the picture. I noticed a strange expression on his face, part affection, part exasperation, and part relief.

Those two photos show the fault line in our family more clearly than anything else could. I'd looked at this black-and-white snap many times and never seen the deadness in my father's eyes as he looked at his wife. Nor had I seen that Adrian was already looking past our mother as the object of his attention.

Eva most often appointed herself family photographer, although her composition usually was askew or the image blurry. I imagined she didn't really look through the viewfinder or that her hand shook as she triggered the shutter. How had I not registered that her picture-taking, like her version of the past, was out of focus?

———

Life felt very isolated after Adrian went away to school, three months before I turned fourteen. Adrian and Duncan, two very different points of gravity on either side of me, were both gone. I learned to play the piano then, whiling away many late afternoons after school playing ballads, learning a Chopin étude, attempting a Bach concerto. The music washed away the silence, the absence of my brothers' voices. Thirteen seemed the most tragic, wasted age. Everything seemed either an end or an enemy, my own transforming body included.

Turning fourteen released me. Ninth grade meant a new school, new friends, even a boyfriend. My gawky self suddenly morphed from grace-less goose into graceful swan. After Adrian had come and gone for a year, I paid him scarce attention when he came back for visits. My life was with my friends. But I forgot nothing, not Duncan's vanishing, not the shat-tered door the last winter Adrian lived at home, and not the fractured dreams that followed. But I discovered that for Adrian attention was the elixir of life. To deny him that grieved him more than anything I could actually do or say.

Duncan stayed in my heart. Sometimes I touched the place on my side where my ribs ended and the soft flesh of my waist began and felt a strange sensitivity. It was there, I thought, that the physical essence of Duncan had broken away from me. The tissue remembered and mourned him with a dull ache.

During Adrian's second visit, at Christmas, he snagged me as I went out to plug in the car's head-bolt heater so that the engine would be warm enough to start the next day when I needed to drive into town.

"Manda, wait," he panted, high-stepping through the snow between the house and the garage. "I'll do that for you," he said.

"I'm getting good at it." I'd already popped the hood and had the electrical cord in hand. Those winters in the seventies were severe on the plains, "global warming" a term a few decades from colloquial use.

I opened the garage door and then sat in the car. The heater hadn't had time to warm the engine but the motor roared to life. Our '64 Buick had the constitution of a tank, weatherproofed and impervious.

Adrian jumped into the front seat with me. I cranked up the heat and we sat there together. I had just gotten my driver's license; back then, rural kids got learner's permits at thirteen and licenses the following year.

We sat for a while in silence. I felt Adrian's eyes studying me, but I stubbornly kept my face forward. Eyes on the future; that was my mantra as I waited for the time I could graduate and leave home.

"You're different," Adrian finally said.

"Oh? How?"

"You seem more confident, that's all."

I turned to him. "I was elected class vice president this year."

"Congratulations." Adrian pulled at the tips of his gloves with his teeth. "Look, we never talk anymore."

The wind had flushed his cheeks and nose making his face look very young. "You don't live here anymore, that's why." I tried for a reasonable tone, but I was aware of the thrumming of my heart through the layers of clothes I wore. The air seemed thin, as if we were at altitude, or maybe Adrian's heavy breaths depleted the oxygen in the car.

"Yeah. I don't miss it much, either." His nose looked pinched as he squinted straight in front of him. "But I miss you sometimes."

I didn't say anything.

"I think about you, Manda." Adrian shifted, his parka making a swooshing sound against the Naugahyde seat of the Buick.

"Me too," I muttered.

Adrian's voice was wheedling. "I hope someday you'll be able to trust me again."

I felt the hair prickle at the base of my neck. He reminded me of our mother, treating trust as a currency you could easily bank or withdraw.

"Trust has to be earned, Adrian."

His laugh had a raw sound. "I could say the same about you."

"What do you mean?"

"Look, you're the weird one. You're the one who sleeps like a dead person and walks around the house like a zombie, trying to get out in the middle of the night."

Adrian had often made fun of the sleepwalking I'd done when I was younger. "I don't do that anymore," I said sharply. "And at least I don't break down doors when people are sleeping. If I wandered around, I didn't take anyone else with me."

"It was only a door," he muttered, his throat mottling an ugly red. "Your imagination was on overdrive."

That was the family line about the night Adrian battered down the apartment door. And, since I couldn't remember anything from that night after I saw his furious face bearing down on me, it was the one that stuck.

"*Overdrive*. Right." I turned off the motor and opened the car door. "If you want me to trust you, tell me what happened at the pond when Duncan died."

Adrian's hand strayed to his forehead. "We've gone over that so many times."

"Have we? Then why don't I know how it happened?" I punched Adrian lightly on the shoulder. "'Cuz I don't know."

Recoiling from my touch, Adrian straightened. "You know what I know."

"What's that supposed to mean? You were there, I wasn't."

Adrian's gray eyes looked bleak. "I'm not sure I remember."

The low, muffled ticking of my brother's Timex made me aware of the pounding of my heart; it jumped and lurched like a rodent in a cage. "Yeah," I said, as a phrase popped into my mind, something our freshman English teacher had read to us that week: "And I'm the queen of Romania."

"You don't understand anything. You're just a kid." Adrian opened his door and slid out, then he slammed the door so hard the car rocked. The chassis swayed slightly over the tires and then settled back like the dead thing it was.

16

A casual mention of Teresa performing onstage precipitated a barrage of e-mails from Babs. My old friend thought it utterly implausible that a financial client of mine would be acting in *Betrayal*. "Somehow, dear Amanda, this could only happen to you."

In late May, Babs called to tell me she wanted to come for a visit.

"The *Betrayal* connection is just plain spooky," she said, between bites of something crunchy. "What are the odds you'd meet someone associated with *that* play and then find out they went to graduate school with Sarah Moore and Marta Conway? Oh, and even more strange, that somehow this person *knew*—as if by osmosis—that you were Sarah's student?"

I ignored her. I'd already uncomfortably dismissed the same thoughts from my mind several times. "What are you eating?"

"Carrots. I'm trying to lose weight." Babs groaned, a sound both breathy and musical. "If I were an opera singer, my signature aria would be a lament to heaven about the burden of the body. Something like *corpulum rotundum*," she added, managing to sound both morose and clinical at the same time.

She immediately gave a snort of laughter. "Or, how about this? The greedy dentata—if I didn't have a good set of choppers, think how much better off I'd be."

When Babs laughed at her own jokes, I didn't have to. "But if you were an opera singer, maybe you wouldn't care. Isn't there some correspondence between chest size and vocal resonance?"

"But I do care, I'm not an opera singer, and I have no idea." Babs coughed. "And I'm sick of carrots."

"Things not going well?"

Babs was still in upstate New York—she'd moved from Albany to Ithaca five years earlier to teach at Cornell. "I'm getting stir-crazy up here. It's supposed to be almost summer and we've gone straight from mud season to cool and rainy. Forget May flowers. It's muddier than ever. And there's no sun."

"It's too hot in this place." I checked the thermometer on the other side of the French doors. "It's 6:00 p.m. and it's still ninety-two degrees outside."

"Sounds good."

"So when are you coming?" I asked.

I heard pages turning. "I'm absolutely free all of June," she said. "How about the middle of the month?"

"Bring shorts," I said. "And a swimsuit."

"I suppose that means more carrots," Babs said. "Oh, hell, what's the point? I'm past forty-five. Why torture myself over how I look?"

We both laughed at this. "You have to torture yourself about something. Which reminds me, how is your book coming?" I knew she'd been chained to her desk writing a book about the French writer Madame de Staël.

Babs's tone warmed immediately. "I'm in heaven. My editor loves the new biography. I won't get the revision notes—absolutely minor, she promised—until July. That's why visiting you in June is so perfect. I feel utterly free for the first time in five years."

I heard a muffled *thunk*, possibly Babs hurling her carrot across the room, before she continued. "You know, when I started this I was simply fascinated by the fact that a woman born in the eighteenth-century was so powerful that she was exiled by the greatest ruler of her age. Just think— Napoleon literally thought his position was unsafe with her onshore!"

"And now?"

"Well, that's just one in a string of amazing things." She happily launched into the intellectual achievements and romantic preoccupations of her current focus.

"Babs . . ." I broke in after a few minutes. "You just reminded me of something . . ."

"Hang on, let me finish." A rare grumpy note crept in at this interruption of her mini-lecture.

"Go on." I winced at my impatience.

After a pause, she resumed her discourse on her heroine, ending with: "She's really your kind of person. For instance, she said this . . ." Babs's voice became fuller: "'In matters of the heart, nothing is true except the improbable.' Okay, you can talk now."

"Are you sure? You probably just want to hang up, I'm such a terrible listener."

Babs seemed to have regained her good humor. "Actually, you're not a bad listener. You just have a short fuse when you're onto something. So, spill it."

I resolved to monitor more carefully my reliance on my generous friend. "It can wait for another time. Tell me more about your book."

"I'm done. Really. If you don't tell me, I'll have to go back to work."

"Believe it or not, this is actually related to what you were just talking about. You mentioned the salon de Staël held in Paris. Wasn't she a consummate actress? I don't mean professionally, but in her everyday life?"

"Well, she was very dramatic, especially compared to her mother, another brilliant woman. The mother was a great beauty, the daughter not so celebrated in that department. So, perhaps, being flamboyant early on was a compensation. . . . Why?"

The words *dramatic* and *flamboyant* pulled my brain onto a familiar track. "Don't think me obsessed, but meeting Teresa has made me think about Sarah again. What do you remember most about her?"

A muffled snort greeted this question. "Did I hear you right—did you actually say, *Don't think me obsessed?* You forget who you're talking to. I know something about obsession—the note cards are so deep on this table, there's nowhere to eat. But back to *your* fixation—have you ever noticed how one's own preoccupations are so much more imperative than other people's?"

I laughed and considered dropping the subject when Babs added, "I didn't know her very well."

"Maybe not. But you met her several times. What did you first notice about her?"

"I'm assuming you mean her appearance." Babs's voice slid into a maddening measured, analytical tone. "She had regular features, but I wouldn't call her beautiful. Yet she was striking wherever she was. Dramatic, decidedly. I hope you don't think I should write a biography of her next. There's just no material . . ."

"Be serious. No, I was trying to describe her appeal to my therapist. And I realized I just couldn't do it."

"No," Babs mused. "I suppose not. That's because you saw her differently from how most people did."

"What do you mean?"

"Well, I admired her but I never trusted her. When I looked at her I saw a very polished person, but one with a hidden core. Something not quite there."

Babs's tone was dismissive—the vocal equivalent of a shrug. "That—I don't know if I can call emptiness a quality, but that aspect of her—affected my view of everything about her, including her looks."

"You don't think there is something about my behavior that reminds you of her?"

"Oh, God, no." Babs's affectionate giggle hit my ear like the merry tinkle of wind chimes on a breezy spring day. "What a funny little person you are, Amanda. When you hide, you have a perfectly good reason. Sarah seemed to take a strange pleasure in the patina of mystery. Calculated intrigue I'd call it, and that's never been your MO, if you know what I mean."

I wasn't sure if I did but I hesitated to say so. The rustling of papers sifted through the line. I imagined Babs reaching for her special grading pen. "I suppose you're already sick of this subject."

"Ah, no. But there was a time when the mention of Sarah Moore brought a certain weariness. I'll admit that."

I didn't blame her. I'd been relentless in my focus on Sarah and Marta as an undergraduate. I tracked their opinions, read the books they were reading, and second-guessed every comment they'd made in my hearing. It amazed me that Babs hadn't categorized me as a total bore in those days. Or perhaps she did, but given her capacious mind, she merely observed and classified my fixations.

And then Babs spoke unexpectedly. "I was thinking of Marta Conway the other day. You remember for a long time you were trying to find her? I heard that she's head of a performing arts program in Georgia somewhere."

"How is she?"

"That I don't know. I assume well enough to function. This new development of yours—Teresa Baron—she interests me. I hope I meet her."

"Yes." I looked at my watch. "Actually, I'm seeing her this evening for dinner. I'll mention you're coming. You know, Babs, I used to feel you thought me trivial for being so interested in every movement of people like Sarah or Marta. But maybe I was wrong." I stifled a laugh. "Maybe you're not immune to 'dining out,' as you call it yourself."

"Ha." Babs's voice abruptly shifted pitch: "Oh, Lord. Gotta go. Mister has cornered a bird outside. I'll call you in a day or two."

17

I met Teresa in a small bistro downtown on Colorado Street at seven. Although we'd talked on the phone, we hadn't seen each other since dinner at her house. She'd phoned twice, suggesting a movie the first time and an outdoor concert the next. I'd begged off on the pretext of traveling for work. I had accompanied John to Dallas for meetings with a couple of clients, that was true, and I had been busy—I'd begun to paint again—but I also didn't want to see Teresa until I felt I could be with her without immediately thinking of Sarah. Or Marta.

That day hadn't come and so when she called again and invited me to dinner, I'd accepted. Babs's comment that I only hid when I had a reason to resonated. I was hiding from Teresa, or shielding myself from painful feelings. Probably both.

The street was almost deserted when I parked, but the restaurant, a renovated warehouse, was three-quarters full. I arrived first and, taking a table near the back of the long, narrow room, was able to watch everyone who entered. The rough limestone wall next to my table had once formed the building's exterior and lent the room a warm, earthy texture.

Teresa, arriving exactly five minutes past our agreed meeting time, looked lovely in fawn-colored silk trousers and a cream tank top. Her hair looked longer, fuller, than I'd remembered. We hugged somewhat awkwardly.

"I'm free!" she said as she sat down opposite me.

"Oh?" I asked cautiously.

"The play. It's over. Thank God."

I felt relieved to be on familiar ground. "It's a lot of pressure."

"Well, it's that." She picked up a menu, holding it lightly between thumb and forefinger. A slim silver bracelet glinted against one wrist. "The fact is, I couldn't take those people anymore. Remember the man I told you about who played Robert? I started to feel a creeping fury in his manner, as if the role of the betrayed husband was one he carried beyond the world of the play. He began to treat me in a familiar way—as if we really were married. Unhappily so."

In a pivotal scene in *Betrayal* Robert finds out from a stray letter that Emma has been sleeping with his best friend for years. The spouses are locked in the confined space of a hotel room in Italy. Emma lies on the bed and Robert stalks her with his words. Robert's rage, quiet but vicious, spills off the stage into the audience. Will he strike her? Force her to have sex with him? He does neither, he has other ways of retaliating as we see, but the audience holds its collective breath.

Revisited by how much that character had scared me, his anger as unpredictable as my brother's, my own breath stuck like a hard bubble in my chest. "Insinuating men are difficult," I managed.

A server delivered salads to a table nearby and strolled over to ours. He asked about wine. "White or red?" I asked Teresa.

"White."

I sent the waiter off for a bottle of Sonoma-Cutrer. I took a breath and released it. "The actor, wasn't his name Dale? Maybe the role was just soaking too deeply under his skin. I've seen it happen."

Teresa looked at me soberly. "I know you dislike the play."

The wine came and I indicated that Teresa should taste it. After the cork was removed and she'd had a sip, Teresa waved the waiter away with a smile and poured it herself.

I welcomed the excuse to drink. Cool and full, the Chardonnay was buttery on my tongue. "No, that's not true. I'm fascinated by it. But its themes make me anxious."

"Too many memories?" Teresa took a sip, then a long swallow.

Before I could answer, she launched into a slightly different subject. "I've heard from Marta Conway."

"When?" I asked, struck by the oddity of this second mention of Marta in one day.

"Just last week. She phoned on Friday. Unfortunately I wasn't home—she left a message." Teresa lifted up a small brown leather bag, fiddled with the fastener, and then dropped it again. Ex-smoker, but not completely out of the habit, I suspected.

"Is it so unusual to hear from her?" I topped off both our glasses.

"Didn't I tell you? We haven't been in touch since I moved to Austin. It's been five years at least since I've heard a word."

Five years. The length of time since I'd seen Adrian. The old foggy feeling returned as I tried to calculate the whereabouts of all of us in the years since Sarah died. "But Sarah died fourteen years ago."

"Well, yes," Teresa said patiently. "What does that have to do with it?"

I wanted to ask if she and Marta saw Sarah back then, but I feared the question would take me through a door I wasn't ready to enter.

I lifted the hair off the back of my neck; the air was humid and heavy. "I don't know. It seems like yesterday to me. And yet, it's a lifetime ago. I'm forty-two years old." I stared into my wineglass, overcome by an old sadness. "Sarah didn't even live that long."

Teresa took my hand. "I'm upsetting you with all this talk about the past. I don't mean to. I guess what I'm thinking about is survival—I'm so glad Marta is still here. She's had such a tough time. There were times I didn't think she would make it."

I left my hand where it was for a few moments, then gently withdrew it. "You know, your history is a total blank to me. That's really what I'm feeling."

"I suppose I've been cautious . . ." Teresa said haltingly. "It's just that . . . I'm not very good at trusting people." Teresa rushed on before I could respond. "I could tell when you were at my house that you wondered about my friendship with Marta. And your instinct was partly right. We became good friends after she and Sarah broke up."

Teresa looked away and I saw a flash of annoyance in the set of her mouth. "It's not what you think," she said. "We were close but we were never partners."

I nodded, wondering why that information had been so hard to share. "I've been very frank with you about my life," I said, trying not to accuse her of anything.

Teresa looked at me, her hazel eyes flecked with gold, reflecting the wine in front of her. *She's such a chameleon,* I thought, *like a wild forest creature, striking and yet camouflaged in any surrounding.* The image of Narcissus gazing into a pool visited me briefly, yet Teresa didn't seem overly self-conscious. Not nearly as much as I felt myself to be at that moment.

"I'm not sure that's true," she said.

I turned to see the waiter delivering an order to the table next to us. I leaned forward over the table. "Well, I didn't tell you that Sarah came into my life again in a startling way right before her death. But of course you knew. Marta knew, didn't she?"

She nodded. "She knew everything about Sarah. I never understood it. Sarah hurt her more than anyone ever had. Marta hated her, in a way, but couldn't break off contact either. They talked on the phone all the time. They kept in close touch. When Sarah's stepmother died, it was Marta she called."

I sat upright in my chair. "You're telling me that Sarah and Marta were still in each other's lives at the time of Sarah's death."

"Oh yes."

I felt off balance, as if I'd stepped in a slight depression in the earth, expecting a momentary unsteadiness and instead finding myself hurtling downward through a tunnel. So many things I'd assumed about Sarah when we met in Minneapolis—that she was unattached, healthy, and free from her old Minnesota past—seemed untrue.

As I looked at Teresa's face, so open, I made a decision. "I'm surprised. You see, right before Sarah died she and I had begun an affair. To me, it was an affair; to her, it was probably just a fling. If it registered at all." I flushed, surprised after all these years that my statement could still cause fresh pain.

"The thing is . . . I found out that at the same time, she was apparently seeing my brother, Adrian."

Teresa's face registered no recognition. "Adrian?"

"Adrian Ferguson. I think you might have taught with him at Amherst."

Teresa frowned, fine lines framing her lips. "That name sounds familiar. Amherst is a small place. . . . What did Adrian look like as a young man?"

"Very handsome, regular features. Blond." *Like a sculpture,* I thought. *A bronze one, with skin that feels hard and cold.*

"Adrian Ferguson," she repeated and her eyes cleared. "Yes, I remember. Anthropology. We were at a new faculty seminar together. Such ancient history now—that must have been the late seventies." She appraised me. "Your brother, Amanda, is quite a piece of work. Or was then."

I felt relieved for a moment then old family conditioning kicked in. I sat back, feeling suddenly proprietary about Adrian. I might criticize him endlessly, yet I felt a surprising resistance to hearing Teresa's negative view. "Well, yes, he can be difficult."

Teresa turned to watch a man and a woman leaving the table to her right, and when she turned back, she spoke thoughtfully. "I didn't really know him. Just remember him being opinionated, and kind of abrupt. Testy. Not unusual qualities for men in academia. What is odd is the idea of Sarah attaching herself to him. She liked people who were malleable. Not rigid personalities like your brother. You're sure he's not just torturing you?" Her tone was light, but I felt her words were probing just the same.

"I think he fancied you." I told Teresa that I'd noticed Adrian's eyes tracking her on the lawn of the college all those years ago, the way he'd run after her to talk to her.

Teresa looked puzzled. "I don't recall. I don't think he ever called me. It was so long ago. You remember the late seventies. Everyone was after everyone else."

I felt a sudden constriction in my throat. "I guess I need you to tell me that Adrian really meant nothing to you."

"But, Amanda, I just did." Teresa's forehead creased with concern.

"Please understand. His connection to Sarah torments me. Of all the people she could have been with during that time. Well, that it was Adrian . . ."

Teresa's teeth gnawed at the inside of her mouth. "Adrian," she repeated and suddenly looked stricken. "That's very strange."

"Tell me."

"I hesitate to even bring this up. . . . I barely knew your brother. But now I remember Marta speaking of a friend that she was seeing a lot of, and that she and Sarah spent time with him. The friend's name was Adrian, I'm sure of it."

Teresa's right hand rested on the table. She clenched and unclenched her fist. "It's very spooky if it's the same person. If it's your brother, I mean."

Spooky. The word Babs had used the last time we'd talked about Teresa and *Betrayal.*

I felt a slow rise of excitement. "That makes sense. Adrian called me and said he needed to find Marta after Sarah's memorial. I was surprised he knew anything about Marta." I laughed uneasily. "I was surprised to hear from him. He didn't know how to reach her and he seemed almost frantic about it."

"God." Teresa's jaw tightened.

"You remember something?" I feared I sounded too desperate for information.

"I just had a thought. I've gone over and over in my mind what could have driven Sarah to attempt suicide. She had to have been surrounded by a situation that was out of her control and it had to affect something bedrock in her life. And who was more a part of her life than Marta? The two had been through so much. They really loved each other once, I know, even though at times their relationship could appear punitive, especially to Marta . . ."

She stopped. I noticed that the more affected by something Teresa was, the more guarded she became. Now, her face was deathly pale, almost expressionless. "I wondered at the time, by the way Marta talked, if she had resumed her relationship with Sarah. But there was something else . . ."

I waited, not sure what to think. "You weren't around them then, were you?" I blurted out the question I'd long wanted answered.

Teresa shook her head. "I hadn't seen Sarah for years, since we were all in Champaign-Urbana. There is something about this that nags at me."

"Sarah's state of mind," I said, remembering that Sarah had been very frightened when she'd phoned me. Being involved again with Marta might be unsettling, but I didn't think it could lead to the kind of fear I'd heard in Sarah's voice and seen in her face.

Teresa leaned forward. "Don't think I'm crazy. But what if your brother was actually attached to Marta, not Sarah? Wouldn't that explain why Sarah never mentioned her relationship with him to you? Maybe she didn't have one; not the one you imagined at least."

"Marta and Adrian . . ." I spoke quickly, feeling disturbed. "I took

Adrian at face value when he said he was involved with Sarah, but I'm not sure why I did . . ."

"There's some connection among the three of them. I'm almost certain of it. As to chemistry—" Teresa shrugged helplessly. "Look, we don't know what Sarah's feelings really were about Marta. She could be very possessive, even when she was through with someone. She always had to be the one who said good-bye. So, seeing Marta with Adrian might have been very disturbing to her."

I felt light-headed. We needed to order food very soon. "When Sarah phoned me, she was upset. Ragged, not herself at all. That's why I saw her right before she died. I drove down to Chicago to see her because she told me she was afraid of someone and that she wanted me to come."

"Surely not Marta?"

"No, she distinctly said *he*. She said, *I need you to come here before he does*. I've never been able to get those words out of my mind."

"And when you arrived?"

"Adrian was in her house. I was so startled, I ran away."

Teresa looked longingly at her empty glass. "We need more wine. Maybe my hunch is all wrong. Because if your brother was close to Marta, why wouldn't he know where she was after Sarah died?"

I watched Teresa's eyes. "Yes, why? Maybe because Sarah was dead and her death could be seen as suspicious. If so, someone was to blame. It's just too strange that Marta disappeared then. My instinct is that she was afraid, too."

"But of what? Or should I say who? Surely not Adrian?" Teresa looked around the room and leaned forward, her voice very low. "It all gives me the willies."

Adrian's shadow looming on the wall flashed into my mind. But I didn't want to talk about my recent dreams. Not yet. "I don't know what he's capable of," I said slowly. "And that's the truth. Besides, we've spent very little time together since we were young."

Teresa breathed out slowly. "It's a riddle. An excruciating puzzle. It seems impossible for us to reconstruct it now."

I managed to get our waiter's eye and we quickly ordered. Both of us chose the special, grilled salmon. Our bodies craved food but our minds roamed elsewhere, tantalized by details that beckoned like flashing lights over a dark sea. It was impossible to know how far away they were or how near.

"I have a feeling you're right," I said as more wine and a basket of bread appeared in front of us. "As improbable as it seems, there's a history between Marta and Adrian."

"Yes." Teresa's voice had an edge. "You see, I lost touch with Marta after Sarah died. And for about six months before that Marta was very preoccupied. We talked only rarely on the phone. I was trying again to make it as an actress in New York; she had moved to Chicago."

"Why? To be near Sarah?"

"I don't really know. Interesting that Sarah and Adrian were there. She was very busy, she said. She'd only talk a bit about work—she was back teaching—and then ask me what I was doing."

Our salads arrived. I devoured mine, but Teresa only moved the greens around on the plate with her fork. "Then I heard Sarah died." Teresa's eyes, in this light a murky green, looked almost frightened. "Marta wasn't the person who told me. In fact, I didn't hear from Marta again for six years."

"Do you know where she had gone?"

Teresa shook her head. "It was like a chunk of time fell into the ocean. Because the next time I talked to her she refused to talk about it."

"But you've seen her since?"

"No. Only the occasional phone call." Teresa sounded uneasy. She smiled uncertainly when the waiter came and asked if he could remove her plate. "Not yet," she said finally, as he stood hesitant with one arm outstretched.

I waited until the waiter withdrew. "You mean you haven't seen her in fourteen years? Since before Sarah died?"

She looked dazed. "It seems impossible."

I stared at her. "Isn't it odd? I mean, here the two of us are now. We met only a few months ago. And yet because of our connection to Sarah and Marta it's almost as if we've known each other for all these years."

"Time slips in just that way," she said slowly.

I took a deep breath. "Could you possibly ask her about Adrian now?"

Teresa sucked in air, making her cheekbones look overly pronounced, her face strained. "But it's been so long since we've talked. I wouldn't know where to start. And I don't know where she is. Out of the blue, she'll call me. I'm always surprised."

"What if you invite Marta here? And the three of us talked?"

"Oh, sweetheart, it's not that simple." Teresa looked genuinely distressed.

Suddenly exhausted, I slumped in my chair; I realized then how much I was asking of her. "I'm sorry. I don't mean for you to take this on."

"I want to help," she said, lifting her napkin and refolding it before placing it back in her lap. "Amanda. Please believe me. I don't know any more than you do about this. As for contacting Marta . . . well, she's only available when she wants to be. I don't know how to reach her."

I did believe her. For the first time, I felt if I could just be patient, she would come closer, like a plant turning slowly but inexorably toward a source of light. I knew if I pushed, she'd recede. A thought I'd had earlier in the evening intruded. "Isn't it odd that Marta should leave a message now? After being absent for so long?"

Teresa looked tense. "It is odd. And that I haven't actually seen her since Sarah's death now seems even stranger. I wonder why she is being so elusive. And the odd phone call followed by years of silence—I almost feel she's playing a game of cat and mouse." Her lips pressed together in an expression of displeasure. "With me in the role of mouse."

I nodded. "Yes, why leave a message now?"

Teresa's eyes darted around the room and then back to my face. "I have to tell you, this makes me very nervous. I don't like it. And the thought of going back to that awful time of Sarah's death . . ."

"I don't like the thought of that either." I realized, talking with her, that I'd never been out of that time. "I often wish it were possible to leave it all behind. If only it were as simple as moving to another place—you don't have to revisit a house you once lived in, but a vivid time in your past threads through your whole life."

"You'd have to unravel yourself to remove it." She sat back in her chair as if to push away from the subject, but I felt we'd sliced through an invisible membrane of distance. "Adrian." She said his name as if tasting it. "This brother. He haunts you. And frightens you."

"He has a habit of being with people I care about just before they leave life behind." I opened my bag and brought out the small photo of Duncan I carried with me. "This was Duncan. My other brother."

126

Teresa took the photo almost tenderly from me and studied it. "Your twin." Her voice sounded wistful. "That's extraordinary."

"What? The resemblance?"

"Well, that too. But the fact of him." Her eyes grew soft. "That there could be two of you."

Teresa's forehead crumpled. She ducked her head, fumbled in her purse, and brushed a tissue over her eyes. "I'm sorry. I had a sister just a year older who died. I was only six. I remember how my body felt empty after she was gone. I often fantasized that we had been twins."

She clutched the table as the waiter came bearing down on us with more food. "I want to tell you about Sylvie. And I'd like to hear more about Duncan."

I nodded. "I thought you were an only child."

"It's a protection, isn't it? I wondered the same about you."

18

The summer Duncan and I were ten, Adrian used to take us out in a beat-up rowboat on a small lake not far from town. Our dad had painted this sorry craft white several times, but no matter how he primed it, the paint always began to peel soon after. In six months or so its surface returned to a comfortable weather-beaten gray. The boat was clumsy and broad-bottomed, but it didn't leak and there was plenty of room for the three of us.

We didn't have much of a purpose when we went, just to be out on the water. Duncan brought a rod and a line and a few worms, insisting this was his summer to be a fisherman. But the worms usually ended up crisping in the sun in their small pail at the bottom of the boat. The rod, tucked under the middle seat, would trail off the side, limp and forgotten. Duncan was more interested in tracking snapping turtles and the occasional heron that swooped by. Birds especially fascinated him, and I teased him that he was more bird than boy.

"Black-crowned night heron," he'd say as a chunky swirl of gray and white flashed above. "Cool!" Or, "Look at that great blue take off from the bank. On land it's gawky, but in flight"—he turned his arms into graceful wings—"it's like a poem." I mimed Duncan's attempt at flight, and the two of us swayed gently side-to-side, arms gliding out and back.

"If you shut your eyes, you're really flying," I'd say.

"Cut it out, you two, you're messing up my rhythm," Adrian grumped. Adrian was good with the oars; he was able to guide the boat around buoys and stands of weeds, something that eluded me, and so he always sat in the rear, or the stern, as he insisted on calling it. Terms like fore and aft, stern and bow tended to make my brain glaze as much as later in our lives when Adrian tried to teach me to tie those intricate sailor's knots he became so fond of.

Eva had made us ham sandwiches and deviled eggs for lunch. I remember Duncan fed most of the ham in his sandwich to the fish. At one point, he stood up and swung his arms above his head and hurled chunks of meat out over the water. "Come and get it!" he sang.

"Hey, Dunc, stop it!" Adrian's voice was gruff and tense. "You're rocking the boat."

"You need someone to shake you up," Duncan teased, deliberately teetering from one leg to the other to make the wallowing vessel sway more.

Adrian scrambled forward and grabbed Duncan's right ankle. "I said stop it. I mean it."

Duncan squinted at his older brother, his dark eyebrows standing out against his honey-colored hair. He sat back down. "Okay. It's no big deal. It's not life or death."

"Well, it could be." Adrian released Duncan's ankle and peered over the side, straightening into a semi-crouch. "It's deep here. I don't even know how deep. And there're rocks all over the place down there. Remember some kid went diving near here last year and cracked his head?"

"Craig Johnson?" Duncan looked sad. "He was in my class."

"Then listen up. Keep your center of gravity down. See the sides of the boat? If you're going to squirm around, keep the bulk of your body weight below. Besides, you don't have very good sea legs."

Duncan's head was round, his cheeks plump. As Adrian's lean face loomed over him, he looked small and soft, almost babyish next to his brother. Duncan pointed at Adrian. "You're standing up now. And you're heavy. If you lose your balance, we'd be swamped in a minute."

"Yeah, but I won't." Annoyed, Adrian retreated and settled back down in the stern.

"So, if you had to choose," Duncan said unexpectedly, "you know, if the boat turned over and you could only go after one of us, who would you save, me or Amanda?"

I'd been ignoring them, finishing my lunch and trying to read a mystery I'd found at the library, a story of two boys searching for a lost will in their grandmother's house. But Duncan's tone alerted me and I looked up with interest. "Yeah, which one of us would you save, Adrian?"

Adrian flushed. "That's a stupid question."

"Is it?" I closed my book. "It seems pretty important to me."

Adrian licked his lips; they looked chapped. He brushed a fly away from his hair and I noticed he had an angry cut on his wrist. His eyes darted from me to Duncan and then away; he looked panicked.

Duncan stared at him curiously. "What's the matter—are you seeing double?" He laughed, his high voice trilling over the water and startling a group of turtles sunning on a flat rock into a sudden dive.

Duncan used to tease Adrian about not being able to see straight when he looked at the two of us. "Which one is the real twin?" Duncan would ask him.

"I wouldn't be able to choose," Adrian said and leaned forward, applying his shoulders to the oars.

"Oh, great, you'd let us both drown," I said.

Adrian shook his head. His hairline beaded with sweat as he turned the boat around. I wondered why he seemed to take Duncan's scenario seriously.

"I don't know how to save anyone," he said, his voice morose.

"What do you mean?" Duncan asked.

But Adrian just pursed his lips, lowered his head, and pulled hard, first with one arm and then the other. He was only fifteen, but already I could see his biceps bunching under the skin, the play of tendon and muscle around his shoulder joint.

I must have looked surprised or disappointed because after a few minutes Duncan said, "Don't worry, Manda. I'll save you."

———

At my next session, I related this story to Helen. "Maybe Adrian had a premonition that day on the water."

"But Duncan didn't drown," she said reasonably. "Didn't you say it was the frigid water that got him? It was his heart."

"That's what our mother said."

Helen leaned forward in her chair, her wrists dangling between her knees. She was large-boned but thin, and her hands were large. Competent hands, I always thought, the kind that knew how to calm a kitten or a child, change a tire, plant a row of corn.

"Amanda?"

"I'm here. Just thinking about Adrian and Eva and Duncan."

Helen cleared her throat. "What was your mother doing down by the frozen pond the day Duncan died? You've never said."

I shivered. "That's just what I was thinking about. I don't know. I've never known. Duncan and Adrian went out skating alone. But, somehow, when Duncan was taken out of the water, Eva was there. She helped Adrian carry Duncan home. And she was wet and covered with dirt."

Helen's tone was gentle but persistent. "You never asked her?"

I felt a sudden fear. "I did. But she never talked about that day."

"But you wanted to?"

"Oh, yes." An old hunger twisted my insides. "I would give almost anything to know what happened to Duncan." I almost said, *my Duncan*. "But Eva said it upset her too much to talk about it. *Losing him almost killed me,* she'd say, or, *It was the worst day of my life.*"

"But it was the worst day of many people's lives—your father's, Adrian's, and, of course, yours."

Tears flooded my eyes; I willed them back. "You don't know my mother. What happens to her is always worse than what happens to other people. She can't help herself."

Helen nodded. "And that's why you call her Eva and not Mother or Mom?"

"I don't know."

"Maybe she doesn't feel like a mother to you in the way we tend to think—as a parent who nurtures us. When you say, 'She can't help herself,' it makes me think you don't feel she takes responsibility for her actions, which is a job we assign to parents. So, maybe to you she feels like something or someone else."

"We all tried to make her feel better afterward."

"Your father, too?"

"He worked a lot then. I . . . don't remember seeing very much of him. But I know the little time he had he spent with Eva. She'd shut herself in their room and he'd try to comfort her. She was so upset she'd let the boys go out on the ice without her. She'd wring her hands and say the same things over and over again. I heard her call out for Duncan in her sleep."

Saying these words brought back the misery of that time, as if I'd unleashed an echo in a cave. Once vocalized, my words reverberated on and on. "Nothing seemed to bring her out of it."

"I'm sure she was devastated." Helen's voice was firm. "But she was the adult. She wasn't the only one who was grieving. It was her job to help you come to terms with losing Duncan."

"It's hard to talk about 'jobs' when someone is crazy with grief," I muttered. It was unlike Helen to sound so judgmental.

"Do you mean her or you?"

I thought a moment. "Maybe we all were crazy. And that was the problem."

"You weren't crazy, Amanda. You made it through."

"Which parts of me made it, though?" I felt my face crack in a strained smile. I could hardly allow myself to believe Helen, so fragile was my claim to survival—without Duncan—in my own mind. "I'm not sure my mother made it at all. Sometimes I think she's trapped in that time. Funny, isn't it? She didn't seem really there when it happened and yet now that's where she lives."

I exhaled, emptying my lungs fully, then breathed in the quiet of Helen's office. Pillows were stacked against the walls, a yellow rose stood on the table, the light was soothing. Everything about the room smothered sound and harsh angles. Yet the past huffed at the door and at the walls, swirling up from the floor and rushing through the air like a gale; I felt its raw force. "My mother wasn't there," I said simply.

Helen sighed. "Yes. Sometimes we have nothing left over for others. I'm sorry about your mother's pain. But your mother isn't my client. You are. The fact is you were a child and you had nowhere to turn."

I knew Helen had two children. For a moment, and not for the first time, I envied them.

I shook my head. "I'm forty-two years old. I can't change her. I can't change the past. I have to accept it."

Helen tilted her head to one side. The skin on her neck creased; she suddenly looked older. Her voice was low and sad. "That doesn't mean you don't wish for things to be different." Helen watched me for a few moments. "Can I sit beside you?"

"Yes," I said.

Helen perched on the arm of my chair and put her arm around my shoulders. She felt solid and safe. "You know," she said, "there were many times I wanted another mother than the one I had, too. Mine was very ill most of the time when I was growing up. She couldn't sleep during the night, and was rarely alert during the day. We were under orders not to disturb her."

I imagined Helen's mother wandering their house at night. Did her footsteps wake—or scare—her family? Adrian's wiry body prowling the halls and stopping at the door to my room popped into my mind. I shook my head, willing the image to fade, as I focused on Helen. I imagined her as a child sitting by herself in a large room with white walls. There were no shadows, and no place to hide.

"It's very lonely," she said, "when your mother isn't really there. It's like a deep hole at the center. It will never be filled up, no matter how rich our lives."

I wanted to say something but the tears were coming too fast. The two of us sat together, propping each other up, for it seemed a long time. Then, Helen handed me a tissue and went back to her chair.

"My mother spent her days in her dark bedroom," Helen said quietly, her voice distant, almost as if she were reporting on someone she didn't know well.

I wanted to ask, *How did you spend your days?* But the paleness of her face, turned inward and far away, stopped me.

Helen's eyes glistened. She focused on me once more. "What made you feel better during that time?"

I turned toward the one window in the room; the wood blinds were slanted downward only slightly and I noticed the dark shape of clouds reflected in the pond between Helen's building and the next one. Drops splashed against the window and the wind churned the trees. A leaf skidded across the water and plastered itself against the rim of the concrete enclosure.

"I suppose this is strange, but it was Duncan. He helped me. I thought of him all the time. I like to think he was thinking of me too."

19

Babs arrived in the intense heat of mid-June. The pavement shimmered with it, the car seethed in it, and when I picked my friend up, she basked in it. "Oh, I love the way the sun soaks into my back here." Her broad face looked hot and happy.

"I hope it soaks into you and leaves the rest of us cooler." I tossed Babs's luggage into the backseat and we took off. "You look like life is treating you well."

Babs's brown hair was shorter; instead of bunched untidily on the nape of her neck, it grazed her shoulders and shone with highlights I'd never noticed before. She turned to the backseat, tucked her purse against the side of her suitcase, and then looked forward, her face tranquil. "I've met someone."

I was amazed. In all the years I'd known her, Babs had been solitary. She had dated, but I'd never known her to partner with anyone. Of course, I didn't know everything about Babs. She was fully capable of living several quiet lives at once. "Tell me."

"His name is Dan," she said, as if that one syllable explained everything.

"Why didn't you bring him?"

Babs drew her head away from me like a startled bird. "Oh, I don't think we're at the meeting friends stage yet."

I laughed. "You mean you're afraid of what he might think when he meets me?"

"No, you goose. I mean what I said. Things are too new." She peered out the window. "This place is growing. And sprawling."

"Yeah, I know. Look, I'm so glad you're here."

"Me too." Babs's tone shifted into a mysterious register. "I brought something for us." She reached into the back and patted her briefcase. The creased brown leather had a warm patina.

Babs noted my gaze. "No, it's not the same one I've had since we met. It's getting harder to hunt down this model. Some people obsess about shoes. For me it's the perfect case—you know, roomy and solid. It feels like an extension of my arm. Dan says this one matches my eyes." She settled back into her seat and smiled.

When we got to my house, I showed Babs her bedroom, a small L-shaped room off the back deck. I'd bought the house just under a year ago, and Babs hadn't seen it before. Like a teenager, she dropped her bags inside the door and immediately tested the bed, flopping on the spread. I noticed she was wearing bright red sneakers. Color had entered Babs's life—in her shoes as well as her hair. I decided that Dan was good for her.

"Nice," she said. "You know, this house isn't as tiny as you said."

"In Austin, this is called a bungalow. In St. Cloud it would rent out as a guest cottage, or possibly an office." I pointed to the small backyard, other houses clearly visible beyond the cedar fence. "This neighborhood was built after World War II—standard GI housing, two bedrooms, one bath, and a tiny formal dining room. The first thing I did was add a second bath. And a study."

Babs nodded. "I like it. You know me, cozy is best."

"How can you say that when the places you've lived in are all spread out, more like rabbit warrens or a maze? Rooms leading into rooms. Passages going every which way, like your thoughts."

My friend frowned and tapped her foot. "Thoughts are one thing—and mine explore *possibilities*, by the way, not rushing 'every which way.' But in my life I like to think I have some order. Although you have a point— too many square angles make me anxious."

I threw up my hands. "The amazing thing is you can always find your way around. And your mind, unlike most people's, has a category for everything."

"Exactly. Hence the rabbit warren. I need lots of odd spaces, dim corners, and a hidden cupboard or two for filing. But look, we have more important things to do." She seized her briefcase and hefted it off the floor. "Let's go to the table. Speaking of files, I have some you'll like."

I brought iced tea in frosted glasses to my dining room table and sat down while Babs unpacked her case. She did indeed have files, and also a couple of old yearbooks.

"Okay, let's look at the Marta question first." Still standing, she opened a manila-colored envelope and spread several photos out in a star pattern. "I found these in a box of stuff from St. Cloud that I never had the energy to go through. So I kept moving it from place to place. Remember, I took that photography class when you were working on *Betrayal?* Well, when I'd go to rehearsals, I'd bring the camera along."

Several of the photos had been taken on breaks at rehearsals—people milling around onstage, scripts flung on set pieces or the deeply scarred floor to be picked up later. I noticed as I always did how dusty and decrepit most stages looked without the magic of stage lights.

Babs tapped a fingernail on a picture of two women smoking in the back of the theater, in the last row.

"Sarah and Marta," I said. The two brunette heads were fairly close together as they slouched in their seats. Both of them were laughing.

"Yes. But do you notice anything odd?"

I looked more closely at the print, which was just slightly out of focus. Both women were wearing jeans and sweatshirts and white tennis shoes, both were smoking similar cigarettes.

"They're dressed alike, I guess," I said, "but that doesn't mean anything. Everyone wore clothes like that to rehearsal." I put on my reading glasses and moved my face closer to the photo. "It's not the greatest picture."

Babs plopped another one next to it, same two people, but clearer and closer. I could see their teeth and hair gleaming in the light from the flash.

"Yeah. They're dressed alike. And?" Babs prodded. She was being patient, but I felt the pressure of her mind speeding past me.

"Your students must be nervous wrecks keeping up with your expectations. I give—I don't think I have the right answer. What is it?"

"Simple. Tell me which one is Marta, which one is Sarah."

"What?"

"Elementary, my dear Watson, you're thinking? Fine. So which is which?"

I cleared my throat. "They must have gone to the same hairdresser the day before or something." It was eerie: both women were the same height; both had close-cropped brown hair, pale skin, and fine features. I'd known this of course, but in the flat perspective of the photograph, their physical resemblance seemed more obvious. I pointed to the figure on the left whose wrist seemed unnaturally stiff as she held her cigarette. "That's Sarah. She always had kind of locked wrists. Don't ask me why I noticed that."

Babs flipped the photo over. Marked on the back was the date—November 1, 1979, and the identification—Marta Conway (left) with Sarah Moore (right).

Babs made a flat buzzer noise. "Wrong."

"Let me see the other photo." I grabbed the picture less in focus. They were both smoking short, unfiltered cigarettes. "So they're both smoking Sarah's Camels. Marta usually smoked filtered cigarettes but that's no help here. I don't get this—it must be because they're laughing. Or poor resolution on these prints. I don't remember them looking this much alike."

Babs plopped in a chair and thrust out her sneakered feet. "But you know, I do. I remember coming out of the 7-Eleven on Washington one afternoon in the winter and Sarah's white Honda pulled in beside me. She had on a ski cap, kind of perched back on her head. I waved but she didn't see me. But when she got out of the car, she took off the cap and shook out her hair. It wasn't Sarah, it was Marta."

"How can you be sure when you think they looked so similar?"

"I noticed Marta's ring when she locked the car. Remember she wore that huge opal ring on the middle finger of her right hand? I remember seeing it when you invited me to your acting class to watch your final projects." Babs tapped her front teeth with her index finger. I noticed she wore no rings on either hand.

"Okay, but Sarah could have been wearing Marta's opal ring. Just playing devil's advocate," I added.

"Exactly." Babs's pecan-colored eyes were hooded. She looked half-asleep.

Opposite her, I crossed my legs carefully under the table, thinking about what consummate performers both of these women had been. After all, each of us gave off many cues of physical mannerisms, voice, and aura that separately weren't so remarkable, but that in accumulation made us recognizable as unique beings. If these cues were manipulated, the boundaries of personhood were blurred. "You're making me nervous."

She nodded. "The point is they could look alike, very alike. It's like all those old movies. What was the one with Bette Davis? *Dead Ringer*. The twin sisters no one could tell apart. Both played by Davis, of course."

"Which one is the real twin?" I said.

"Hmm?"

"Oh, just something Duncan used to say to torment Adrian, as if our older brother was too obtuse to know who he was talking to."

Babs tipped her glass to her lips and drank a third of her iced tea. When she set the glass down, finger marks were clearly visible on the sweating glass until the beads of moisture gradually obliterated them. "Or maybe you looked that much alike. In certain situations."

"What kind of situations?"

"Oh, maybe in the water, swimming? Or from a distance? Wearing a hat? There are lots of possibilities."

I felt a stubborn resistance. "I don't think so. But you're forgetting something—Sarah's voice. It was like no one else's."

Babs's lips stretched in a slow smile. "Like almost no one else's. Have you forgotten those after-production parties you dragged me to?"

Confused, I shook my head. "What do you mean?"

"Come on. Who had the most uncanny Sarah Moore imitation you've ever heard?"

My heart sank. "Marta, of course." Everyone else would try, but no one was able to produce Sarah's low, peculiarly accented cadences, part Southern, part elocutionary. No one but Marta Conway. "I'd forgotten what a great mimic she was."

"A dead ringer. For Sarah Moore, anyway."

My mind floated back to Duncan, what he must have looked like in the water the day Adrian found him. I didn't like to think he would have looked like me at all.

"What are you thinking about?" Babs asked.

"Oh, nothing. I told you Adrian called me looking for Marta shortly after Sarah died."

"He thought he was looking for Marta," Babs said, her voice soft.

I laughed uneasily. "It's only in movies that they identify the wrong person. Sarah died. It was her they found in her bed."

Babs touched the photos again, lined up their edges against the edge of the table. "I'm sure you're right. It's not so much that Sarah's death is in question. It's that what if Sarah and Marta played games with Adrian? Maybe he didn't know them very well after all."

"Teresa said Marta mentioned spending time with Sarah and someone named Adrian at about that time." My voice sounded slow and stupid. "But I don't get it. Why would they play games with Adrian about who they were?"

Babs slipped the pictures back into her envelope and secured its metal fastener. She folded her arms and tilted her head to one side. "I honestly don't know. Maybe because they could?"

20

I traveled several times to Chicago after Sarah died, drawn to explore the last place she had lived. The mystery of what had happened to her after I saw her on that rainy night for the last time kept me going back.

There was also the question of Adrian. I craved details about Adrian's relationship with Sarah and any scattered scraps I could collect about his life in general at that time. But when I called his house three weeks after I'd talked to him on my birthday, his phone had been disconnected. A bit later I got a card from him: *Pulled up stakes*, it said. *On a long trip. New address coming when I land.* Soon after, I found out from my mother that Adrian's lecturer position at Chicago had been a three-year contract, one he didn't try to renew. Adrian, like Marta, made contact only on his own terms.

A few of Sarah's colleagues at the theater she'd worked in talked to me on the first trip I made after her death. But I didn't learn very much from those interviews. The managing director who had discovered Sarah's body, Susan Rule, didn't want to see me. But I haunted the administrative offices of her company until one afternoon I found her drinking coffee alone after her secretary had left. My appearance in her doorway appeared to startle her because she sloshed coffee on her desk and all over the spreading piles of paper that covered it. She made no move to blot the liquid, just pushed that particular stack farther back on the desk.

"I have nothing to say," she said immediately when I told her my name. "I told you that when you called." She looked to be in her late thirties; a single vertical furrow split the skin of her forehead as she turned toward me.

"I'm sorry to be a pest." I stood expectantly until she motioned me to a chair.

"I don't think you are sorry." She wore half-frame glasses in bright green plastic. She took them off. Like every other managing director I'd ever seen, she looked weary, her eyes slightly inflamed, the lids papery.

"Sarah was a close friend," I told her.

"Well, then you knew her better than I did. I should be interviewing you." She didn't crack a smile. "I'm late getting out of here. I really can't talk."

"I just want to ask one question . . ." At her impatient but grudging nod, I continued. "Sarah often collaborated with an acting teacher, a specialist in voice. Her name was Marta Conway. I'm curious whether they worked together on anything here." I sat forward in my chair, feet planted, ready to leave. I expected a blank look or a shrug.

But Susan Rule put her glasses back on. She looked at me closely. "As a matter of fact, Sarah was thinking about hiring her."

"Oh?"

"Dr. Moore hadn't been feeling well. She was in the middle of preproduction on a new play. She mentioned that Conway was interested in guest directing."

"You met her then? Conway?"

Susan pulled her long blonde hair off her neck and twisted it to one side. "Yes, I did."

Her tone was so careful that I was uncertain how to proceed. "Um, she was terrific with actors when I knew her."

She nodded. "That's what Sarah said." She cleared her throat and reached for her calendar. "Actually, I'd worked with Marta Conway before."

"Ah."

She took off her glasses and wiped them. "Great sense of humor."

"Oh. I think so too. And very intuitive—she could get things from actors no one else could."

"That's true," she said, as if this was an insight that had never occurred to her. "I was an actor when I worked with her." She thought a moment and then added, it seemed grudgingly: "A little theater in Wisconsin. Stevens Point—you might know it. She had a way of getting us out of our heads. Completely." A faint smile. "I think it scared me. I quit acting after that."

I digested this. "For some people, being onstage is addictive. You know, they want to see how much further they can go."

She nodded. "That's how I knew acting really wasn't for me." She looked at her watch. "Look, I have a rehearsal in an hour, and I need to eat first."

It was clear her remark wasn't an invitation to dinner. "I appreciate your time. If you don't mind my asking . . . after Sarah died, did you hire Marta?"

"We were about to sign a contract. But you know, it never happened."

I tried to look only mildly interested, even though inside I almost vibrated with curiosity. "Oh?" I managed.

"The day after Sarah died, I walked into her office. Marta was sitting in the chair reading a script. She gave me quite a start." Susan reached compulsively for a cigarette from a pack by the phone and turned it over and over in her hands. "The angle of her neck, the way she sat there—composed and yet relaxed." Susan laughed shakily. "It was eerie. I thought for a moment it was Sarah."

I didn't say anything, just picked up my bag from the floor and held on to it, slight anchor though it was.

Susan tapped the cigarette against her desk, suddenly forthcoming. "I never saw her again after that. It was so odd—Conway just disappeared. I phoned her several times but her number was apparently disconnected." She shook her head, her hair falling around her shoulders in a fine spray. "There was so much turmoil when Sarah died. By the time my head was above water again and I realized what a bind we were in, it was too late." She shrugged tensely. "We muddled through."

"It is odd." I hadn't smoked for years, but I had to forcibly keep my hands from snatching the cigarette from Susan's hand. I braced myself. There was something I had to know. "The play Conway was going to direct. It wasn't by any chance Harold Pinter's *Betrayal*, was it?"

"No," she said very quickly. "But funny you should ask."

I kept my eyes glued to the cigarette, now beginning to look a bit frayed at the filter tip.

"Sarah had suggested it for the next year's season," she volunteered. "She said she and Marta were going to work on a new production of it together."

I nodded. "So, it's on the season still?"

"If we can find a director. Myself, I'm not that fond of it. Or of Pinter either."

A tiny voice inside me clamored to volunteer. But a much cannier part, the intuitive mind that watched my back, squelched that impulse. "I'm sure you'll find someone" is all I said.

"I don't suppose you know where Marta Conway is?" She looked at me intently.

"No . . . no. I was hoping you knew."

Susan looked sad. "Sarah left a few things for her. I thought if you knew how to locate Dr. Conway, I'd give them to you."

I opened my mouth to amend my words. My fingers itched to see the items. I frantically tried to think of a reason I could legitimately claim them. I hesitated just a moment too long, because she said, "I suppose I should wait a bit longer, to see if she comes back."

I stood up and backed toward the door, conscious of a missed opportunity. "If I hear, I'll let you know." I retraced my steps, remembering to offer my hand.

"All right." Susan rose and stepped toward me. A tired woman, I thought, overworked and not too happy.

We shook hands and I left.

———

I told Teresa and Babs that story when the three of us had drinks on my back deck the second night after Babs's arrival. It was a hot, overcast evening, one of those frequent summer days in Central Texas when the heavy air signaled a storm but the relief of rain never arrived. The unceasing racket of cicadas, as much a part of summer in Austin as the blooming crape myrtles, made the heat feel more intense.

"I'm sure Susan was fooled by that profile—so eerily like Sarah's," I said.

"Marta was such a chameleon," Teresa said, lifting her arms to catch a whisper of breeze. She wore a short green tee and khaki crop pants. Even Babs had broken down and put on shorts, a cargo model with enough pockets for a carpenter to frame a small house.

"That's why she was such a good actor," I said.

"*Was?*" Babs said. "I assumed this woman is very much with us."

Teresa smiled. "Yes, it's just that neither of us has seen her in so long."

"But you've talked with her?" Babs persisted. She lifted her glass. "Do you have any more of these lovely margaritas?"

"Is this an interrogation?" I asked mildly when I returned from inside with the pitcher and a plate piled with limes and coarse salt. I did think Babs had missed her calling as a defense attorney or maybe a private investigator.

Babs frowned. "I suppose in a way it is. The two of you are looking for answers. You're the experts on Marta and Sarah. Who knows, maybe you know just enough details to confuse yourselves. I'm just trying to ask questions that might reveal things you haven't thought of. Clear the muddy path, so to speak."

Babs had become her maddeningly cerebral self again. I opened my mouth to say so but before I could utter a word, Teresa interrupted me.

"Exactly," Teresa said. "And we're grateful to you, believe me." She turned toward Babs, who grinned like the child I imagined she once was—the one who was always the smartest kid in the room.

"But you asked about talking to her. Yes, I have, but I haven't *seen* her since Sarah died."

Babs, who had been rocking in a spring chair, grew still. "That is significant," she said.

The three of us had already scrutinized Babs's photos and pored over some yearbook pages she'd earmarked of faculty productions in St. Cloud. "The voice thing," I said.

"Not just that. You recall what Susan Rule told you about the physical similarities." Babs had resumed rocking, her large feet in brown Birkenstocks planted squarely in front of her. The pumping of her feet and the steady tapping of her fingers on the chair arms belied the absolute calm of her voice.

"Is this when the anxious detectives call for an exhumation of the body?" Teresa asked nervously. Her face was pale, her lips chapped and slightly parted.

"I don't know." I turned to Babs. "You don't think it's possible, do you?"

"What?"

"Oh, the dead ringer thing. Just reassure me—Sarah did die, didn't she?"

Babs gnawed on the salt of her margarita glass. "Jesus, I hope so. I doubt there was an autopsy, though. Didn't this Susan person find the body initially? And she didn't raise your antennae, did she?"

"You mean is she a nutcase?" I shrugged helplessly. "I imagine she acted in good faith. But, she wouldn't have been the person to identify the body, I don't imagine. Sarah was an only child, but her father was still alive. And her stepmother." I turned to Teresa. "Who do you think would have been the next in line as a witness?"

Teresa spoke slowly. "I don't know. Sarah's father was very ill when Sarah died, and died soon after. Marta, possibly? They had many legal entanglements. She may have even been listed as executor of Sarah's estate."

The moisture gathering on the back of my neck felt suddenly intolerable. I swiped at it with a tissue from my pocket and closed my fist around the soggy fibers.

"But surely Susan knew who she had found?" Babs frowned. "Why would she muddy the waters?"

Teresa sat forward in the Adirondack chair. "I can't imagine."

"Unless Susan assumed she'd found Sarah, but she was mistaken." Improbably, Babs had an almost enchanted smile on her face. "Here's the thing. The mere fact that we're sitting here thinking about this tells me it's possible. There are some very eerie ways in which Marta Conway and Sarah Moore are the same person."

I balked at this. "Hardly . . ."

Babs held up a firm hand. "Yes, I know that for you Sarah walked on water and Marta merely drank it. But how many other people have been confused by them? We talked about what a great mimic Marta was. What about Sarah? Could she impersonate Marta?"

A memory crept across a dim recess of my consciousness and came into view. A few days before I graduated, I walked into Marta's office to turn in a take-home exam. "Just leave it in the basket," Marta said with characteristic impatience. Shoulders hunched, she was crouched by the bookcase in the corner by the window, searching through a pile of papers. Then she turned. "Oh, it's you," Sarah said with a smile, her voice relaxing. "I thought it was the same student who's phoned twice today."

I turned to Babs and said reluctantly, "I remember them laughing at parties about how they could fool their families on the phone, even their mothers. A fact that impressed me at the time. They made jokes about how easy it was for one or the other to cover for the other—canceling a meeting with the department chair for instance—and how no one had a clue."

Teresa unwound her arms from where they tensely hugged her body. "I didn't know Sarah well," she said slowly. "Only Marta. Who had— has—a kind of perverse satisfaction in playing roles. Throwing a temper tantrum out of nowhere just to see how people would react, pretending to be devastated about something she didn't give a damn about. I've seen gifted comedians do this. It's some kind of protective covering."

"A magic cloak," Babs offered. "It keeps her invisible."

"Exactly," Teresa nodded. "She liked to keep people guessing. I don't know if Sarah was that way too."

Babs jumped in: "I don't know about Sarah. But this reminds me of that case Clarence Darrow defended in Chicago in the twenties. You know, Leopold and Loeb. Those two kids who committed the perfect crime, they thought. They were so smart, so talented. They could do anything. It made them overreach. The thrill was in the invention. The consequences never seemed to happen, and so, eventually, they lost sight that there might be any. If you lose that check on reality, it ceases to matter." Babs shook her head. "I don't know. I'm probably reaching, myself."

I refilled everyone's glasses. The cedar elm trees rustled as the birds began to burrow into their inner branches toward dusk. The sound of the cicadas grew more insistent. Teresa picked up one of the yearbooks Babs had brought and paged through it. Her hands, markedly petite at the end of her long, slender arms, hesitated on one page—a theater department faculty picture on the stage of the Mansfield just after the space had been renovated. The wood floor gleamed, its soft maple finish not yet scuffed and scarred from scores of shuffling feet as their owners scrambled for lines. The refurbished floor told me this photograph was at least a year older than the ones Babs and I had puzzled over earlier.

"One thing is clear," Teresa said, tapping her index finger at the top of the page, "no matter how much the two women looked alike or sounded the same—there were two of them."

146

"There were." Babs nodded. "And now? One. Or," she turned to me with an enigmatic smile, "still two?"

I felt the space around my heart contract. "What do you mean?"

"Well, Sarah created acolytes, didn't she? Young women who cut their hair like hers, tried to enunciate vowels as she did, gestured like her . . . like your friend Ellen."

"Ye-es," I agreed reluctantly. "I hope you're not putting me in that category."

Teresa laughed, but Babs just said, "Don't be such a goose. We aren't talking about you." Her lips settled into an indulgent smile. "Just this once."

"Are you saying someone like Ellen is impersonating Sarah? Or died and was taken for Sarah while Sarah is off somewhere with Marta?"

"And with Adrian. Don't forget about him." Babs shook her head. "But the idea that Sarah could be alive is just a fantasy, isn't it? The Chicago police aren't that gullible."

Teresa stared at Babs, her hazel eyes a golden brown in the early evening light. "No, they probably aren't. But doesn't it depend—again—on who was notified of the death? Who provided the dental records, the identifying scars, and so forth?"

"Sarah and Marta went to the same dentist," I said, aware of a stubborn note in my voice. "And wore each other's clothes."

"But not each other's skin," Babs said, an odd and macabre remark, I thought.

"I wonder," Teresa said, staring down at the rough cedar deck, her hands clutching each other in her lap.

———

Babs went to bed early. As I saw Teresa to the door, I kissed her on the cheek and impulsively said, "Why don't you stay."

Teresa put her arms around me and hugged me tightly. Then she pulled away and smoothed the hair away from my forehead. "I feel self-conscious."

"About me?"

"No, about your friend being here. Babs. She's very protective of you."

She smiled. "A she-lion. And you're her cub. Lucky you. She's a very reassuring person but I confess I'd have trouble forgetting she's here, somewhere in the house. Maybe you should come to my place."

I hesitated and she said, "You told me Babs leaves Saturday. Let's get together that evening." Then she brushed her lips against my cheek. "I think that would be best."

Saturday was only three days away. "All right."

Teresa walked to her car, backed out of the drive, and as her headlights swept in an arc over my street, I felt lighter and more hopeful than I had in a long time.

21

Two days later, in a session with Helen, the lightness had receded and I reverted to obsessing about the conversation we'd had on my deck. "I can't stop thinking about the idea of Marta and Sarah as two parts of the same person. What if the woman who greeted me in Chicago the evening Adrian was there wasn't Sarah at all? What if it was Marta? That would explain why she seemed not to know why I was there."

"Yes, but how would that explain the tension and fear you saw in Sarah? If the person you saw was Marta, why wouldn't she have simply been dismissive? But not necessarily under strain at all."

"Don't you see? It all has to do with Adrian. If Marta was delivering a command performance, trying to get rid of me, and Adrian was watching—always a pressure, believe me—that would explain it. I hardly recognized Sarah that night." My hands clenched around the arms of the chair I sat in.

"All right," Helen said, her voice deepening. "Let's look at this. There's no way to know exactly what happened. Not with the amount of information you have."

I pushed my hand deep into the hair around my forehead and tugged. "Everything I thought I knew is called into question. The horrible rejection I felt from Sarah that night. The shock of seeing Adrian standing behind her. Nothing was as it seemed. And then my grief about Sarah. I've relived it all many times."

"Of course. The experience was traumatizing for you. Loss brings back other losses. But despite Adrian's presence, or whatever really happened between him and Sarah, or Sarah and Marta . . . your feelings for Sarah were real. Are real." Helen put her notebook aside on the arm of her chair and leaned forward. "Is it the uncertainty about what happened to Sarah that is so disturbing, or is it your brother?"

I nodded slowly. "Adrian. I can't get the image of him standing behind Sarah out of my mind."

Helen nodded. "You view him as a predator. So much of your experience with him reinforces that. He even haunts your dreams."

"I can't get past it. He manages to possess everything I've ever wanted," I said sadly.

"Duncan too?" Helen asked.

"Yes, of course Duncan!" My voice sounded harsh in the quiet room. "He was the reason Duncan died, wasn't he?"

"But you don't know for sure," Helen persisted.

"No, not for sure. We know precious little in life that is 'for sure.' What matters is how we feel about what happens to us. You've taught me that. And I feel that Adrian has claimed so much of what is important to me— my mother's attention, Duncan, Sarah. My poor father's sanity."

Helen didn't say anything right away when I finished. "When did you last talk to Adrian?" she finally asked.

"I don't know," I said without thinking. But of course I knew.

When Eva turned seventy, five years earlier, Adrian and I went to Minnesota and threw a party for her. She was living in a graduated living community then, but she was still healthy, her memory still largely intact. Most of her friends still lived nearby, she went out to dinner once or twice a week, took the occasional trip. She volunteered at the local library, arranging programs in the children's section. My mother loved children in her older age, reading to them, tying their shoes.

Adrian and I held the party in the clubroom at the complex where Eva lived. We'd hired a band that played the old swoony forties tunes she loved, and at least forty people were there. Candles on the tables cast a flattering light on weathered skin. The room, festooned with balloons and banners, reminded me of the kind of place where we went to dances in high school, plain and squarish, animated only by the twirling couples on the dance floor. In this case, the dancers had wrinkles and moved less smoothly, but they all wore bright colors and the ripples of talk and laughter made the air more festive than those teen dances of my memory. Back then everyone aimed at a studied cool, anything to mask the agony of trying to pass as someone who didn't care whether or not she was chosen, or the misery of disguising that he really didn't know how to dance.

The band was playing a medley of Andrews Sisters' numbers when Adrian asked Eva to dance. She curtsied in front of him and happily let him lead her onto the floor. Adrian had on black slacks and a soft camel hair sport coat. Eva wore an electric-blue dress and high heels. My mother's legs were still good, the calves toned and shapely.

They quickly claimed the floor with a respectable jitterbug. Adrian often appeared stiff and removed, but as he danced with Eva his spine seemed to loosen and his feet to find a happy slide. He reached an arm high in the air, making a wide arc for Eva to twirl into. I found myself lulled by their ease. They grinned at each other as the music ended, and Eva stepped to one side and did a little bow. Two of her friends watching from the floor clapped and cheered.

They came back to our table flushed and pleased with themselves. Adrian went to the bar and came back with two gin and tonics. My glass was empty. Adrian lowered the drinks onto the table and moved to sit before he noticed. He rose and asked me what he could get me.

"Glenlivet, if they have it. And a rock or two."

While Adrian was gone, Eva leaned in to me and said, "You know, one of my friends said to me, *You and Adrian look almost the same age.*" Eva winked at me. "That's always happening to us. People wonder if we're a couple."

I recoiled from her. "Really?" I couldn't hide the disbelief in my voice. Even though Eva was one of those people who tended to look younger than she was—she'd always been vain about that—and Adrian at forty-three was sufficiently underweight and intense-looking to tack on a few years if one didn't look closely, I couldn't imagine anyone not seeing them as a generation apart.

Eva ignored me. She flashed a wistful smile at Adrian as he resumed his seat and slid my drink in front of me.

"Thank you," I said.

He nodded and then stood as Eva got up and excused herself to go to the powder room as she still called it.

When he sat back down, he pronounced that the music "wasn't bad" and then lapsed into silence. He frowned and studied his drink.

After Eva was completely out of view, I stared at his profile until he looked at me. "Adrian, I need to know something. Did you harm Sarah?"

He didn't look as shocked by my question as I had hoped. I'd imagined my words to have the force of a bullet shot out of an executioner's gun.

"Why don't you ask if she harmed me?"

I had to hand it to my brother. He was always quick, able to keep his footing on any terrain even when he didn't know where the potholes or sudden drop-offs might be.

"Because she's dead. And you're here."

He stared at me, his face a mask, the candlelight darkening his gray eyes to a midnight blue. Then he swallowed and I imagined a glitter of feeling—pain?—in those eyes, like a tiny flaw in a perfect gem.

"Sarah isn't, wasn't, who you think she was," he said.

"I wish you'd stop making these mystical pronouncements. You're like an oracle that only answers a question by repeating the words of the questioner. 'Sarah wasn't who you think she was.' How do you know?"

He placed his hand on my arm, his fingers hot on my skin. "Because I was there."

"Adrian . . ." I moved my arm on the pretext of taking a drink. "That's why I'm asking you. I know you were there. At least you were there the day before Sarah died."

Adrian stared at the musicians, the fingers of one hand keeping time on the table to the beat. "I don't know what happened to Sarah," he said finally.

"Ah." Of course he would tell me that he didn't know.

"It's not what you think," he said quickly.

"Of course not." I picked up my purse from the extra chair at the table. I'd decided to leave. Eva would just have to cope when she came back from the restroom and found me gone. Or perhaps she wouldn't notice.

The muscles around Adrian's jaw bunched in a reflex that I'd only noticed in the faces of men, as if they were chewing on the carcass of something, or wanted to rip it to shreds. "Look, I wasn't exactly honest with you. I really didn't know Sarah all that well."

"What?" I shut my eyes, reminding myself that Adrian was a master at throwing me off my guard. Even so, I felt unnerved, as though yet another false bottom had dropped out of the cage I shared with him over the years. It was as if the two of us were in a continuous magic trick, one that lasted decades. The problem was that I never knew who was the audience and who the magician, what was the trick and who the trickster.

"Look," I began. "If you didn't know Sarah well, why were you in her town house the day before her death?"

Adrian's eyes shuttered for a moment, and my memory of that evening expanded. As I stood on the stoop of Sarah's house, the light was fading, and just after Adrian stepped into the frame of the door, I'd looked up. A shift in the curtains of a window on the second floor had caught my attention. Or maybe I was desperate to look at anything rather than Sarah or my brother. But I had glanced upward and just for a moment, the drapes slid to one side and I'd seen a face in the window. The glimpse was as fleeting as an afterimage floating on the eye after exposure to bright light. I'd blinked, and when I looked again, the face was gone.

"You probably assumed that I had been seeing Marta." Adrian cleared his throat. "Didn't you?"

My voice sounded dogged and dull. "No, that never occurred to me. Not until this minute. Because someone else besides you and Sarah was in that house, weren't they?"

When he didn't answer, I said, "I couldn't figure out why you called me after Sarah died, looking for Marta. Wondering if I knew where she was. She'd left you, hadn't she?"

He thought a moment then nodded. "She disappeared, yes. As you know."

"But you didn't know it, did you? Not right away? You couldn't imagine she would just leave." I stared at the part in my brother's hair, a sharp crease on the left side of his head. But hadn't he always parted his hair on the other side?

I didn't believe my brother was involved with Marta. It seemed too convenient, an easy way to divert my attention away from Sarah. He'd stood behind Sarah so possessively the night I'd arrived that I felt sure there was something between them.

I rephrased my question. "Did you know Marta was going to leave?"

"I'm afraid something happened to her." Adrian's face stiffened as he caught sight of Eva across the room. She'd stopped to talk to two women at a table.

Adrian grabbed my wrist. "Manda. We don't have much time. Believe me. I'm not responsible for what happened to Sarah. When I left her house that night she was still alive."

My wrist stung from Adrian's grip. I attempted to pull my arm away, but he didn't release his hold. Feeling the old mix of panic and fury, I put my other hand on top of his and dug my nails into his skin. He quickly let go. "I suppose you're saying Marta Conway is a murderer."

"Jesus . . ." he muttered.

I put my lips to Adrian's ear and whispered, "It must be nice. It must be unbelievably fabulous, in fact, that nothing is ever your fault." Adrian's head jerked away from me. He winced and rubbed his ear as if I'd just nicked it with a tiny dart.

Eva, walking quickly, reached our table and smiled at us. She grabbed the back of a chair with both hands as if to steady herself. I wondered if she'd been drinking too much. "That was Hilda and her daughter. Remember them? Such nice people. What are you two conspiring about?"

"Nothing, Mother." I pulled my sweater over my wrist, the one Adrian had been clutching, to hide the chafed and mottled skin. "We were just talking about someone we used to know. Someone rotten things used to happen to. We disagree about her. I think she's a sad case and feel sorry for her. Adrian thinks she deserves whatever she gets."

———

Helen dropped her notebook in her lap. She tapped her gold pen against her chin. "Was Adrian telling the truth about Marta? That he was involved with her? You didn't mention that you shared that detail with Babs or Teresa the other night."

I shook my head. "No, I didn't tell them. Although Teresa thought that might be a possibility another time we talked. Babs and I haven't talked about Adrian, we just keep cycling on details of how much Marta and Sarah resembled each other. Absorbing the shock of that fact, really."

My hands were tightly squeezed between my knees. I shook them out and tried to relax. "You probably think this is strange, but I'd almost forgotten that talk with Adrian at Eva's party. What hit me so strongly during our conversation was the memory of that face at the window upstairs at Sarah's the night before her death."

"But you didn't tell your friends about the person on the second floor, either?" Helen pressed about this incident as if commanding me to remember.

"No. I didn't trust the memory. Did I really see a face in the window? Or was I trying to make sense of Adrian asking me if I assumed he and Marta were together?" I shook my head. "I don't know if it happened."

"Yet you remember clearly what Sarah said to you. And that she seemed afraid."

I nodded. "Oh, yes, she was afraid. But since Babs and Teresa and I talked, I've been replaying that image of the face on the second floor of Sarah's house over and over. The only thing that makes sense is that I think Marta and Sarah were both in the house the night I came to the door."

Helen's voice was cautious. "And you think Sarah was the face upstairs at the window?"

"Yes." I uncrossed my legs. My right leg tingled from the rigidity of my posture. "I don't know what to think. I mean, if she was upstairs, why didn't she come downstairs to see me? She'd asked me to come." My stomach felt both hollow and nauseous, my head unsteady, as if on the verge of seasickness.

Helen spoke slowly, like a child learning to count. "So the woman who greeted you on the steps of Sarah's town house, the woman who was so edgy and afraid, wasn't Sarah at all? You think it was Marta impersonating Sarah?"

"That's what I think. At this moment. I've just put it all together. It's the only thing that makes sense." I stared into Helen's earnest blue eyes. "Don't you see? That's why when Sarah greeted me she seemed so disconnected, so surprised to see me. It wasn't Sarah at all." I clasped my hands together tightly, the pressure on the bones felt reassuring. "I know this seems crazy."

Helen shifted her feet on the round rug. Her green pullover matched the rug's weave. She smiled. "The *situation* is crazy. That makes everything seem suspect—and off-kilter—and makes you doubt what you had perceived. I think it's entirely possible what you're saying. After all, Sarah called you and wanted you to come. She was asking for your help. Yet when you arrived, she acted like she had no idea why you were there."

"I wasn't able to help her. That haunts me."

"She acted surprised to see you. In effect, you were dismissed. You had no way of knowing at that moment how you could help." Helen shook her head. "I don't know what you could have done. Not with Adrian there. But why was Sarah upstairs? Do you think she was ill?"

"I think she was a prisoner."

Helen's face looked pensive. "Like the lady in the tower in the poem."

"Like all the ladies in all the towers. Trapped. Waiting for rescue." I picked at a silver button on my blouse. "It's not so easy to be rescued when you're trapped in the tower."

Helen nodded. "Especially in real life."

I thought about the night Adrian broke down the door when I was asleep. "In real life you don't always have an escape hatch."

"Traditionally, if you're trapped in a tower, someone has locked you in." Helen spoke incisively as she looked across the room at a wall of books. I knew she was a student of myth and folklore. The lower planks of the built-in bookcases contained rows of oversized hardcover volumes. The dust jackets on many were faded and ripped.

"I don't think Sarah was locked in. It was her house. She had the key. But a key's no use if, like her, you have nowhere to go." I resisted the urge to go pick up the copy of Grimm's fairy tales that I'd seen on the bottom shelf across from me. "You have three options when you're trapped in your own house. You can lock yourself in. You can try to run. Or you can jump."

"And Sarah?"

"She gave up. She locked herself in."

Helen frowned. "Yet, there is the fact of the overdose. By taking the pills, you could say she also jumped—the effect was the same."

"Yes. Unless she tried to run but was pushed. Maybe she didn't choose to take the pills."

"The pills were forced down her throat?"

"What if she had no other option but to take them? In looking at the difference between suicide and murder, intention is everything." For the first time, I wondered if Sarah had felt her life worth living.

"Yes." Helen's voice was thoughtful. "It's very complicated. There's her intention and then the possible intention of the person who was with her."

"Her murderer." As I said this, a thought came: *Or her rescuer.*

22

B abs left early on Saturday afternoon. "I'll miss you." I crushed her wonderfully round self against my slighter one. "What if I don't let you go?" Babs's body, solid and low to the ground, bolstered my spirits. My frame was the flexible one, reedy and able to bend in the wind, while Babs anchored my bones with her sturdy flesh. Together we could weather anything.

"You keep me from drowning in the stagnant pond of my routine." Her voice was gruff. "I'm such an old fuddy-duddy academic on my own. Set in my ways like the school of spinster poets from the turn of the last century."

"You're too earthy to be taken for a maiden aunt. But maybe you should write more poetry. 'Stagnant pond of my routine' is a pretty good line."

My old friend extended the handle of her rolling bag. "Come see me soon. I think it would be good for you to get out of here." She peered at me through a fringe of frosted hair. "You can bring Teresa if you want."

"Do you like her?"

"Very much." The skin around Babs's eyes pleated pleasantly, making the broad planes of her face more prominent. "What's bothering you?"

I sidestepped her question. "I feel as though we were obsessed with the past while you were here. We didn't talk much about Dan, or your new book . . ."

"But I was obsessed right along with you! How often do we have such an intriguing real-life mystery to chew on? Plus, I talk about my book all the time." She gave me a sidelong look. "As you know. And Dan, well, I don't need to talk about him. I just need to spend more time with him."

"As long as you don't feel neglected."

"Ha. With the kind of food you've been cooking for me? Not to worry. I am a very simple woman—I only need food, wine, talk, and sleep. I've been full since I got here." Babs patted her stomach then suddenly looked tense. "God, I hate flying. I'd better get through security."

I hugged her again. "Okay, sweetie. There's something I wanted to ask you, but I can't remember what it is."

Babs tightened her grip on her luggage. "About Teresa? Yes, I think you can trust her. I know it's pretty wild that she moves here and then shows up in your life and is connected to all of this mess, but the world—your world, our world—is small. We all met in academia, and that universe is tiny. It's as closed as a gothic novel—there's only one road in and one road out." Babs looked thoughtful, and I sensed a new essay brewing in her brain.

I waggled my fingers at my friend and blew her a kiss. As usual, Babs was ahead of me—she was already on the road out while I was still on my way in.

Holloway met me as I came through the door, and I swooped her vibrating little body up into my arms. I put her on the counter with three heart-shaped Pounce treats. "You liked Babs, too, didn't you?" She cocked her head to one side and squinted at me. In truth, Holloway liked routine and was probably glad to have the house back. Unlike her human. For me, Babs's presence was a part of nature's bounty that I never quite got enough of.

The hard afternoon light streamed through my bedroom as I stepped out of my clothes and headed for the bathroom and a long soak. Except for the steady gushing of water into the tub, the house was quiet. Outside, a sparrow pecked experimentally at the bathroom window, then, disappointed in the lack of nutritional possibilities, flew off.

I submerged myself in the water scented with lavender and thought about what Babs said about Teresa. She'd tapped the very nerve in my psyche that was sensitive. Could I trust Teresa, given her connections to Sarah and Marta, and, peripherally, Adrian? Was it all just a wild set of coincidences? I placed a hot washcloth over my face and breathed deeply. The steam opened more than my sinuses. I glimpsed myself on a path that veered sharply upward and to the left, and I knew that without further excavating the past, I couldn't go forward. Teresa was my one road in.

———

That evening Teresa arrived with a bottle of wine and a fragrant covered pan of something. "Chicken enchiladas," she said.

"How did you know I was going to order takeout?" I took the bottle from her and led her into the kitchen. Holloway peered out from a corner near the refrigerator, green eyes stark and staring, and then vanished into the utility room.

"I know how it is after you've had a guest. This is comfort food."

The wine was red Bordeaux. I poured two glasses, placed the dish in the oven, and led the way to the living room. "Babs is easy," I said. "But we did trash the kitchen." I looked at the living room, every surface still littered with newspapers and books from Babs's habitation.

"I'll bet you had a delightful time doing it." We sat on opposite corners of the sofa. Teresa slipped one foot out of its shoe and tucked her leg beneath her. The gesture instantly made her belong to the room. She inclined her glass toward me and took a sip.

"It was like old times. You know, she and I haven't lived in the same city for over twenty years, but it doesn't seem to matter."

Teresa nodded. "Old times carry through to the present."

"Funny you should say that. Do you ever feel so constrained by the past that you don't feel like you are even in the present?"

She nodded. "I do. I hate it." Teresa turned more fully toward me. "I want to live my life, not just think about it."

Before I could say anything, she went on. "When my sister, Sylvie, died, I just stopped. That was forty-five years ago. Of course, I kept going, stayed in school, finished college, went to graduate school, became an actress, went back to grad school then started teaching. It's just that a part of me stayed back there, with her."

Tears pricked at my eyelids. This December will be the thirty-first anniversary of Duncan's death.

I had to ask, but a part of me dreaded her answer. "How did Sylvie die?"

Teresa stared into her glass. "She suffocated. In our beach house. It was April and still cold. The cottage was heated by propane."

When she didn't go on, I prodded: "A gas leak?"

Teresa uncoiled the leg that rested beneath her and massaged her foot as if to bring it back to life. "My parents and I were outside in the yard, cleaning up broken branches and leaves that had accumulated since autumn. Sylvie had a cold and my mother wanted her to rest."

This time when she stopped talking, I didn't say anything. I just listened to the quiet growing thicker in the room until the gears in the old clock in the hall made a muffled grinding sound at the half hour. The clock's chime had gone mute a decade ago, but the sound reminded me to take a breath.

"I don't quite understand how it happened so fast." Her eyes were almost dreamy. "But when we went back inside, Sylvie wasn't breathing. My dad tried to resuscitate her while my mom called the ambulance. I remember running around the room opening windows and turning on the ceiling fans."

I could imagine a small and frantic Teresa tugging at swollen window frames. "You said you were only six. You must have been terrified."

Heavy frown lines rippled across Teresa's forehead. "I thought it was my fault. You see, I'd loved having my parents all to myself that afternoon. Sylvie was only seven but still she was older. And so pretty. My parents adored her." She stretched her glass toward me and I filled it.

"They must have adored both of you." I spoke softly, so as not to disturb her.

"I don't know." Teresa's body retreated into the sofa corner. "My mother didn't talk to me for a long time after that."

"Oh?" I shivered, thinking of Eva.

"She didn't talk to anyone." Teresa's hair fell across her face as she leaned forward to put her glass on the table in front of us. "She was hospitalized for six months. My mother was a fragile creature. The randomness of life tortured her in general. And then came this disaster, so impossible to predict. She couldn't adjust."

"Her eldest child . . ." I began, but I didn't know what I was going to say. Instead, I saw Eva as she cradled Adrian in the kitchen the day Duncan died, her body bent around her son as if to shield him from the world's harsh turns. She'd absorbed one cruel blow and was determined to block the next. I'd always thought of Eva as a powerhouse, not fragile at all. But what if her vulnerability drove her to hold on to the ever-diminishing fixed points of her life? Her version of the past . . . her memory of her husband and "happy" early family life when she was young . . . her surviving son.

"I'm so sorry, Teresa."

"I know you can imagine what it was like," she said. "And that's comforting, because I feel so lonely when I think of my family."

I slid over to her and gently pulled her toward me. "Yes. There's nothing more lonely than a household that's filled with the presence of someone who is gone."

She looked up at me, her hazel eyes gold in the light of the lamp. "The odd thing is that although Sylvie was the absent one, I always felt that she was with me. It was my mother. She was the one who was missing, even though I saw her almost every day of my childhood."

She kissed me then. A first kiss floods the lips with flavors, nuances of pressure and urgency. Teresa's lips had a tangy freshness, reminding me of ocean breeze and salt. Lingering underneath the taste of promise was a trace of longing and loss. Her kiss released me. My worries about whether or not to trust—or to take a chance—drained away. For the first time in many years, I felt excitement about what was to come.

I remembered Duncan's delight in the fairy tale where the frog turns into a prince from just a kiss. I had been lurking in the reeds and muck for a long time, hiding from the sun and the unfettered view of the sky. I smiled into Teresa's neck. For these few moments, I felt like a princess.

The knowledge of death can unite two separate selves as powerfully as memories of joy or pleasure. Beginnings and endings both sprout from the same seed. I felt a communal history with Teresa, a twinship of experience and of regret that neither of us had been present during the defining moment of our young lives. As children, neither of us had saved our beloved. A trick of fate had brought us together as firmly as an earlier one severed us from the sibling who was our anchor.

"I often wondered after Duncan died if I could exist without him. Things often only seemed real because he was there to share them. Or just to touch me and say, yes, that particular thing did occur, and no I hadn't imagined it. He and I were witnesses for each other."

Lying on her back in my bed, one leg slung over my hip, Teresa nodded. "Maybe it's true and a part of you doesn't exist."

I touched the furrowed skin of her forehead. "It hasn't. Until now." I stopped, embarrassed. What was I saying?

She just smiled and squeezed my other hand, the one resting on her thigh. "It's all right with me."

"What?"

"To feel close." She turned on her side, her face level with mine. I felt a shock seeing her so near. How had I not noticed how sad her eyes were? "We can know each other through hearing about each other's past. I believe that." Her voice took on a note of fierceness. "I feel like I know Duncan because I know you. That's real."

I put the palm of her hand against the soft flesh where my rib cage ended. A tightness that I often felt there seemed to ease. "Do you feel you must live for Sylvie as well as for yourself?"

Teresa's eyes closed. "Sometimes that's all that's kept me alive."

23

Soon after Teresa and I started sleeping together, my dreams about Adrian changed. The nightmares of Adrian's nocturnal visitations to my room, when he sometimes choked me and always scared me with threats of snakes and monsters, ceased. But the dream of the teenage Adrian pounding at the door and crashing upstairs became more insistent. Adrian knocked frequently at the door to my psyche. I imagined opening the door before he could break it down, gliding by him into the frigid January air like a wraith surrounded by a bubble of heat, my aura so hot he couldn't touch me.

The old pain in my left shoulder returned. Malcolm, my massage therapist, suggested moist heat, then physical therapy, and then patience. The pain abated when Teresa, alive and vibrant, was with me and emerged sharply when I was alone. Pain crept into the room in the dead of night, settling on my flesh like a shroud, sending tendrils of fear burrowing into my bones and my dreams. Staircases appeared and multiplied in these nightmares; they led to the second floor of the farmhouse, to the cramped apartment where we'd lived that one winter, to Sarah's room in her town house, to the scuffed stage of the theater where we'd worked so ardently on *Betrayal* all those years ago.

"The second story is your higher self," Helen told me one day in late August. "In this higher consciousness, there is more than one way to look at things—there's *another story*. But downstairs, especially below the ground floor of daily life, is the repository of the unconscious, in your case a kind of burial ground of memory and sensation. In it are raw sensations, primitive feelings, possibly an unseen truth."

I turned away as she raised a cup of tea to her mouth, seeing the basement of the North Dakota farmhouse, the dank root cellar with its weathered door. The door was warped and hung so unevenly that it scraped the dirt floor and had to be forced open and closed. It took just long enough for that plank of wood to clear the threshold that phantom fears and dread had time to crowd in behind it. By the time I pushed it open, I held my breath, light-headed with apprehension. As a child I'd imagined skeletal creatures dressed in tattered cloth with howling mouths awaiting me, their bony fingers scratching my scalp and twisting my hair.

I pushed those memories away. The root cellar door, needing to be pried open and shut, reminded me of so much of my past. I didn't mention that to Helen. Instead, I clung to a thread of control over that time. "I had a magic elevator in the basement. It kept me away from those hidden truths. I didn't face anything I didn't want to see. I just disappeared."

"You think you disappeared. But believe me, wherever you think you were, you were *there*. Those events we've put away into the attic or the basement, long ignored, are the stuff of our dreams."

Helen's brown hair had sprouted silver threads along her part in the last few weeks. The strands seemed electric, powerful, and I imagined that touching them would set off sparks.

"Your hair is beautiful."

"Thank you. I've decided to let the gray win out." Helen's face broke into a fleeting smile, her clear blue eyes shielded by new glasses with round tortoiseshell frames. "Back to your magic elevator. It must have felt wonderful, to be able to escape. To be whisked away."

"Yes. But I always had to come back, didn't I? You're right about the stuff of dreams." I hesitated. "Duncan sometimes enters my dreams. He's older than when he died, about eighteen, the age Adrian was when he broke down the door. I had that dream again recently about Adrian but this time this older Duncan was standing beside the sofa where I was sleeping. He beckoned to me to get up and come with him."

Helen leaned forward, forearms on her knees, the purple sleeves of her top draping over the bones of her wrists. "That part of you, the Duncan who is older than either of you were when he died, knows something."

"I keep hoping that when Duncan appears again he'll show me what happened the day he died." I heard the air-conditioning switch on. Cool air crept along my arms and shoulders. "This humidity is killing me." I lifted my hair off my neck.

"Does the Duncan who is older in the dream resemble Adrian at all?" Helen asked after a moment.

The thought startled me. "No . . . not really. You can tell they are related, but . . ." I rarely considered resemblances between my brothers, and I began to wonder if the Duncan in the dream was more of a presence than an actual physical representation.

"I was just thinking about you and Duncan being twins. And wondering if Duncan and Adrian, side by side—"

"Could look like twins?" I shook my head vigorously. "No. Not ever."

Helen nodded slowly and then changed directions. "Do you want to try EMDR therapy around the dream?"

EMDR—eye movement desensitization and reprocessing—was developed to treat post-traumatic stress victims, including Vietnam War vets, in the late 1980s and then spread into mental health practice. EMDR makes use of bilateral stimulation, sometimes visual, sometimes tactile, to stimulate both sides of the brain. The stimulation releases emotional responses trapped in the nervous system. The client tracks a light—or the therapist's moving finger—from side to side with her eyes while visualizing a traumatic event, frequently pausing to share images or feelings. The technique has the potential to allow the client to access long-buried trauma, often enabling feelings of resolution or emotional relief. In the process, wordless memories of suffering are given a voice. Ideally, integration takes place and the client begins to feel a sense of control over what had happened to her back when she had no power or agency. The process reminded me a little of lucid dreaming, where the dreamer learns to engage the conscious mind and change the course of a dream.

Helen sometimes used a TheraTapper, a handheld device that alternated measured vibrations between left and right hands. We'd worked with this technique before on my memories of the day Duncan died. The images of that day were still jarring and raw, like a series of still pictures violently juxtaposed.

"Shall I try to visualize the dream of Adrian coming up the stairs?"

"Yes, and if you like, with this older Duncan present. Remember, you can stop whenever you need to. You have the power to remake the events. And to complete the action."

I nodded uneasily. The truth was that just thinking of the night Adrian entered the apartment leached any feeling of control from my brain.

"Here, these are new. They attach to your ear and you control the rhythm and intensity of sensation." Helen handed me two ear clips for my earlobes attached to a control box. At first overly aware of the electrical current on the soft tissue of my ears, I adjusted the rate of the sensation to match my heart rate.

"Tell me what you see," Helen's voice intruded.

"Nothing." I let the electric stimulation pulse back and forth, feeling lulled by it. "I'm not sure I can go there today."

"Take your time. Maybe just picture the space you were in."

My mind skittered from the cellar to the fields around our farmhouse and then to the streets of our little town. I remembered a bank of windows above a small dress shop on Fifth Street. The apartment my parents had rented that winter so long ago was on that second story. I let myself enter the small living room. A lifeless beige carpet covered the floor. The paint on the walls was such a pale green that it looked pasty. A sofa that opened into a bed, a coffee table, two end tables, a few lamps, and a simple land-scape painting filled the room. For a long while my mind panned that stark space, then fixated on a view of it from above, like a still from the opening shot of a movie. After each breath I hesitated, gathering courage to stare into the face of the past.

Abruptly, Adrian's red face emerged from the corner of the room, his body rocketing into the space with the pressure of his rage. He seemed to grow larger as I watched until his bulk almost obscured the slender form that was my thirteen-year-old body. That young Amanda crouched in a corner of the sleeper sofa, a pillow held vertically against her chest so that it obscured her mouth.

"I hate you," Adrian shouted.

"I hate you," Amanda echoed in a quiet voice, as if she had no words of her own. She held the pillow out in front of her like a shield.

"Get up!" Adrian punched at the pillow.

"I can't get up." Amanda shrank back, pale and stiff.

The two figures froze. I held my breath.

My eyes flew open as my brain fled the apparition of this Amanda and

Adrian, trapped in time and space. I appealed to Helen. "I feel removed."
In reality, I couldn't get far enough away. My heart had sped up so that by
contrast the electrical charge of the clips on my ears seemed to slow way
down.

"I just want to run away," I told her.

"Then do it. Imagine yourself running away."

Adrian appeared frozen as the young Amanda on the sofa levitated and
leaped to one side, sprinting for the hall closet. Once there, she locked
herself in, breathing in the thick scent of wool coats, nylon parkas, earth-
caked boots.

"Come out of there or I'll come in and get you," Adrian growled.

Part of me watched from a distance the stiff, quivering bar of Adrian's
shoulders squared against the closet door, and then I left Adrian behind
and slipped inside the closet where Amanda hid behind Dad's tan trench
coat. I stood quietly behind her in the dark, stuffy space. A sliver of light
crept under the door and slid across Amanda's bare feet.

Shhhh, it's all right, I imagined telling her. *This is a magic door. He can't
come in.*

In the dim, muffled space of the closet, buffered by fabric, I could no
longer hear Adrian. My eyes snapped open to the bland comfort of Hel-
en's office. "What if I refuse to see or hear him?"

Helen sat, feet planted, still and alert. "That's fine."

I shut my eyes and began to hum to the child hiding among the coats,
a tuneless ditty I remembered my mother mouthing as she did the dishes.
Time went by. Adrian's fists pounded on the door, but the sound was curiously muted. The closet, a nest of textures and smells, transported us to a
separate world. Then I heard the rapid steps of someone moving around
the room, and then retreating footfalls down the stairs.

I thought I heard Duncan's voice calling, trying to coax me out:
"Amanda . . . He's cleared out now." Or did he say, "It's all clear now"?
After a short while, I took the young Amanda's hand and we opened the
closet and peered out carefully as a unit, like a tortoise reluctantly extend-
ing its head from its shell. Adrian was nowhere to be seen. We walked to
the living room window and looked out. Outside under the light of the
streetlamp, fresh footprints marked the snow. *Amanda,* I heard Duncan's
voice again, far away. But Duncan had vanished.

The room lost its charge and melted from my awareness. The field of my memory was suddenly blank, like a vivid painting whose colors and lines abruptly evaporated into whiteness.

I blinked rapidly, adjusting the dial on the box that controlled the current to an even slower pace. "I don't know."

"What don't you know?"

"If that could ever happen. That Adrian in a rage could just vanish."

Helen looked at me. "It just did happen."

"Yes, but that's because I don't want to let his anger come out anywhere near me."

"I think that's healthy. You don't have to allow that ever again."

I frowned. "I just can't remember." I rubbed my upper stomach near the diaphragm. "I can feel the punch to the pillow, pushing into me. I don't know how I survived that night."

"Can you live with that?"

"I have lived with it for almost thirty years. But I feel incomplete. Like there's something there I need to know."

"But how did it feel to be with your younger self in that closet and feel safe?"

"Not exactly safe. Maybe insulated, like there was another layer between me and Adrian."

"Maybe insulated is all you can have for now."

I took off the clips. "I felt something new." The tightness in my stomach constricted my chest. I concentrated on breathing steadily.

Helen waited for me. The circular clock above Helen's chair ticked slowly, reminding me of a steady heartbeat, not the fluttery, uncertain one I identified so often in Helen's office as the one living in my chest.

I was almost afraid to tell her what I was thinking. "A part of me, well . . . I almost felt sorry for Adrian. So stiff, so angry, so unhappy, so shut out. For the first time, I felt he wanted me to push back, somehow put him in line. The footsteps going back down the stairs were a hollow echo of what they usually sounded like. They seemed forlorn, lost."

"Do you feel lost?"

"Not right now. But oh, yes, I know what lost feels like. You want to break out of yourself, but there's nowhere to go. Maybe that's why Adrian is so angry."

Helen removed her glasses and sat back. Her eyelids looked faintly pink. "He didn't know how to soothe himself. You were too inexperienced to be of much help. And too frightened."

A silence fell as I digested this. Helen's large, melancholy eyes rested on me, those eyes that told me she had seen—and I suspected, had experienced—so much pain. I heard my voice, sounding wistful like the young Amanda I had just witnessed: "I wonder where my parents were. Where they ever were."

24

The day that Teresa walked so easily into the financial planning office six months ago, I'd felt a premonition of change flow through the room in her wake. Her being, that vibration of matter, collided with my own. It was as if the uncompromising brick and mortar that held my life together transformed into something supple and resilient. New possibilities swept aside the careful containment of my routine.

Another seismic change occurred a week after I'd seen Helen. It was September and still blistering hot. Teresa came into my house one late afternoon. I heard the refrigerator door open several times as she put away groceries she'd gone to purchase for dinner. A few minutes later, she found me at the computer in my study, kissed me, and waved a piece of paper in the air. She hesitated before speaking, as if aware that talking about the thing that had so stirred her—her face was flushed, the swing of her arms as she strode into the room exuded energy—would make it real.

"Marta is directing a new production." Teresa held the paper out to me as if it too was hot. It was a printout of an e-mail she'd received from Marta. The paper was recycled, with smudges and crossed-out words on one side and a short message on the other, printed on a machine whose cartridge was beginning to fade.

She dropped the paper on my desk. "Marta invited me to the opening."

I watched Teresa's hazel eyes, a murky brown today, as she relinquished the paper. "In Chicago," I said, without looking at it.

"How did you know?" She sounded winded, as if she had been racing through the scorched streets. In Central Texas, summer tended to grind on as a slow burn, with September as its crowning glory. All week the temperatures had hovered at just over one hundred degrees. The mornings were humid, the day drying out as the mercury rose steadily until five o'clock, the hottest part of the day. By then, the heat scorched your skin and seemed to suck the air out of your lungs before it could grudgingly relinquish any oxygen. It was easy to feel out of breath.

Uneasiness made my own breath shallow. "I don't know. Just a hunch. And the play . . ." A nauseating certainty seized me and I was aware of folding my hands in my lap, becoming very still. "I have a strange feeling that Marta's directing *Betrayal*."

Teresa looked uncertain. "The e-mail just says 'a Pinter play.' But the name of the theater is here—Division Street. Something new I think. We can look the title up." She bit her lip. "It would be a little too strange if it were *Betrayal*, wouldn't it?"

We spent a few minutes looking up the theater on the web. Division Street Playhouse was west of downtown and aptly named. There's a part of Oak Park that's affluent and privileged, and a part that's not. The membrane between them, as in so many towns, is very thin. Just like the membrane I felt between the present and the past. In my case, it was easy to go back in time but not so easy to return. I often got lost retracing the streets of what did happen, with occasional detours down the alleyways of what might have been. Or, maybe I couldn't tell the difference.

A few screens later, the season of the small theater came up. "It is *Betrayal*." Teresa managed a listless smile. "That word just broadcasts *stay away*, doesn't it? It feels too strange . . ."

Teresa impulsively seized my hand and held it between both of hers. I wanted to tell her under no circumstances must she go anywhere near this production. A part of me didn't believe it existed. Or Marta either.

Teresa squeezed my hand before she released it. "The other odd thing is that I also heard about this project from an old friend today."

"Who is this friend?"

"Connie Stephen. From U of Illinois days."

"She knew Sarah and Marta then?"

Teresa leaned against the desk as if her back ached and couldn't support her. "Yes. We used to see each other at theater festivals. Until I began to go to literature conferences instead. A few years before I moved here and took this job." Teresa pushed herself straight and sat down abruptly on the sofa. "Connie lives in Chicago and is a big supporter of new theaters. And of Marta."

My mouth was dry. "You're tempted to go, aren't you?"

Teresa's shoulders slumped. She kneaded her forehead. "When Connie suggested I come up, I thought of course not. But now . . ." Her expression was concentrated, almost piercing in its intensity. "You know, Amanda, maybe this is an opportunity. You're haunted by Sarah. I'm haunted by Marta's breakdown when Sarah left her, and when Sarah died. Marta is the link to that time. If I go, maybe I'll find some answers to our questions."

Hearing this filled me with a peculiar mix of doubt and relief. "I can hardly imagine putting all that to rest. But you're right, it would be the best thing for me . . . and us."

Teresa looked at the printout again. "You don't think she's just playing a prank, do you?"

I shook my head. "It sounds to me like Marta is sending you a message, and using Connie to emphasize its urgency."

A flush spread across Teresa's cheekbones. "What are you saying?" She rose from the sofa and went to the window, impatiently adjusting the blinds against the afternoon sun. She turned around to face me. "Amanda, this room isn't big enough to pace in!"

I gestured at the yard. "We could go outside. The beauty of this heat is that it melts tension." At her nervous head shake, I asked, "How much do you trust Connie?"

"We're not close. I hear from her from time to time. She's always been a Marta groupie. I'm sure she's thrilled Marta is directing again. Sometimes Connie produces new plays as well. She doesn't confine herself to a specific theater. New work—it's a small world, even in Chicago. It wouldn't be surprising if Marta has been in touch with her."

As we talked, I felt the shadow that was Marta Conway expanding, creeping closer. "Marta knows you've met me. You told her that, didn't you?"

"Yes, of course I told her when we talked those months ago. But since then, I've heard nothing from her. But she knows I performed in *Betrayal* fairly recently, because it was during the production that she phoned me."

We looked at each other, both of us struck by how very odd it was that

Betrayal and Marta were connected once again. "I don't know what to think." Teresa sat down again on the sofa, kicked off her sandals, and stretched out.

"She knows this play is loaded. For both of us." I stared at the computer screen; the website was divisionstreet.org. As I went through the links, I found e-mail addresses for staff members, but nothing for any guest directors. Marta had used the general Division Street e-mail account for her message to Teresa.

"Something just struck me. Remember when I told you and Babs how I went back to Chicago and talked to the artistic director of the theater where Sarah worked? And how at that moment she was looking for a guest director for *Betrayal*? It's almost like Marta is calling our attention back to the time when Sarah died. Almost as if she's stepped into Sarah's shoes. It's eerie. She *is* sending a message. But I don't think she cares about me. Only you."

Teresa spoke slowly. "Are you implying that somehow Marta wants me to know about this production to comment on my relationship with you? That she is saying I've betrayed her?" She shook her head. "No, not after all this time. Plus, we were never lovers."

I shrugged helplessly. The word *betrayal* echoed in the room. I didn't want it to pollute what I had with Teresa. "I don't know how she thinks. How do we know what she really wants from you? Maybe she blames me in some way for what happened to Sarah. Or suspects that I caused her breakup with Sarah. But that's ridiculous. I was, in the end, nothing to Sarah."

A bitter note crept into Teresa's voice. "Just as I am nothing—obviously—to Marta. I don't know why I even care." She folded her arms. "You're right that it's all eerie. I keep feeling like the past is knocking at the door."

Involuntarily, I listened for a moment. The air conditioner switched off abruptly; without its hum the air seemed suddenly too still, dead. "It's just so very strange, isn't it? Unless . . . God, Teresa, back then I felt like a pawn in some game that Sarah was playing. Marta didn't really figure into the equation at all. But now that Sarah's dead . . . I can't help but feel Marta's toying with us, letting us know she's watching and that she can enter into our lives at any time."

I tried to laugh but it came out sounding more like a hack. "Or are we just inflating our own self-importance in assuming that she's thinking about us at all?"

I watched Teresa chew on her lower lip. She stood and reached for the printout of the e-mail. She turned it over and pushed it to the edge of my desk. Her voice was hoarse. "This appears to be proof that she's thinking about us. But we don't have to respond to it. And I can just tell Connie it's not convenient for me to come." She thought a moment. "If I go, you have to come with me."

Light-headed at the thought, I nodded. "I want to. I'd worry too much if you went alone." I knew I'd worry whether I went or stayed home, but if I went I'd at least be at Teresa's side.

Her eyes glistened and a deep crease appeared between her eyes. "I think you could be right, that Marta's using Connie. Connie always admired her, thought she was the most talented of our generation at school." Teresa resumed her seat and leaned forward. "You know, in the old days, I trusted Marta. We were good friends. But now, well, I have no idea who she is. She hasn't been in my life for a very long time. I shouldn't let her back in, should I?"

I didn't want to answer that, didn't want her to think I was influencing her in any way about Marta. I'd made the mistake before of getting between old friends. Instead, I asked, "Did you answer this e-mail?"

"Yes, but I'll be surprised if I hear back."

"Why?"

"Because that's how it's gone with Marta for years now. It's like she drops in and then drops out. She doesn't continue the exchange."

"No dialogue. Just a monologue."

"Yes."

My mind flashed on Adrian, much more comfortable with monologue himself. "Would you say that's even more true since Sarah's death?"

She nodded.

"I was just thinking of my brother. So if Adrian and Marta spent any time together, they would both be talking. But who would be listening?"

———

I put this question to Babs when I called her the next morning. Papers rustled and I heard the clack of her ceramic coffee mug hitting the table. Babs most likely was devouring her morning dose of newsprint. I imagined her rubbing a smudge off her index finger as she replied: "For some people, the lovely sound of their own voice is enough. Marta's an actress. If she *appeared* to be listening, wouldn't that make Adrian perfectly happy?"

"I suppose. I have a hard time imagining him happy."

"You sound pretty grumpy yourself." Babs cleared her throat, took a sip of something. "So you're going." There was no inflection in her voice.

"To Chicago?"

"Ummmm. Let's be more precise—to the play."

I looked up at the ceiling in my dining room, noticing a hairline crack jagging down from one corner and threading into the baseboard above the floor. "Do you ever find yourself in a situation where you see two clear paths in front of you, a clear choice, but you know in your gut that there isn't a choice, there's only one way that you're compelled to go?"

"All the time," Babs said, and I thought my friend sounded both sad and resigned. "You're telling me there's no other possibility—if Teresa goes, you'll go."

"Yeah."

"Well, that does suck the proverbial mop." Babs's coffee cup clattered on the table again and then I heard the scuffling of footsteps. I could see Babs refilling her cup and hauling it, along with another biscotti or some other dunkable snack, back to the table.

"Oh?" I held my breath.

"I can hardly bring myself to think about leaving the Northeast during the one decent time of year," she said with a cough.

I felt enormous relief. "You mean you'll meet me there?"

A mirthless laugh sounded sharply in my ear. "You know how it is. I don't feel that I have a choice."

"You don't have to do this, dear friend." I wanted to cry.

Babs reverted to gruffness. "Oh for heaven's sake. You'd never forgive me if I didn't."

I thought I heard a note of weariness in my friend's voice. The week before, Babs had told me she and Dan had had an argument. Suddenly, what I needed felt far beside the point. "How are things with Dan?"

"Okay," she said. When I waited, she added: "Really, one of those early relational tiffs. I found out I'm not perfect. Again. But we're fine."

She didn't sound fine. "Babs, tell me something I can do for you."

Babs stifled a sneeze, a funny wheezing sound. She didn't say anything for a bit. Then she spoke very softly. "I don't think you can imagine what you give me all the time. You save me from my predictable life. Without you, I'd be one of those caricatures mystery writers are always going on about, pottering about her bookshelves, spilling tea—and bourbon—on the pages of her latest drivel, laughing at her own jokes." Babs paused, I assumed to picture herself in this improbable role. Then she sighed. "To be honest, I'm at loose ends right now on the writing front. And, if you think I'm going to miss seeing the elusive and improbable Marta Conway . . ."

"I can't imagine you ever missing anything," I said quickly. I swallowed a giggle. "Babs, I hate to tell you this, but I laugh at my own jokes all the time."

"You always did," she answered. "In you it seems charming. But I can't afford to, in public anyway—it would just be more proof of the perils of spinsterhood, I suppose. I'm not excluding men from this problem. My colleague Mallory is always sniggering into his tea and when I look around, I realize no one has spoken but him."

"Spinsterhood? I don't think so. You'll never be the dry, chaste, Miss Grundy type. And now—"

But Babs chose that moment to tune me out. "Wait a minute." I heard footsteps again and more rustling on the counter. "Damn. What a mess. There's water all over the place. I wondered how Mister's paws had gotten so wet—he just strolled across my paper and gouged a chunk out of the op-ed page. I think this coffeepot is leaking."

"How old is it?"

"Probably fifteen years, why?"

I laughed. "It's just exhausted. That's all."

"Is there anything worse than a worthless appliance? Somehow it knew I'd gotten a meager royalty statement on my last book. Never let an appliance know you have a few extra dollars. Oh, forget it. Look, e-mail me when you and Teresa pick your flight times. And your hotel. Oh," she said as if struck by a sudden inspiration, "and send me any photos you have of Adrian."

"I have lots and I found a fairly recent one on the web when he received a research award awhile back."

"Good." Babs didn't ask why I was trawling the net for my brother's photo. She was a consummate researcher, so she probably assumed everyone was scouring any easy sources for crumbs of data at all times.

I could sense Babs was about to ring off. As if I were hailing a taxi after having sprinted a half mile, I suddenly felt winded. "But wait, there's something else."

I heard her murmuring something to her cat and then she said, "Hmm?"

"Adrian. What if he's at the performance? What if he and Marta are just sitting in their spider web, tugging on some little filament and waiting for us to crawl inside and get stuck?"

"A possibility." Babs spoke almost sharply: "We shouldn't think about him too much. It's dangerous to concentrate on energy you don't want to attract into your life."

I wondered what event in her life my friend was referencing or if she were quoting someone. Before I could ask her, she continued: "Let's think about the play. The magic triangle. Whenever three people know one another well and the axis of love shifts—as it does when someone starts sleeping with his best friend's wife, for example—their intricate dance is unbalanced. The force field connecting the three collapses. The person who is left out—the abandoned husband, for example—is left with tremendous feelings of envy and passion and nowhere to put them. His emotion is like a tidal wave that curls back upon itself, barrels at him with tremendous force, and swamps him."

Mystified, I said, "Are you talking about Adrian?"

"Of course I am. Suppose he and Sarah and Marta were some kind of unit. When Sarah dies and then Marta—who he told you he was involved with—disappears, where does that leave him?"

I shook my head. "No, by now Adrian has found her. If he wanted to find her, that is."

"Suppose he has found her. What does he do? He creates a new triangle, that's what he does. That's why you must go with Teresa. It's dangerous to allow her to be swept into the vacant position of the triangle. She is at risk, I think." I heard Babs back at the sink, pouring water.

A ripple of alarm swept over me. "Teresa? Babs, the three people in this triangle were Sarah, Marta, and Adrian."

"Might have been. Until Sarah died."

"Her death doesn't mean she's not part of the equation." I thought of the talk that Helen and I had about the woman trapped in the tower. "Energy remains even when someone isn't physically present."

"Yes, and that force can be active or passive."

I thought of myself as a child in my family. "Passive," I echoed. "In my family, that was me, always there, listening, watching."

"Always enabling?" Babs asked shrewdly. "There are many triangles here: you, Duncan, and Adrian for example. We've talked about this before: two sides join forces to pressure the third."

"Until the third gives way?" I tried to imagine how this worked in my family. And then I thought of Eva and Adrian as two very weighty points of the configuration, and the rest of us: my dad, or me, or Duncan facing them one by one on the other side. Oddly, I never saw the three of us as making up the same kind of triangle. For one thing, I didn't see Duncan as separate enough from me—we took up one space, not two.

Babs's comment about enabling told me this position was familiar to her. I knew she was the eldest of four children and I was about to ask her a question when she said:

"Amanda, what does the theater allow adults to do safely that they don't always have the sanction to do anywhere else?"

"Act out?"

"Well, yes. But I was thinking about wearing masks. We've always loved plays because what people seem to be—what they appear to be—might not be who they are. It's very easy to hide behind another's face and words."

"Uh-huh." I wondered where this was going.

"Where is Marta hiding by directing a play about betrayal, I ask myself," Babs said thoughtfully. "What does this particular play allow her to do, or become? That's our central question."

"In this play everyone wears the mask of the friend or lover—or mother or father—and the characters aren't sure about the genuine impulses behind those guises. Just as in life." Eva and Adrian, their faces turned toward each other expectantly, rose into my mind. At times they'd seemed overly possessive of each other, almost as if they were intimate partners. I recalled my father and Adrian, circling each other warily when Eva was present, competing for her attention in the manner of male lions vying for a desirable female.

"There's something revealing here about how Marta felt about Sarah." Babs's voice intruded on these uncomfortable thoughts. "If we could only see it."

I was still occupied by how the triangle joined two people and left out the third. "Isn't it possible that if we create a square, we could dismember the power of the triangle? For instance, Jerry's absent wife in *Betrayal*. She's mentioned but she's off the page, never onstage. We only see three players and their shifting loyalties. And hence, there's never stability."

"You and Teresa, Adrian and Marta form a square, too." Babs yawned. "We could go on with this forever. However, in these squares, someone always drops out."

"Or dies," I said.

———

That night I sketched in the journal Helen kept urging me to keep. Using colored pencils I drew a picture about a dream I'd had. Adrian and Duncan and I were sitting at a table in a café with my father. Eva didn't appear. But because she wasn't there, her presence at the table was strong. This sense of lack robbed the square table of its solidity and wholeness. Our longing made Eva materialize. Dad kept turning around as if expecting someone.

"I miss my wife," I thought he said. A plate shattered, voices rose, and it was hard to hear.

"What?" Adrian asked.

"I miss my *life*," Dad said.

25

I dreamed that Adrian stabbed Sarah in the chest and left her lying on the sidewalk. I arrived at the curb in a white taxicab right after it happened. I hadn't directed the cab to this destination, but when the car stopped, I stepped out. Before I could pay the driver, the car sped off. The place was a dark, deserted wasteland without streetlamps or parked cars. Sarah's body, slight and lifeless, stretched before Adrian's long, narrow feet on the pockmarked pavement. My brother stood above her with his arms extended, as if he wanted to fly away. Blood pooled around the outline of her torso. His left foot, encased in burnished brown leather, pointed at her hip.

Adrian began to walk away. I clutched at his arm until he turned around and faced me. His eyes, hooded in deep sockets, were unreadable.

"Am I next?" I asked him, my voice calm.

The house was quiet around me when I woke from the nightmare. Teresa slept beside me, her breath soft and even. Holloway was nestled between us, her ears twitching as she felt me stir. I put a hand on my chest, certain that I'd feel my heart leaping under the skin, but I felt only a thin film of sweat. My ribs strained as I held my breath. Perhaps my heart was waiting until it was safe to beat again. Lying there, desperately thirsty, I wondered why I hadn't voiced this fear to Helen in any of our sessions. I sensed Adrian's predator self coming closer. Duncan had died, and then Sarah. As Eva's memory had failed, I was now the one living repository of Adrian's history.

———

During the last two years of Duncan's life, he and I spent many Saturday nights watching horror films with Adrian when my parents traveled to my dad's music gigs or joined friends for the evening. Duncan's favorites were vampire movies, the gorier and the more laden with fogs and scarlet capes and smooth throats the better.

At eleven he became fascinated with the idea of the brides of Dracula hovering over and attacking young men as they slept.

"That's so creepy," Adrian would say as the pinched, keenly alert face of Peter Cushing would appear on the screen examining yet another punctured throat of a helpless male.

Duncan focused not only on the grotesque images of blood-streaked lips and leaking wounds but Adrian's interest in the various voluptuous brides. It struck Duncan as hilarious when his older brother got very quiet during erotic scenes. The very red lips of the vampires hovered over pale young throats, nibbling at the savory flesh. At the first puncture, the victim swooned in ecstatic agony.

"Big brother, you better breathe!" he'd crow.

"Shut up." Adrian's voice climbed a half register as his eyes devoured the screen.

"The vampire killed them by draining all their blood. But they don't stay dead. They come back, not alive or dead," Duncan said. "That's the scary part. They're undead." He turned to me, his eyes narrow and dark. "Think about it, Manda. They're in between. Never at rest but never in the world either."

Adrian strained to hear Christopher Lee's funereal voice on the screen. "Cool it, Duncan. Leave it."

But Duncan followed me into the kitchen and watched while I made popcorn. "What would being in between be like?"

"How would I know?" The oil sizzled in the pan and smoked a little. "Be careful. Stand back. This stupid pan spits all over the place. You'll get burned."

"If I were undead it wouldn't matter." Duncan's face was earnest, his lips tightly pressed together.

After a bit, the corn erupted into rapid-fire reports, and before I noticed, began to scorch. "Damn it."

This got Duncan's attention. It always cheered him up when Adrian or I would swear. For some reason, he never did. "Way to go, Manda."

I shook the popcorn into an old bowl of my grandmother's that she'd given us, a white ceramic one with tiny yellow flowers painted on it. It was both solid and attractive, just as she was. Duncan grabbed a handful and I almost dropped the bowl. "Be careful!" I couldn't imagine ever making popcorn again if the bowl shattered. It was deep and oversized, my small hands barely able to support it without wobbling.

"But what if I were?" His nose pointed at me, practically quivering with persistence. His face lapsed into a wide-eyed, frozen mask. "Undead," he breathed hoarsely, coming toward me in a stiff-kneed lurch.

"And what if I dropped this bowl on your head?" I chased Duncan around the room, my feet slipping on the linoleum floor. Miraculously, the bowl survived.

I still have it. The sight of it in the dish drain comforted me when I walked into the kitchen when I couldn't go back to sleep after the nightmare of Adrian stabbing Sarah. The undead. That's what all the uneasy spirits were, Duncan and Sarah included.

I drank a glass of milk as I stood at the counter. The digital numbers on the microwave announced 3:30. Perhaps Sylvie's spirit was restive too. I felt that I'd absorbed some of Teresa's grief over her sister. Between us were these three deaths. A triangle of lost loves, each unrelated to the other. As soon as this thought occurred, Adrian popped into my mind and anchored at one point of a triangle, connected to both Sarah and Duncan, his weight pulling the other two out of their orbits, pushing them onto another plane entirely.

The glass trembled in my hand. It disturbed me that I had compared Sarah's death to those of Duncan and Sylvie. Sarah had lived a full life. A short one by modern standards, but one that at least had a trajectory. But my brother and Teresa's sister only had nineteen years of life between them.

Again, I heard Duncan intone *Undead,* his young voice expelling the word into the air in such a way as to capture both awe and dread. Duncan's obsession with the creatures of the night that could never rest struck me as a strange corollary to the dream I'd just had. My brother's spirit was not quiet. A part of him was still restless, still seeking, and his unrest lived in my psyche as well. He was, for me, in between, not gone from the world even though I couldn't bring him back into it.

Until we let them go, all those we have lost are undead to us. The mystery of Sarah's death animated my dreams. Like Duncan, she had vanished as surely as if time had bent around her and continued without her. She might be at peace somewhere, but those of us who saw her life as unfinished kept her with us. I stood next to that space she'd left behind, marking it with sadness and regret. What had I read somewhere about the dead? *Our grief is their presence.* I poured more milk, drained the glass, left it on the counter next to the fridge. I'd go back to bed, try to sleep, and the next weekend, go to Chicago.

———

The next day, I saw Helen in the afternoon. September was creeping to a close, but the run of high temperatures hadn't broken. In fact, at four o'clock the bank's temperature monitor on the corner near my house announced 104 degrees. A hot wind swept the city, further fanning the flames of the heat rather than giving relief.

I described my dream of coming upon Adrian right after he had stabbed Sarah.

"The dark street, the white taxi," Helen mused. "A stark world, one of sharp contrasts. The dark is the shadow—and in many ways I think Adrian represents the shadow side of your psyche. Cold, calculating, bold, aggressive."

She tilted her head to one side as she regarded me. "Those are not ways you come across. But you possess all those qualities somewhere. We all do. If we look at the dream and see each image representing a part of your distributed self, Adrian acts out of one place in the unconscious. He kills Sarah, quickly, brutally. Sarah hurt you badly. Your anger, even if you've submerged it all these years, is powerful just the same. A part of you may have wanted to retaliate and strike at her. You may never actually *do* such a thing in your waking moments, but the impulse is there just the same."

Less imprisoned by the impact of the dream by now, I regarded it more critically. "The dream reminded me of a film noir movie," I replied. "Except for the brown shoes."

"The shoes are the one grounding image—brown, earthy, planted." From the pad on the table next to her chair Helen picked up a pen and scrawled a note. She tapped the pen on the paper. "Perhaps this violent, buried part of you feels desolate, like the barren city street where he stabs her. It's dark, dreary—negative. What is that term? A camera obscura."

I sighed and shifted in my chair, my low back stiff and achy. "That's the world I feel surrounds me when I think of going to Chicago. Not violent exactly. But desolate. And the black-and-white décor—it *is* like going into the past for me."

"But there might be something you can learn there," Helen spoke thoughtfully. "And so in that sense, going back there might be a way of going forward."

I nodded. "That's a positive way of looking at it."

Helen's face turned toward the window, toward the dry, rustling leaves as they stirred against the pane. "You don't have to go."

"Oh, but I do. I can't imagine letting Teresa go without me. All I'd do is worry. And if something happened to her . . ."

"But Amanda, Teresa doesn't have to go either."

The vivid afterimage of my dream held me captive once more. "I know. Neither of us *has* to. But we must. Don't you see—it's like a play. It's as if the script has been written and we have to act out our parts even though we don't know the ending." I raised my shoulders and let them drop. "I can't explain it. I'm sure it doesn't make sense. It doesn't make sense to me."

Helen's lips curved with sad understanding. "If only our emotions made sense. Of course, then you wouldn't be here."

I rubbed my fingers over the soft leather of my chair. Tiny cracks radiated along the chair arm where hands had worried at the material, perhaps seeking grounding in the midst of turbulent emotions. Stroking worn leather was comforting, its texture so like skin. "But it's not like just any play. It's particularly like *Betrayal*, which starts in the present when the love affair is over, and then takes us back to its beginning when there was only passion and hope. Showing the plot in reverse like that creates an illusion of inevitability about what happens."

"I'm not sure I'm following you." Helen's eyes drifted to her bookshelves as if searching for a copy of the play.

"I just mean that for any of us, our past sets us on a collision course with the future, which culminates in a present moment when the future becomes now. It's as though we've been walking slowly toward the far-flung horizon of what is to come and one day it's not off in the distance anymore—instead, we're living in it. I'm just saying that my history with Sarah, Adrian, and Marta has created the possibility of now. And so I have a feeling of inevitability about going to Chicago. My friend Babs wrote an essay about Henry James's fiction in which she talks about how he creates 'an aura of destiny' around his characters. That's what I'm feeling." I blushed. "I suppose I'm taking myself awfully seriously."

Helen didn't react to this, except to say, "Well, the situation is dramatic, in every sense of the word."

My fingers thrummed rhythmically on my thigh, and I suppressed the urge to keep up the pattern, a kind of metronomic ticking as anxiety leaked from my body into the atmosphere. "I feel afraid and yet excited. I wish I understood it."

"I think if you choose the recognition that you're on a path where there is something you will discover, something you need to know, you will feel more in control. I can remember times in my life when I had to do something. In a way, it's like falling in love. You don't really think about it, you just do it."

"You turn to meet your fate," I said.

"What?" She looked startled.

"In the tarot, there's a major card called the Wheel of Fortune that symbolizes the cycles of fate. Fortunes rise and fall and each of us is responsible for our destiny. Babs used to read my cards. I got that one a lot. Falling in love is like that. It's a risk but one you don't weigh at the time. You just seize it—you turn to meet it. It's compulsive in a way. Like gambling."

A line of tension deepened between Helen's eyes. "Amanda, given your history, I want to urge you to realize that you can protect yourself. If things feel too frightening or too uncertain, you can withdraw. You do have the power to get on a plane and come home. Whatever Teresa does. That is a choice you have."

Helen's intensity startled me. "I see that," I said, even while the idea of 'choice' seemed far away. "And I know I'm not alone. Teresa and I may be influenced by old feelings. But Babs is joining us and she has a cool head. The three of us will support one another and if one of us feels at risk, I'm confident the other two will step in."

"That's good. None of you is without resources at this point in your lives. Or without judgment. You, Teresa, Babs—together you're quite a formidable group, from what you've told me."

"A triangle. A functional one."

"I read *Betrayal* last night," Helen said. "It held my attention. I found it stark and disturbing."

"Those two words describe my dream."

"Your dream is much more direct, though. The violence is explicit. In Pinter's drama the three people are very civilized on the surface. But their shadow selves are needy and hungry. Unsatisfied."

Helen's eyes were focused inward. For a moment she looked like a professor pausing in a lecture. "Well, it really taps into something, doesn't it? Three affluent people who on the surface have everything—education, resources, positions of influence—but at the core are terribly empty."

"Yes, isn't it strange? I can hardly think of Sarah or Marta without thinking of that play. I'd say that characterizes them too."

"Let's go back to your dream again. Is there a part of yourself that Sarah represents?"

I saw again the lifeless body lying at Adrian's feet. "Well, she's his victim. I felt such grief for her lying there. It's odd, I'd always thought of her as strong, active—until the night at her townhouse when I saw Adrian standing behind her. The woman I saw that night, whom I thought at the time was Sarah, seemed helpless that last evening. And in the dream, I only see her after she's fallen onto the pavement. She appears passive there as well, and fragile, a bystander to her own death."

"The passivity. That's important. When you think of Adrian, do you feel that he's typically in control? Of other people and events?"

I saw where she was going with this. "When I was younger, Adrian seemed to hold all the cards. I played defense most of the time. I didn't know how to handle his power. But now that we're both adults . . ." I shook my head. "I'm afraid I still feel at a disadvantage when I interact with him. He always seems to have a strategy. Or maybe it's that he's determined to move forward and I'm used to stepping back when confronted by him." I couldn't help but wonder why, after all these years, I so often didn't work out a clear plan for dealing with him. Wasn't it my fault that I wasn't prepared? Aloud, I said: "I don't act around him. I react. I'd like to change that."

"That brings up something I've wanted to ask you," Helen interjected as if she'd been waiting for just this moment. "About your career in theater. Would you say it ended—or rather you ended it—when Sarah died?"

Taken by surprise, I found myself without a response. My mind refused to process the question. It was all a jumble—the day Sarah died versus the last play I directed, when I'd withdrawn from the production company, and when I'd ceased translating everything I read into how it would look, and sound, on a stage. Performance was second nature to me then, as automatic as registering the temperature of a room. Until it wasn't.

Once I withdrew, I imagined that I'd been in a bubble all those years working in theater, and that one day, I'd simply stepped through the membrane of the bubble and it had popped. The space was no longer there to return to.

"Amanda?" Helen prompted after some time had passed.

Perspiration gathered between my breasts even though the temperature of Helen's office resembled the inside of a walk-in freezer. "Oh, I was just reminded of how many times Adrian has told me that I'm afraid of success. He used to point out that just when I reach a certain mastery I change careers." I added hastily: "I don't think what he says is true, at least not of me. It seems to me that when you've achieved your goals is precisely the time to search for new challenges. So I don't agree with him. I think we're different in this way. But what you're saying . . . about the why of my leaving theater . . . I'm trying to think it through."

The light from the lamp glinted on Helen's glasses, cast a golden glow on her skin. She relaxed her posture and leaned back. I sensed my answer was significant for her.

"I loved theater. But after Sarah died, I wondered if I had just followed in her footsteps rather than deciding for myself. She had always encouraged me to become a director. I wondered if I'd chosen directing as a career as a way to feel a sense of relationship with her. It's clear to me I had wanted her approval, even after she and Ellen got involved, and even when I could see the damage she'd done to Marta. I didn't trust her, yet I wanted to feel close to her."

"Yes. I can't help but think, now that you mention footsteps, that the name you and your friends gave your company was Footprints. A coincidence, perhaps, but interesting just the same." Helen looked at me sympathetically and I was aware of the heat rushing into my face.

I was embarrassed by how much I had craved Sarah's good opinion. A memory of the intense desire I'd felt for Sarah's attention startled me. "I'm ashamed to say that I was hungry for Sarah's approval. I felt empty without it. What you said about the characters in *Betrayal*—their core emptiness—reminds me of me then. Looking back, I see that my neediness was pathetic. Who was I trying to be successful for—her or me? I didn't know."

"And after her death?"

"I couldn't tolerate how conflicted I felt. About Sarah and theater, about my life in college, graduate school, the company we'd started." The memory of that turmoil lived in my body. I suddenly felt as if I were running in place—my heart raced, my breath sounded ragged in my ears. I dropped my hand and reached for my tote bag near the chair. I wanted to hurl it across the room. "Don't you see? Pride, desperation, loathing, love—all of it was tied up together! I felt like everything I'd done had been polluted. What was real, what was artifice? I didn't know."

I slumped in my chair then, the frisson of walled-up emotion draining from every joint. I wanted to go home and go to sleep. For a very, very long time.

"Amanda, listen to me. In your family you didn't have the approval or attention that every child desires. You're a very imaginative and talented person. Of course you wanted someone to notice what you could do, to encourage you to excellence. That's what we all do—we look for mentors, for someone who can bring us along into our true work. It's not your fault that your mentor betrayed you."

I closed my eyes. "But I chose her. I persistently refused to see who she really was. In some way, I made the betrayal possible. Don't you see? It's like my relationship with Adrian. I had no strategy around those two people who had a very clear sense of what they wanted."

"Yes, and you were all of eighteen years old when you met Sarah. You were a student. You were young, inexperienced." Helen bit her lip and crossed her arms. She sounded angry and troubled, and beneath her words I sensed something personal. "We all need a time of incubation when we can be safe. A time when we don't have a strategy; we just need to explore. Isn't that what a good undergraduate education provides in a sense? A student is someone who is a beginner, not a master. And the adults around a student, like a parent with their children, take responsibility and make sure there are boundaries. That is their job."

The muscles on the left side of my neck throbbed. I was certain if I tried to turn my head I wouldn't be able to. "Thank you," I whispered. But inside, a pool of lethargy swamped my spirits.

Helen observed me closely. "There will come a time," she said very slowly, "when you will forgive yourself." She didn't utter the words *I hope* but I thought I saw the whisper of them form on her lips.

I looked at the clock, slightly askew on the wall but ticking regularly just the same. "I'd like to make an appointment for the week we come back from Chicago."

———

Driving home, I thought about how I'd begun to paint when I left the world of theater. And how as I'd learned and experimented, I hadn't had any ambitions about the work I did. I'd just loved doing it, the daily routine of it, handling my implements, mixing color, assessing light. Oils, acrylics, pastels, each allowed me to produce different textures. If I'd been hungry in those years, it was only to find time to work. Yes, I'd enjoyed the times I'd exhibited my work, and the occasional moments when someone had praised it. But more than receiving accolades for what I'd made, I'd found that it fed me to face the blank canvas and transform it using my mind and spirit into something new. I didn't experience the self-consciousness, the craving for approval that I'd always felt performing or directing. I deliberately abandoned the imperative of external validation that had been so stifling to me in my years in academia. It had been one of the hardest things I'd ever done, like breaking an addiction to alcohol or sex. Yet my continuing preoccupation with Marta, and Sarah, and even *Betrayal* itself, showed me I was only recovering after all, I wasn't cured. I realized that painting was essential to my continuing recovery.

My grandmother, my mother's mother, had made my study of art possible financially. But her inheritance went beyond the resources she'd left me. Her persona itself had served as a template. Unabashedly frank, her enjoyment of life a tangible presence in any room she occupied, she had always been herself. An ability to take pleasure in daily life was her gift and, through the many hours I'd spent in her presence, she'd made me appreciate how precious that gift was. As an adult I'd searched to find a place in my life where I felt that well-being, that pure pleasure in the moment that seemed to inform much of her life. In our time together, I wasn't inhibited by the weight of her expectations of me. When I painted, I found some of that joy—the empty space in front of me became pure possibility.

I vowed to get back to thinking about, and doing, art. My hands at that moment itched to hold tubes of paint, test the texture of each brush against my fingertips, gauge the grain of paper or canvas. Since I'd worked with John, I'd set aside my daily discipline of drawing, taking classes, setting up my easel, even my close observation of the natural world. When the gallery that had shown my work had folded, I'd assumed that the closing was a referendum on my work. I'd perceived the fate of the gallery as a sign, rather than the pragmatic business decision by the owner it had no doubt been. Worse, I'd taken it all personally, an assumption I'd warned my students to resist when they received criticism.

Making art was, I realized, my true work, to use the phrase Helen had chosen. It was satisfying, nourishing, not tainted with my desire to be noticed—or watched—which I'd felt the first time I'd met Sarah. That wasn't Sarah's fault, of course. Like Psyche, who gazed at Cupid in the light of a candle when he'd told her the one thing forbidden her was to look upon him, I'd been unable to keep myself from wanting the one thing Sarah couldn't give me—intimacy. My need had been like the drop of candle wax that shattered Cupid's slumber and sent Psyche into a life of trial. Sarah's gifts had been many—charm, intelligence, insight about ideas. Her practice of using the stage as a laboratory had cemented her professional reputation. Yet emotionally she had been remote. I never penetrated her armor, but I'd surrendered my own too willingly.

Turning into my gravel driveway, I sat in the car with the air-conditioning blasting around me. I stared at the square of the green garage door as if it were a canvas in a museum that might offer up its secrets. My eyes lost focus while my brain searched for clarity. At the time in my life when I'd met Sarah, my inner being was housed in the most porous of membranes.

And in the years afterward, one mystery had preoccupied me: why had I willingly offered myself up to someone that I feared had wounded so many others?

I remembered Ellen calling Sarah a witch when we were in college. But that was much too simple. After all, no one has to let the witch inside when she knocks on the door. No, she has to be invited inside in order to exercise her power.

I heard Babs's voice in my ear. *The sanctum sanctorum. We all have a place that is ours alone. No one has the right to violate that place.* I'd always admired that about Babs. She hadn't given herself away. She had an inner core that belonged only to her. If I had a daughter, I would give her that advice. I would tell her not just once, but many times: *There is a special part of every person that contains their essence. You can choose to share it, but never, ever give it away.*

26

We flew to Chicago on the first Saturday in October. Teresa insisted on splurging for the occasion and so we checked into the venerable Drake Hotel on East Walton. We arrived a couple of hours before Babs was due in from the East Coast. The lobby, burnished by old wood, high ceilings, and sparkling chandeliers, felt grand, just as it had when I saw it on my first trip to Chicago with my mother and her friend thirty years before. The carpet, with its hues of gold and red against royal blue, animated our steps and propelled our feet in a forward glide. Afternoon tea, an occasion at the Drake as ornate as the lobby, was proceeding at a magisterial pace as we walked to the elevators.

"My mother and I had tea here once when I was a kid. Eva had this friend, Sophia Martin. We were close. In fact, I thought of her as my aunt. I remembered one of my greatest fantasies was to go and live with Sophia. When I first met you, you reminded me of her. A much younger version, of course."

Teresa gave me a tender smile. "What a lovely compliment. Thank you. You don't know how much I like the name Sophia. I always wanted that to be my name."

"Why?"

"Oh, I liked the sound on my lips when I was young. And then I discovered that Sophia was the goddess of wisdom."

"*The keeper of knowledge,* my grandmother used to say."

"Hmm." Teresa grabbed the handle of her bag as the elevator stopped on the sixth floor. "Those two aren't necessarily the same thing, are they? I think of wisdom as something beyond knowledge."

"Maybe you are lucky enough to possess both."

"Even without having been given the name Sophia?"

I linked my arm in hers. "The spirit of the name might have to be enough for you."

———

The first thing that attracted my attention when we entered the theater that night was a red jacket lying on the floor in the aisle five rows from the stage. The garment had spilled off the back of the seat to make a crimson pool on the gray carpet. The space was small, no more than a hundred chairs, and our tickets did not give us assigned seating. Gravitating to the splash of red, I led Teresa and Babs to the middle of the fifth row.

When he was ten, Duncan had persuaded Eva to buy him a pair of rubber galoshes a scalding shade of red. I can't imagine where she found them. He had mittens and a scarf that matched. A year later, he was still talking about "red" days and "purple" ones. He'd come into the world a born eccentric. If Duncan had lived, I'm not sure what he'd have become, but I was certain he would have made his life a work of art, rife with color, verve, and instinct.

As we settled into our seats, I imagined Duncan sitting beside me as if he had regained those thirty lost years and attained the age of forty-two, lines firmly etched from his nose to his mouth, his eyes like a depth charge of blue against his creamy skin. For a moment, I let myself entertain the comfort and pleasure of having my twin next to me again. I registered the fine-tuned ease of having my right shoulder graze his left, my heart and brain bolstered by the oneness of two.

Right about then, perhaps three minutes before curtain, I saw the back of Adrian's head in the second row. And next to him, coming up to his shoulder, was a finely molded head, the dark hair streaked with gray. I drew in a slow breath. Sarah Moore's head had looked that way from the rear, floating on her neck in perfect equipoise.

I touched Teresa's knee and felt her instant alertness. Of course she would feel the panic that leaked from the tip of my finger. "Is that Marta or Sarah?" I whispered, surprised I had any voice at all.

She frowned, following the line of my vision, but didn't look alarmed.

"I can't tell." She was humoring me, I thought. Teresa had no doubts that Sarah had died.

My own thoughts about Duncan a moment ago came back to me, the oneness of two, how I felt that Duncan was still in this world because I was. Sarah and Marta, those two linked selves, perhaps weren't so very different. The presence of one contained the shadow of the other. I thought of the technique of chiaroscuro in a painting or the halo around the moon on a dark night. One brushstroke or object highlighted another. I wondered in the larger scheme of things if we were all projections of someone else, united through a trick of time, the path of light. As long as Marta was alive, Sarah's shadow stood next to her or behind her. As the small head turned toward Adrian, I noticed the downturn of the lips, seductive yet severe.

Babs, alert to the tremor rippling through our row, stood and began to make her way to the aisle. She walked down toward the stage, very deliberately as if to hail a friend in the first row. Reaching the end of the walkway, she assumed a look of surprise as if she'd mistaken the person for someone else and walked briskly back, threaded through our row once again, and resumed her seat.

"Amanda, your brother is here. And he's sitting with Marta Conway, if I'm not mistaken. But sitting next to her, and I kid you not, is a younger version of Sarah Moore."

"How much younger?"

"Your age. So about ten, eleven years. The haircut, the set of the head on the shoulders, it's amazing."

My mind flashed on Ellen at once, even though I hadn't seen her since we were twenty-one and in college. Who else would have made her life's study becoming the perfect acolyte of her obsession? "You're sure that's not Sarah sitting beside Adrian?"

Teresa intervened: "This other person must look like a younger sister of Marta as well. And look," she leaned toward me to whisper," there's another woman farther down the row with the same haircut."

At that moment, the first younger woman turned around and I could see that it wasn't Ellen, but some other appendage attracted into the Marta-Sarah orbit. A familiar ache crept along the ridge of my eye sockets and weariness invaded my body. I was too tired to enter into the high drama of the past. "Let's just go," I said.

194

"Are you utterly starkers?" Babs looked at me in astonishment. "After all this?"

"Shhhh," Teresa said as the lights went dark and then came up on Jerry and Emma seated in the pub in the first scene.

I closed my eyes and listened to the still-familiar words as Emma follows their first words of greeting with "You look well," and Jerry says, "Well, I'm not all that well, really."

No, I thought, *we're none of us all that well. Not really.* I opened my eyes just to see what the woman playing Emma looked like. She was tall, auburn-haired, like Patricia Hodge, who had played the role in the film version. Then, fighting a ripple of nausea, I closed them again. The words in the scene unspooled in front of me, too familiar, too treacherous. I didn't think I could sit and listen to them again. "I'll be right back," I whispered to Teresa.

The show had no intermission and I considered waiting out the ninety minutes or so of its playing time in the small lobby, but that space felt too claustrophobic and exposed. I stepped outside, turned right, and stopped at a small pub halfway down the street. Its plain brown brick front was anonymous and appealing. I went in and sat at the bar, staring at the back of the slender bartender and noting how the mirror I faced seemed to magnify the circles under my eyes. I studied the long rows of multicolored bottles arranged in an appealing display of shapes and labels, trying to avoid my reflection.

As Jerry did in the middle of *Betrayal* during an awkward lunch with Robert, I ordered a scotch, neat. It arrived in a squat square glass and I tipped the entire two-and-a-half fingers of its contents down the back of my throat at once. The burn startled me awake. Even the faces reflected in the mirror in front of me appeared less wavy and indistinct. The dark room, roughly half-full, came into focus. Two women sat at a table in the corner, their heads close together. One swabbed at her face with tissues as if wiping away tears. As a man walked toward the empty barstool next to me, I quickly paid and left before he arrived.

Reluctant to go back to the theater, I hesitated in the middle of the block. Any sense of excitement I'd had before the trip had evaporated. In its place was the sense that the Adrian-Marta-Sarah conundrum would remain a puzzle, no matter how much more I might see, hear, or learn. New facts would simply beget more possibilities.

Babs and Teresa had much more objectivity than I did anyway; let them find—and follow—the breadcrumbs leading out of this section of the woods. *Betrayal* was like a prism turning slowly in an open doorway, refracting the world through its crystalline eye. The mirror it offered up to its audience, like the one in the bar I'd just left, revealed a stark human craving that most of us didn't want to face. It was much easier to dismiss it as a distorted, idiosyncratic view. This thought tore through a protective shield over my senses and I began to walk again. What if the impulse to betray was truly a human appetite, as basic as love or hate or possession? Maybe love led to possessiveness, which led to fear of loss of the beloved, which led to betrayal? Maybe the sequence simply had a momentum of its own. That would explain why in every life there is betrayal, even down to the lies and self-deception that allow us to reassure ourselves in the darkest times.

My brooding about the play weighed on my shoulders like a heavy cloak. No, it was more like a dark bird had perched there, piercing the skin with its talons in its effort to hold on. Small wonder that at points in western history drama was viewed as a suspect art, seen to be as wildly inflated as the thundering edifice of Oz, and that those who manipulated its glittering surfaces were either shunned or rejected as flimflam.

A few minutes later, having successfully made it back into Division Street, I splashed water on my face in the ladies' room, avoiding the mirror, and let my skin air-dry. I checked my watch—amazingly, I'd managed to kill forty minutes.

As I cracked open the door, I saw a tall man with tense, broad shoulders prowling in the lobby. It was Adrian, dressed in black pants and jacket with a maroon shirt buttoned to the throat. Surreptitiously, he took a drag off a cigarette and stubbed out the butt in a fern plant by the door. As he leaned over the planter, I noticed that his face had become leaner and sharper. Age had been kind to my brother, marking him lightly. Only the telltale small fold of flesh sagging under his chin indicated he was in his late forties. He leaned into the door and pushed out of the theater, turning right, the direction of the bar I'd just vacated. I didn't think. I just followed.

For a couple of blocks, Adrian walked swiftly, arms swinging, as if working to dispel a head of steam. Or anxiety. He'd reach the end of each block as the green turned yellow and keep on going. It had rained since we'd arrived at the theater after dinner, and the mild, humid air felt good on my face. It was at least twenty degrees cooler than Austin was at night. I ran the lights as well to keep up—I didn't hurry, but I kept Adrian in my sight; the synthetic soles of the supple leather flats I wore made little sound.

Fairly quickly, the neighborhood changed and the clubs and coffee shops thinned out. The moonless night had a thick, insulated feel to it, and the headlights of approaching cars glowed with a faint halo as if a fog were setting in. For a moment, the dark street lit by infrequent streetlights during a lull in the traffic so resembled the landscape of my recent dream that I shivered and buttoned the short linen jacket I'd thrown on when I left my seat at the performance.

Adrian stopped abruptly. He turned to a glass storefront, and adjusted his hair in his reflection. The plate glass was wide and he stood in front of it for a long time. His look was so absorbed and intent that I froze in midstep, visited by the urgent sensation that the whole neighborhood, including me, was telescoped in miniature in that window. I began to feel foolish following him—shadowing my brother had been something that had preoccupied me as a child, but what could it possibly accomplish now? And so I turned back toward the theater.

Just as I decided to slink away unnoticed, rapid footsteps sounded behind me and I picked up my pace. I stepped into the doorway to an office supply store, now closed, and kept my back to the street. It was Adrian—I could dimly make him out in the store window—and he hurried past me without a glance in my direction. At first I thought he was looking for me, but he kept glancing at his watch. He reminded me of the White Rabbit, hopelessly late, trying to outstep time. I walked briskly after him, keeping him in view, a difficult task in the tedious drizzle. My watch told me the production was within ten minutes of its curtain. I needed to find Teresa and Babs, and hopefully get them away from the theater, away from Marta and Adrian and this part of town, and safely into the lounge at our hotel.

Adrian stopped for a moment to light a cigarette, and when he pulled the lighter from his jacket pocket, a small square of paper fluttered out. When he resumed walking, I picked it up and carefully unfolded the fragment of yellow legal paper: *Have the car ready by the entrance.* I assumed the note was from Marta, but I wasn't sure; the headlong, hasty scrawl seemed reminiscent of margin notes on college papers. The message logically could have referred to another evening or city, yet it fueled my rising urgency to collect my friends and head back downtown so I resumed walking at a faster pace.

About two blocks from the playhouse, Adrian crossed in the middle of the block and walked toward a green Volvo parked by the curb. He fumbled in his pants pocket, pulled out a set of keys, and pressed the unlock button. He looked at his watch again before sliding behind the wheel.

I waited for him to start the car, but when he simply sat there, waiting, I continued to walk toward the theater. There was little traffic, but the light fog had turned moist and the drizzle had turned to a light rain. The streets were wet and slick and the sparse streetlamps cast little light; the thick air trapped the filaments of illumination from radiating outward so that there were only isolated pools glowing in the gray murk.

At this point, disoriented in the wet, dark street, I collided with a slender metal pole that supported one of the lights arcing above the pavement, smashing my right shoulder hard enough to spin me half around. My heart accelerated so quickly that my eardrums pounded with blood. Light-headed, I leaned against the lamppost. The thick air swirled around me, occasionally parting to give me a stop-motion view of the action on the street. My body felt insubstantial in the fog, as if I was being absorbed into a cloud.

When I reached the theater, I noticed Adrian had repositioned the green Volvo in a loading zone almost directly across from the playhouse entrance. I wondered if Adrian had circled the car around the block or passed me while I was distracted by my encounter with the streetlamp. He was at the wheel, hunched over the dash and leaning to the right, his shoulders and arms moving as if emptying the glove compartment in search of something. The glow from a light inside the car lit his face. I felt uneasy about Adrian sitting in that car in the pea-soup fog; I imagined another car slamming into the Volvo, its driver unaware that another vehicle was already parked there.

Reluctantly, I left the street and entered the theater lobby, pushing at the interior door just as the applause broke out. The clapping was long and protracted and I stood in the back of the theater as the audience began to file out. About two-thirds of the crowd left in a stream, straggling out the door in single and double columns, causing the room to empty of vitality as a tire deflates from a steady leak. After a few minutes I'd fought the outgoing traffic and made it three-quarters of the way up the right side aisle. About thirty people remained, milling about as the crew set out wineglasses and appetizer trays at the back of the theater, near the exit doors, for a reception.

I skirted the area in front of the drinks table where Marta stood, surrounded by well-wishers. Babs and Teresa were still in their seats in the fifth row.

Teresa's face, creased as she scanned the retreating audience, relaxed as she saw me. "Where've you been?" She looked at Babs as if expecting her to answer for me.

"I went out for a drink."

"All this time?" Teresa said, her tone wavering between concern and annoyance.

I shook my head. "When I got back to the lobby, I saw Adrian heading outside and so I followed him. I'm sorry if you were worried. I wasn't thinking. . . . I'm not sure what he was up to. Maybe he needed some air too. He ended up moving his car closer to the theater. I didn't get a chance to speak to him."

Babs murmured, "Odd how both of you felt claustrophobic in this theater. Or was it the subject matter?"

Unsure how to respond, I asked, "How was the show?"

Teresa's eyes looked glazed. "I don't know," she said. "I was too distracted wondering where you'd gone."

I turned to Babs who tipped her hand back and forth. "It was just fine," she said. "So controlled it made me want to run riot through the aisles." As if composing notes for a future essay, she added, "The character of Robert raises the temperature a bit. There's something pure about him. He wears civility like a mask. Behind it, he's cold and ruthless. A survivor. No matter what it takes."

I thought of the body lying in the street in my dream. Adrian, like the character she spoke of, would always be the last man standing.

My hand strayed to the pocket where I'd placed the note I'd found on the street. "Are you both ready to leave?"

"I'm going to say something to Marta," Teresa said. "Then we can go."

"Don't be long . . ." I wanted to detain her, but she had brushed past me. I noticed the thread of tension across Teresa's shoulders. I couldn't judge her mood exactly, if she was apprehensive at meeting her old friend or put out with me for disappearing earlier. Helplessly, I watched her make her way down the center aisle. The red jacket that had been lying on the floor had vanished, but I filled in its outlines just the same and imagined a scarlet pool in the carpet. I found myself staring at the back of Teresa's shoes as she approached Marta, as if searching for a stain from wading through that crimson puddle.

The thought of Adrian waiting across the street made me feel nervy and impatient. "I really would like to get out of here. What should we do?"

"Wait for her."

"Well, yes, but do you think we should go and stand in line with the rest?"

Babs considered this, her brown eyes fixed on mine. "You might want to do that. I'm going to get a glass of wine. Want some?"

I nodded and trudged down the aisle. Oddly, where I'd seen the jacket there was a blot on the carpet, a rusty-colored smudge as if a patron had spilled something, a slosh of wine perhaps from a glass purchased during an intermission last season.

By now Teresa had moved forward in the line of congratulatory audience members waiting to talk to Marta and the cast, and was standing to the right of the director. I stood at a distance, behind a man with a large mat of curly hair, who was clearly eager to reach Marta's side. His mouth hung open slackly as if in his eagerness he could only take shallow breaths. I felt an old irritation again at the fringe of toadies who inevitably attended theater productions, basking in the reflected glory of the stage lights even though they never set foot on the boards. *Star fuckers*, Ellen had always called them.

The star in this case was Marta Conway, and I didn't need to get any closer to her; I had a perfect view. She looked much the same, hair still brunette, lightly threaded with gray. Still trim, she wore black slacks and a maroon jacket that hugged her hips and emphasized her shoulders. A black braid around the collar gave the jacket a romantic flair. Her face looked fuller around the jaw than I remembered, her posture a trace less erect. But, then, I hadn't seen her since I was a senior in college, twenty-one years ago. I couldn't shake the feeling that I'd stepped into a hole in time. Almost a generation had passed, and to me, a lifetime.

As I examined her every gesture, I realized I was hyperaware of Marta, but wondered whether I'd have noticed her in a crowd on the street in the ordinary course of things. I glanced behind me at the stage curtain and then forward again into the grinning faces surrounding the director, and the thought occurred to me that Marta Conway couldn't have constructed a more perfect setting to launch her reemergence to an old friend like Teresa. My chest constricted as I was overcome by a creeping claustrophobia. The entire evening felt stage-managed. The coincidence of all of us occupying this room at this moment in time appeared suddenly impossible, prompted as it was by this unlikely production that Teresa and I had felt compelled to attend, an event that launched Marta Conway, under the radar for so many years, into our lives once more.

By now Teresa stood chatting with Marta. Marta had grasped my friend's hand and seemed reluctant to let it go. I looked for the oversized opal ring that Babs said Marta always wore on her middle finger of her right hand. It was there, but on the fourth finger, her ring finger, and it appeared to fit snugly. That discrepancy flitted away as I focused on how easy Teresa and Marta seemed in their conversation, their bodies slightly leaning toward each other. The forceful gray eyes studied Teresa's face as if to consume every detail of skin tone and feature. It was obvious the two women knew each other and well.

Had Marta's eyes been the same exact shade of gray that Sarah's had been? Or had they been another color? Babs's old photos had all been in black and white. I tried to remember but all I could see was the woman in front of me.

Amanda, concentrate, Marta Conway had admonished me in the acting class I'd taken with her in college. Her petite body had angled forward as if poised to spring. She placed a hand on my shoulder. *What sensation are you feeling in your body right now?* Fighting resistance, I'd looked into the tight focus that was Marta's gaze when she was working. Dark with large pupils, the eyes were hypnotic.

Teresa continued to talk to Marta. The man with the halo of curls shifted his stance and took a step to the right. I sought Teresa's attention and instead found my eyes locked with Marta Conway's.

Dropping back a few steps, Teresa laid a hand on my arm and drew me forward. "You remember Amanda Ferguson."

Marta grinned, an impish flash of teeth that set mine on edge. The woman was so unflappable, so socially adept, so artfully camouflaged. It was impossible from her expression to know what she was really thinking or feeling. She came toward me, put an arm around my shoulder, and squeezed. "How wonderful to see you!"

Her voice, low and melodic, so like Sarah's, reverberated with the moment I had seen Sarah for the last time, fourteen years ago. My chest felt hollow. I studied Marta's hairline; Sarah had had a small skin discoloration on her neck just behind her right ear that her hair barely covered. My lips had sought out that tender spot on her neck. Marta pushed her bangs out of her eyes, ran a hand under the fine fringe of hair that graced her collar. There, a flash of something. Was it the birthmark? I found myself shivering.

Teresa looked at me, her eyes questioning. "Yes," I said to Marta. "It's been such a long time."

Marta frowned for a moment. "How long *has* it been? I can't begin to calculate—?"

I watched her hands gesture broadly. "Well, Sarah was alive," I began.

A shadow crossed over her features, a ripple of wariness that tightened the mask of her face. "Sarah . . ." she said. And then she turned on me a look of concentrated compassion and sadness. Her face didn't register any guilt, only deep regret. I wondered if she was recalling a part she'd once played, one where she'd had to tell one spouse about the death of the other. It was unnerving that her features could be that mercurial, easily moving from caution and self-concern to empathy. That was it—Marta was purely intuitive, purely empathic. If she desired, if the stakes warranted it, she could mirror any mood presented to her.

"I know how fond you were of Sarah." She cocked her head to one side. Then, as if making a bold move to seize the queen in a game of chess, she added quietly: "Adrian has told me how much she meant to you."

Adrian. The dark gray eyes were unflinching as they bored into my face. My brother's presence filled the room. I remembered his head bent in the green Volvo.

"It was a loss for all of us," I blurted, and then, "Is Adrian coming back?"

Marta ignored my question, or perhaps I'd only thought it and hadn't spoken it out loud. "A loss. Yes."

As she appeared to consider this, the import of her comment struck me—surely she didn't need Adrian to tell her anything about the feelings I'd had for Sarah. Even as an undergraduate, I knew my attachment had been obvious; I'd worn it on my face and in my rapt interest anytime Sarah had been nearby. Plus, Marta had always known who cared about Sarah and how much. She sifted the world through her own alchemical process, absorbing and decoding the vibrations and colors surrounding the people in her orbit. Marta was a magician who juggled the whirling atoms of human behavior, let them catch the light, and reflect back on her.

Marta murmured the word *loss* again as she appeared to calculate the hidden meanings of my attitude and words. Calmly she said, "I believe you saw Sarah fairly close to her death?"

The pale face on the second floor of Sarah's town house, backlit from the low light in the room, appeared in my vision. And suddenly I was certain of what I'd suspected before: Sarah had been a prisoner in the tower. The agitated, fearful woman who had greeted me at the door that night had been a bold and chancy Marta Conway performance. But why had she impersonated Sarah for my benefit?

Marta still had her arm around my shoulders when she suddenly tightened her grip. "It was a terribly unfortunate accident. You know, of course, she was alone in her house?" Her eyes were wide, blank, and chilling. Then she smiled and attempted a light touch, but her voice was colored by a cynical edge. "I know how easy it is for imaginative souls like you and me to conjure up all sorts of complicated scenarios when the truth is simple."

"Simple?" I echoed in a thick voice. Incredulity and the stirrings of anger at this woman's ease in rewriting history—a history that lived in my body—clogged my throat. Marta nodded, but I saw that she was making a decision about me. In the clench of her jaw, the position of her head, the finely wrought tension of her hand resting on the cloth of my jacket, I felt only calculation—how much of a threat did my doubts about Sarah's death pose to her? And in that moment, I was aware she knew perfectly well when I'd last seen Sarah. And I was absolutely certain of one other thing: Marta was linked to Adrian firmly enough that she'd begun to think like him.

Unnerved, I glanced at Teresa, telegraphing my desire to leave. But at that moment Marta released me with a final appraising look, grasped Teresa's arm, and propelled her toward a man in a charcoal suit. "Oh, I want you to meet someone." She turned back to me. "You look well, Amanda."

Without waiting for the two of them to return—indeed, Teresa made a pointed gesture for me to wait for her—I slipped around other patrons, through the tiny lobby, and out into the cool air. I hoped to snag a cab for the three of us but none were empty.

Mist still hung in the air and glazed windshields and sidewalks. The atmosphere was dark and murky, lending an opaque quality to human and inanimate objects alike—it was like everything on the street occupied a life-size game board. And yet the streetlamps highlighted the moisture around the parked cars and gave them a gauzy halo. The heavy air caught in my lungs as I paced down the street for several blocks, then made my way back toward the Division Street Playhouse. No more than five minutes had passed since I'd gone outside.

The green Volvo was still parked across the street, but it now held two people. Adrian was at the wheel. The seat beside him was empty but in the back I could make out the silhouette of a woman with shoulder-length hair. Vapor and raindrops obscured the car windows; they were more reflective than revealing. Uneasy about the identity of the person in the car with Adrian, I strained to see inside. The door to the theater opened and attracted my attention—Marta came through the doorway and began to walk briskly across the street toward the car. It was then that an inconceivable thing happened.

Marta waited in the middle of the street while Adrian began angling the car out of its space. When I'd first seen the car in the loading zone, one car was in front of him and nothing parked to the rear, but a car had since wedged him in from behind. He backed up twice and repositioned the car, but still couldn't clear the rear bumper of the station wagon in front of him. At this moment Marta fished one hand into her coat pocket and pulled something out—a key, a tube of lip gloss?—and looked down at the object in her hand.

While Adrian maneuvered the Volvo once more, a black car, I think a Buick—it had a wide grill like an open mouth—slowly edged up the street, its headlights boring through the fog and scattering the droplets in a silver spray. The car was about two feet from Marta when she walked directly into its path. Even then, I think the car could easily have swerved around her except that she tripped and fell into the diminishing space in front of the Buick's bumper.

I heard a subdued cry from Marta and then the slap of steel against flesh. For a few seconds, time appeared frozen.

The driver jumped out of his car and stood leaning against his door for support. "What the hell!" He straightened up and his arms jerked like marionette limbs dangling from a thread. "Jesus. She walked right into me!"

I stepped off the curb onto the street. The driver had his phone in his hand and wildly punched its buttons. But before he had positioned the phone to his ear, Adrian leaped out of the car, put his arm under Marta's shoulders, and whispered something. Stragglers from the theater crowded around them. "Oh my God!" "Do you need help?" The people pushed closer.

"No, no, we're fine," Adrian said in a commanding voice. Hearing his sharp retort, the group took a step back.

Marta sat up and put a hand to the side of her face then looked at it, as if checking for traces of blood, then sagged back down to the street. My brother lifted her onto her feet; she leaned against him but made her way steadily to the car. Adrian folded her into the front passenger seat, took his place at the wheel, and the car swept into the street. The whole incident flashed in front of me so fast I barely registered it. The startled person in the backseat turned and raised a hand as the car plunged forward. Was she waving? Asking for help? It was impossible to know.

I ventured into the traffic, arms up, trying to stop the car. A sports car veered around me, horn blaring. A rush of air grazed my face. I couldn't see far enough in the rain and fog to see the Volvo's taillights. I stood for a moment in my own private haze and torment, wondering if I'd conjured up the entire scene. Then I spotted the driver, now slumped at the curb with his arms wrapped around his knees.

I helped him to his feet. "I guess she's okay." I aimed for an encouraging tone, but managed only a croak.

He looked at me, eyes watery, a short, slight man with thinning gray hair. "What the hell was that?" His voice was hoarse too.

"Can I call someone for you?" His legs seemed to be holding steady but I still held on to his arm. I wasn't sure which of us was supporting the other.

He shook his head. "I've got to get home. Thanks, lady. I appreciate your stopping."

Desperately thirsty and chilled with damp, I jammed my hands into my coat pockets. The theater was behind me. Who was in that car with Adrian and Marta? Light-headed, I bent over until the world steadied. I had to find Babs.

By this time, only a few strays filtered out of the theater door. I dodged a bulky twosome at the door and slipped inside. The reception table was a ruin of bottles and upended glasses. Only the crew and a few hangers-on were still drinking and vacuuming up the last crumbs of cheese on the platters. Babs stood stolidly by the last row of seats, holding two coats, her eyes glued to the lobby doors.

"Thank God!" She looked pale. Where have you been?"

I looked around wildly. "Where's Teresa?"

"She left with Marta to have a drink. Just one she said, and she'll call us in a few minutes or meet us back at the hotel if all else fails."

"But I just saw Marta leaving the theater alone. Heading toward Adrian's car across the street. There was a woman in the backseat—"

"They went out together and then Marta came back in here—I guess she'd forgotten something—and left again," my friend began.

"Oh God, Teresa was in that car." The *Have the car ready* on the note seemed ominous. Had Marta always planned to whisk Teresa away? The scene I'd just witnessed crowded concern for Teresa. "There's been an accident." I grasped her warm, dry hand with my cold, sweaty one.

I recounted what I'd just seen. "It happened so fast I don't know if Teresa even had time to exit the car. Especially if she wasn't used to the door handles or the lock release." My friend listened closely, squeezing my hand from time to time as if to reassure us both we were still here.

After a time, Babs draped Teresa's coat across a chair back and put hers on. Then she arranged Teresa's coat across her arm once more. It had been mild when we'd come into the playhouse. Teresa had clearly acted on impulse and gone off without it. If she'd gone willingly, that is. As we talked, my eyes strayed to the coat in Babs's arms and followed the line of the drooping fabric down to the floor. On the carpet was a blue cell phone that had slipped out of one of the coat pockets.

I leaned over and picked it up. The small object felt heavy and warm. "She won't be calling us. This is Teresa's phone."

27

Depression blanketed me back at the hotel, as dense and palpable as the fog outside. Part of me was certain I'd never see Teresa again. I already missed her intensely. I realized how I'd come to rely on her buoyancy, her self-possession, her serenity. I collapsed onto the small sofa in our room, my limbs strangely nerveless. The world felt barren and hollow. As if I were trapped at the wrong end of a telescope, everything looked and felt diminished.

Babs had gone to her room to change into other clothes. She'd called to say she was coming up but it was clear she was tired; somehow I convinced her there was nothing for her to do until tomorrow. I opened my laptop to get a list of area hospitals as we planned to call every one in search of Marta, who I suspected had a serious enough head injury that she'd have to seek medical help.

My journal rested by the computer and I fanned through it, noting how the first sparse engagements with Teresa in the spring had proliferated as the weeks progressed. I'd only known Teresa seven months but she was already a bulwark in my life. Even though our time together had encompassed months rather than years, we'd built trust and friendship with care, layer upon layer, until we had fashioned something together. Our common history had cemented our pasts as well. Only four hours ago we'd left this hotel, heading for the theater, anticipating our evening. Now the night had disintegrated around me, and I was left with what I already knew, that in the briefest of moments any world can collapse, no matter how painstakingly made.

Duncan's face emerged in my mind, round-cheeked, expectant. *Manda*, he used to ask over and over when we were waiting for something, *what time is it now?*

The clock by the king-sized bed registered midnight. I had the horrifying thought that Marta had kidnapped Teresa. The possibility was profoundly dramatic, and I realized there were many other simple explanations. She might have just stepped out for that one drink. But the image of the crimson jacket lying on the carpet as we'd first entered the theater stayed with me. More and more it assumed the weight of a portent, a stain that spread over the evening and blotted out everything else.

I closed my eyes, willing Teresa to come back to me. Teresa was not just vital to my current life. She illuminated a path to the future that we could walk together. I realized I could bear all the years of struggling with Adrian's destructive behavior, the unbearable loss of Duncan, the wrenching death of Sarah, if only I could have the solace of this love, this acceptance. Prayer was not my natural reflex, but I prayed.

I was beginning to regret having turned away Babs's offer of comfort. The display on the clock tumbled toward one o'clock, and I continued my vigil, the voice in my ear repeating, *What time is it now?*

Just as I was about to unravel from nervous exhaustion, a key clicked in the lock and the door whispered against the carpet. Teresa walked in. Shoulders slumped, the linen of her pale-green blouse pleated with wrinkles, fine eyes drooping and red-rimmed, she looked all in, yet when she saw me, her lips lifted. I rose from the sofa and went to her.

I enfolded her against me. She felt thin and fragile. "You came back."

"I couldn't wait to get here. What a night. Is there anything to drink?"

I dug into the minibar and came up with two small bottles of Glenlivet that I sloshed into glasses. I pressed one into Teresa's hand and guided her to the sofa. I sat with her, one arm around her shoulders. "I thought perhaps you'd been kidnapped."

"I was, in a way. Marta asked me out for a drink and I thought, foolhardy me, *I'll get to the bottom of this and go with her, talk to her.* You had already left. I didn't know where you'd gone or when you'd be back." Teresa swept her hair off her neck and held it while she stretched her neck from side to side. "Some amateur sleuth I make."

"Were you in the car when—"

"When the car hit her, yes. Your brother half-carried her to the car. I assumed they would go to a hospital. So then I said, *Look, I have to go,* which seemed to make Adrian furious—before I could open the door he gunned the car and we sped down the street!"

"I saw it all."

"You were across the street? If only I'd known. Although it was so hard to see, I don't know how I could have signaled you anyway."

"But you did. You waved to me, didn't you?"

"I tried to clear the fog from the window but I still couldn't see anything."

I saw again the raised arm of the woman in the backseat. And recalled a haunting line from a favorite poem: *Not waving but drowning.*

"What is it?"

"Nothing. My mind is skittering all over the place. I'm just glad you're safe. Please, go on." I got up and grabbed the throw from the bed and spread it over us. Teresa's teeth were chattering with cold.

"Well, then your brother drove like a fiend onto the Kennedy Expressway. I reached for my phone but it wasn't there. I became seriously frightened about then. They started arguing about the accident and what they should do. Adrian left the expressway and began speeding along streets in the fog, dodging around cars. I couldn't look after a while. It was too terrifying and we were going so fast. I thought I was going to be sick in the car. We ended up in some northern suburb."

Teresa sipped her drink; her eyes, murky with fatigue, looked soberly into mine. She grasped my hand. "He didn't slow down. He was a madman. The streets were wet and winding. And that's when Adrian hit a tree."

I recoiled, imagining the impact. "Oh my God. So then what?"

"The front end crumpled. Steam rose from the front of the car. Your brother's head was slumped against the wheel. Marta looked unconscious. I had one of those moments when I wondered if I was still in this world or the next. I was almost afraid to try to find out. But my arms worked, and my legs. Incredibly, I seemed to be all in one piece. Scared almost to death, but still here."

Still here. Fate, miraculously, had spared her. "You were so lucky."

She closed her eyes and nodded.

"*We* are so lucky," I said.

"But Adrian . . ." Sadness rolled into the room with Teresa's sigh, bringing the vision of my brother, injured, crumpled in his car.

Concern for my brother gripped me. Yet in the deep well of my consciousness I found certainty that he was still alive.

Teresa drank again. Her fingers gripped the glass; when she wasn't drinking, she held on to it like a ballast. "I searched Marta's coat for her cell and I called an ambulance."

Teresa took off her shoes and began to massage one of her feet. "Here," I said, moving the blanket aside. I pulled both of her legs onto my lap and began to knead her calves. "And then?"

"Well, the police came too of course and after the paramedics loaded them onto stretchers, I asked for a ride here." Her head drooped forward in weariness. "Marta was babbling after the car hit the tree. She was very confused. But . . ."

I watched Teresa, moved my hands to the soles of her feet. "What?"

Teresa's lips twisted downward. "Oh, Amanda. I feel so terrible."

We both finished our glasses. "I'll find more of this." I turned to her. "I have a bad feeling about what you're going to tell me." I retrieved two more bottles from the minibar. The first bottle wouldn't open easily and the cap cut my finger.

"How did I not see it before?" Teresa said, her head in her hands.

I flinched. "Marta—?"

She shook her head. "Marta isn't Marta. My old friend is dead. I'm positive now."

My head buzzed with fatigue. "But how can you be sure?"

"When she was hit by the car she was in a lot of pain. And very frightened. All of the artifice dropped away, because that's what it had been, a carefully calibrated performance—the refraction of Marta rather than her presence. It would have convinced most people most of the time. But I knew Marta so well, you see."

"What was it, her voice, or what she said?"

Teresa massaged her temples. "I'd been with Marta once when she broke her ankle. Another time we'd gone skiing. She fell and suffered a concussion. I'd seen her when she was ill, with flu or a migraine. Each time she'd become almost catatonic. Very much like a child. Desperate for reassurance. She was terrified, always, of being sick or injured."

Teresa looked up, a half smile on her face. "My sister was like that too. Sylvie got very scared when she didn't feel well. I always tried to reassure her. Sometimes it worked. But with Marta, well, I wasn't able to soothe her, ever."

"So how did the woman in the car act?"

"This woman was furious. She screamed at Adrian, blamed him for the accident, called him every curse word in the world. She started hitting him. And of course, that's when I noticed something else. That's when I was certain."

I thought of the birthmark on Sarah's neck, just under her hairline, and waited.

Teresa shifted so that the cushion behind her back supported her more fully. "She was pounding her fist on your brother's shoulder while he was driving. He just kept driving faster and faster. I was horrified, and transfixed by her hands. It was all I could see. Marta had a wide scar at the base of her right thumb. The skin was very damaged, shriveled, if you knew to look. She'd burned herself as a child. Turned over a pan of scalding water and scorched her hand. It couldn't be covered up with makeup. But the woman in the car had no such mark."

"Sarah." I nodded, struck numb with the truth. "Of course. What is it they say—always hide in plain sight? That's what she did."

I waited for the old keen sense of anticipation, the gripping desire to see Sarah once again that I'd felt at the mere mention of her name. But I felt only weariness. Sarah and Adrian, together. They were, after all, a matched set.

We sat in silence, sipping our second single malt. In my mind, the green Volvo smashed against the tree in slow motion; Adrian and Sarah wobbled like marionettes in the front seats.

"What I don't understand," I said finally, "is why Sarah wanted us to see her. Why invite you to Chicago at any rate, why flagrantly display herself for your scrutiny?"

"Because somehow she knew I would continue to search for Marta if she didn't convince me she was alive. She feared I'd always wonder and wait, that I'd never give up. But if she could convince me, she'd be home free."

I thought of Babs's inquiries into Marta's whereabouts. Had that search alerted Sarah, prompted her to take a bold step?

Teresa continued. "And you too. You were there right before Sarah was supposed to have died. You knew there was something wrong about that night. Sarah was aware that in some part of your mind you didn't believe she was dead. She couldn't resist the opportunity to absolutely put it to rest once and for all—to show you that Marta was oh-so-definitely in the world."

"I still don't understand the advantage of becoming Marta. Was it financial?"

"Sarah was her beneficiary, and Marta's family was wealthy. She must have wanted Adrian for herself. . . ." Teresa kneaded her forehead. "Sarah assumed Marta's identity the way she did so many things. Blatantly and brilliantly. She did it because she could."

I picked up Teresa's right hand and held it. Her skin felt too cool. "Perhaps she couldn't resist the opportunity for the performance of a lifetime."

"There's a way your brother plays into it too. They both wanted to make sure you and I would suspect nothing about their conspiracy. Perhaps so that they could disappear together without a trace. Or maybe they wanted to see you again to be certain of what you knew. Or didn't know."

"Because I was a witness?" I saw again the face at Sarah's door, the darting eyes, the glassy stare, the flinch at the voice behind her.

"Yes, because you were there the night that Marta died." Teresa put her hands on my shoulders. She hesitated. "I don't know if you want to hear this. Your brother Adrian—I think he's very in love with Sarah."

Was it possible Adrian had been smitten all along, ever since I'd introduced them all those years ago after rehearsal? And perhaps Adrian had been the prize Sarah had coveted. Had she cared for me, even for a moment? The old longing of being on the outside flashed through me, the girl with her nose pressed against the window. The sensation passed in a moment. For in truth I no longer envied Adrian or Sarah, those hostages to deception. I turned my attention fully to Teresa. "The woman at the door that night. The one who acted so strangely that I could hardly believe it was Sarah."

Teresa's face looked tense, grappling for the missing piece of that long-ago evening as if she'd been there herself. "Because it wasn't Sarah. It was Marta, off balance, anxious. Terrified for her life. Which I fear she'd already decided to give up—she'd given away control of it to Sarah and possibly to Adrian too. Trapped in the vortex of their orbit, she found life no longer tolerable or worth living. I knew her so well. If she thought she truly would never be free again . . ."

The scene in Chicago replayed in my memory, but this time from a different perspective. The face of the woman on the stoop of the town house, etched with anxiety, turned toward me. "Marta wasn't acting, after all. She was desperate and frightened, just as she'd appeared. And the face at the upstairs window wasn't forlorn as I'd thought, hoping for rescue. It was simply Sarah, staring out the window, waiting for me to leave. Waiting for the next act in the drama. I had it all wrong."

"Just as they'd planned." Teresa picked up her empty glass, rolled it forward and back in both hands. "It was Sarah upstairs waiting and watching. Just as later she waited while Marta swallowed too many pills. Sarah knew Marta was still in love with her, that Marta wouldn't be able to accept her partnership with Adrian. Marta's self-esteem had always been frail. They applied pressure and Marta shattered. I can only imagine the games that must have gone on in that house . . ." She put the glass back on the table. "Adrian and Sarah didn't kill Marta. Not with their own hands anyway."

I thought of the physician's directive: *Do no harm. Help if you can.* "One of them, or both, had no intention of helping or preventing harm. Marta was just a liability." *Do not help. Harm if you can.*

Teresa shut her eyes. "They didn't intervene. Instead they stood by while she took her own life. God knows what life was like with the three of them. The anger, the jealousy, the reproaches. They let her drown in her own despair."

As I absorbed her words, I couldn't help but examine the dynamic of Adrian and Sarah together and wonder who the agent of Marta's destruction was and who the bystander. The history, the recriminations, the painful twists of abandonment and reunion over the years pointed to Sarah as the person with the most motive to want Marta out of the way. I doubted I'd ever know the answer. The events that led to Marta's demise were a conundrum, a labyrinth of motive and fate, a complex of moves now impossible to retrace.

We sat together, the tragedy of Marta between us. I touched the small bone of Teresa's wrist with a fingertip, struck by how fragile it appeared. "You can't imagine how happy I am that you came back to me." I smoothed her hair and framed the sides of her face with my hands. Her skin was chill to the touch but gradually warmed as my hands rested there.

Her eyes, warm as candlelight, swept over my face as she drew me close. "You must know there's nowhere else I'd rather be." After a moment, she said, "My love, you fear that everyone will leave you." Her voice, soft against my ear, whispered, "And don't I know just how you feel."

———

The body in the hospital bed twitched as the woman woke. Her eyes, blurred with sleep and narcotics, struggled to focus.

"Sarah," I said, recalling when the sound of the name caressed my ears, when everything about the woman who bore the name seemed luminous and rare.

The murky eyes, buried in puffy flesh, looked away. "You found me. Amazing. I wouldn't have thought it possible. But you always had an instinct for nuance, for intrigue."

I learned from the master, I thought.

"And you're very hard to hide from. You don't give up very easily." The voice was wry and brittle.

I looked around the spare room for water. There was so much I wanted to know, to ask her. Questions crowded my brain. I blurted out, "Why did you let Marta die?"

She sighed, closed her eyes once more. I pressed a glass of ice water into her hand. I didn't want her to be too parched to speak.

"She never forgave me. She told me I'd taken everything from her. It was unbearable. *She* was unbearable." Sarah's torso twisted as she coughed, a rattling sound deep in her chest. "Imagine. That woman, with all her talent. Most people would be delirious to have half her gifts. But not Marta. The sad thing is that she couldn't take pleasure in her success. A terrible curse."

"What did she mean that you took everything?"

"Women. Men. Students. The accolades that were due her. Who knows what she meant." Sarah greedily drained the glass. "She never got over Ellen, you know. She accused me of stealing her affections away from her."

Ellen? I felt a moment's dislocation. But Ellen had left me for Sarah not Marta. Or had she? Of course Ellen was perfectly capable of having several relationships at once. My face burned—obsessed by my own narrow focus, the wider view had escaped me.

But Sarah was still talking. I leaned forward to hear more clearly. Her lips had thinned, giving her face an ascetic look. "And then Adrian. She accused me of destroying their relationship. A relationship that existed more in her mind than anywhere else. She didn't know Adrian."

My head felt fuzzy. "But wait, if Marta felt you'd stolen her reputation, or the acclaim for her work she thought she should have received, why would you disappear and reemerge as Marta? Why let her live in place of Sarah Moore?"

A momentary glow flooded her face against the too-white bedclothes. "It's quite a feat, isn't it? I can make Marta Conway exactly what she always wanted to be. Or I can make her disappear." She snapped her fingers as if to demonstrate that she had the power to annihilate Marta as simply as a careless shoe crunching a twig underfoot.

"I don't understand. There's something else, something you're not telling me."

Sarah turned her face toward the wall. "She hated me. Do you know what it's like to live with someone's hatred?"

I didn't answer. Of course I knew. It took little to take me back to the time when I entered every room and hallway in our house and listened, too frightened to breathe. Or lay in my room awake until dawn, waiting for the door to fly open and Adrian's furious face to appear.

"You can't imagine what that hatred is like," she continued. "Especially when that someone used to worship you. Intolerable."

Sarah smiled with her old assurance. But now, her heart-shaped face dimmed by illness and pain, the effect was less fatally charming and more a sign of bitterness and regret.

"Many of us tolerate things we'd rather not confront," I told her.

She appeared once again not to hear me. The small form under the bedclothes looked extremely frail, yet somehow her very bones retained their power so that she resembled a once-robust creature with shriveled limbs. Once, I'd seen a cormorant stranded by a storm far up the beach. Its wings broken, the bird struggled over and over through the sand to reach the water. Each time it advanced, a wave knocked it farther back from the shore. It grew weaker and more diminished with each surge of the sea.

My sympathy was shattered when she spoke again. "She didn't deserve to live. Life isn't for the timid, the uncertain, but for the vital, the sure. It belongs to those who seize it by the throat."

"I'm not sure I believe that everyone should have to fight to live."

She raised a finger and pointed it at my chest. "How would you know, you who are so very tenacious? Just remember that I don't give up easily either. I'll always know where you are, Amanda. And if I want to find you, for any reason, I will." The finger, sharp and strong, stabbed at the soft flesh under my breastbone.

I woke then, trembling in the bed, nerves fired by adrenaline. Beside me, Teresa stirred in her sleep. I turned onto my side, one hand touching her warm hip, willing my heartbeat to cease its erratic charge. But the blood rushed to my ears, wild and uncontrollable as a torrent unleashed in a dry arroyo. I waited for the dawn.

The next day we called the hospital in Evanston where the paramedics had told Teresa they'd deliver Sarah and Adrian. There were no patients with the names Marta Conway or Adrian Ferguson. And no one was registered as Sarah Moore, either.

Babs insisted we go to the hospital and check for ourselves. But that effort left us as empty-handed as we were before.

"That woman, and your brother too, are veritable Houdinis," Babs announced with annoyance.

She was right. Not only had Adrian and Sarah escaped, but it was as if they had erased the night on their way out.

"Houdini was brilliant for a long time and then he wasn't. You know the myth of what happened to him." Teresa's voice was troubled. "He drowned in the midst of a trick. It was a terrible death."

Babs nodded. "I know." She added obliquely, "I also know history can always be rewritten."

28

I sipped the ginger tea Helen had given me, comforted by its medicinal flavor. "What does any of it mean? That's what I want to know."

Helen sat quietly. Her energy flowed toward me in an unbroken wave. "What is the worst thing you've imagined during the last few years?"

Without thinking, I said, "Adrian and Sarah together."

"Exactly. And now it has happened, but you're still here. You've survived the thing you dreaded and feared. That means something profound."

I shut my eyes, sensing Helen's presence, hearing the steady ticking of the round clock. Sometimes when I stopped looking and talking, when I ceased *monitoring* the world around me, I could feel the thrum of my nervous system, the tingling of life coursing through my limbs. I registered those things now but didn't feel the clutch of envy or panic or alertness that typically assailed me at the mere mention of Sarah or Adrian.

"Not only have you survived, but you are stronger than ever. And probably happier too." Helen's blue eyes were clear, not shrouded by fatigue as they often were when I saw her. She regarded me steadily. That's why I came to therapy, I realized, to have that gaze, that focus supporting me as I trudged through the dark sac of my unconscious mind, picking up a thread here, discarding one there, knowing all along that someone accompanied me, helping me to make connections or see deeply. Helen was not my friend but my guide, and occasionally simply my companion in the journey during these proscribed hours we spent together.

"I don't really know much more than I did before."

"Oh, but you do. You know why you were so unsettled by the woman who met you at the door that night. Your instincts were utterly correct. It wasn't Sarah and something was terribly wrong."

"No," I spoke slowly. "It wasn't Sarah. But Sarah was not who I thought she was at the time just the same. And I was taken in. Again. I'd thought she cared for me."

Helen wore a sweater of autumn colors, rust and olive and gold. She rubbed her left arm reflexively with her right hand. "So many of your hunches have been right. You knew Adrian and Sarah were attracted to each other early on. And you now know what happened to Marta."

I wanted to weep. "Poor Marta. Lost and abandoned."

"You remember our discussion about the woman in the tower?"

I nodded.

"I can't help but think that a part of you identifies with the woman trapped there."

"Do you mean in a mythological sense?" Over the past months, Helen had loaned me a steady supply of books on psychology, myth, and archetypes. "That a chunk of my life is walled up in that tower, and that I can't go forward unless I release myself?"

"Possibly. But I was thinking more literally. Of that actual night when Adrian answered the door and you looked up and saw the face in the window. You couldn't see it clearly but you said it was a face of longing."

"Yes, I remember. What are you trying to say?"

Helen pushed up the sleeves of her sweater decisively. "I'm saying you sensed that someone was trapped in that house and you recalled exactly how that felt. You were brought face-to-face with your old role of helpless observer. You saw a reflection of yourself looking out the window, yearning to escape."

It was true that the image of the face at the window brought up old feelings of despair. "I'm not changing the subject but you just reminded me of something. Since the night of the play in Chicago, the pain in my shoulder seems less intense. So much passed away that night: any myth that Marta was alive. Or that Sarah was murdered."

"And Adrian?" Helen prompted.

I sat back in the chair. "I saw Adrian. I was this close to him." I extended my arm, indicating the distance from my chair to the door of Helen's office. "He had no power over me. He didn't see me. And really, he's never seen me—he doesn't know me. He wasn't able to detain me. Or involve me in any way."

"But he had Teresa in his car. Someone you value immensely."

My mouth was suddenly dry. "I didn't say I wasn't terrified. I was afraid I'd never see her again."

Helen smiled. "That's your escape from the tower right there. You saw that Adrian isn't all-powerful. He's not capable of keeping you from what you want now. The woman in the tower is passive. She can only watch. But you have reached out and claimed something, someone, you desire very much."

"Isn't that what always happens in fairy tales? Love is the great release and the great healer. If you love truly, you can be free from all manner of things. The patterns of the past. The bogeyman waiting behind the door or in the woods."

"Do you feel that Teresa has saved you?"

I shook my head fiercely. "No. Loving her, choosing her, has changed me, not saved me. I'd like to think I didn't need to be saved, that I was taking care of myself just fine."

Helen smiled. "So much has changed for you. And it's all coming from you. Your search to understand to begin with. And your unwillingness to accept the pain you've been in."

I felt both gratified by her words and assailed by how much more work I had to do. "After what's happened, I'm aware of something significant that is just beyond my reach, but I'm very close to it. I'd like us to try EMDR again to try and access the memory of Adrian breaking down the door."

This time I choose the TheraTappers that fit in my hands, closing my fingers around the slender metal cylinders and adjusting the pulse in my palms to a slower rate than my heartbeat, hoping to retard the impact of the memory on my system.

I didn't feel the usual resistance about going back to that room in that place. Having just seen Adrian, it was almost as if I still followed him down the street in Chicago, but this time he took me back in time to a different street, a particular door, and up a certain hallway into a second-story flat. I fell back into the memory of that night, fully aware and yet physically insulated.

I heard the force of the breaking door reverberate in the room. Once again, heavy footfalls hammered their way up the steps, echoing in the chill hallway.

My thirteen-year-old self was stretched out on the sleeper sofa, asleep, her face twisting from side to side as if fighting off a nightmare. I tried to insert the adult Amanda into the scene, but I couldn't. I hoped that Duncan might appear as he had last time, but there was no trace of him in the room. Instead, the face of the troubled girl grew larger, like a close-up on a screen.

The footsteps grew louder, and then Adrian burst into the room, a mass of energy both tightly coiled and spilling over chaotically. "Manda! Are you crazy?" The furious voice sliced through the air. The girl did not move.

Adrian rushed at the slender figure on the bed. "I was freezing out there. Why didn't you open the door? Goddamn it, why?" His right hand shot out and collided with the girl's left shoulder, pushing her down into the bed.

But the girl said nothing, and I saw something I'd never noticed before, that Adrian's voice was both an accusation and a plea for response. He reacted to being ignored as if he were in agony. His face twisted, and he doubled over as though he had a grinding pain in his gut. He straightened up again.

Once more, his hand grasped her shoulder. "Manda! Get up and listen to me! Do you hear me?" His features, red from cold and rage, loomed over the girl's face. Spittle flew from his mouth onto the pillowcase. "Sit up, sit up or I'll . . ." The full weight of his body bore down on her shoulder. ". . . I'll kill you!"

The girl's eyes snapped open then, cloudy with confusion and fright. "What? What's going on? I'm asleep. I'm asleep." She pulled away from him but he held her shoulder fast and she cried out in pain.

"Stop it! Stop it! I didn't do anything!" She began to scream.

The TheraTappers pulsed in my hands. "Stop," I said aloud. I felt lightheaded, my mouth parched.

In the background I heard Helen say, "You *can* stop . . ." But my nervous system was poised on the precipice of discovery; I couldn't withdraw.

Adrian shook his sister harder with his right arm, while his left hand covered her mouth. The girl's eyes popped wide, her cries were muffled to a whimper; her breath came in fast bursts through her nose. Then, with the speed of a serpent striking, Adrian slid his hand from her mouth to her neck and tightened his grip. The girl flailed for a few moments and then went limp.

Adrian's body recoiled as if he'd been struck. "Manda? Hey!" He took his hand off her throat and poked her. "Wake up! Stop fooling around."

He put his head against her chest and then his head jerked up, his face white. "Come on," he wheedled. "That's enough. Cut it out." He stood and backed away.

The girl on the bed breathed steadily, but did not move. Adrian lay down on top of her, and then put his ear to her chest. The calm rise and fall of her chest continued. He scrambled to his feet and watched her for a moment, his hands twitching.

Adrian hesitated, eyes darting, calculating, and then ran from the room, bent-shouldered, arms plastered to his sides. Steps sounded in the hallway, but softer this time.

Frozen for a moment, I witnessed the scene fade. My chest ached as if under a heavy weight. Again, I felt light-headed. And slightly out of breath. I put my head between my knees, and placed my hand on the back of my neck, which oozed heat and moisture. My heart pinged in my ears, steady but rapid. For a moment I listed deep underwater, the weight of it taking me down and down.

"Ohhhh." The air in my lungs deflated as though I had been punched in the diaphragm. I breathed in again, and at first the air stalled in my throat. I swallowed, coughed, afraid that my lungs could no longer accept air.

I straightened and my chest expanded. Relief, as calming as cool water against my skin, flooded through me when I was fully upright. I was grateful to be sitting in the quiet room.

"That's it," I said when my chest stopped heaving. I opened my eyes to the reassuring solid form of Helen.

Helen waited and then asked, "Can you tell me?"

"I blacked out. That's why I've never been able to remember. Adrian was choking me one minute and then . . . nothing."

"You fell out of consciousness," Helen mused. "For a very long time."

"Adrian thought I was faking at first. But then he was afraid. He shrank from me. I don't know what stopped him, why he didn't choke me to death. Except that Duncan was already dead. Maybe he couldn't stand the thought of being alone. Maybe he felt he needed me to be alive. And yet I think he wanted to kill me, to make me disappear. He just couldn't do it." I massaged my throat. As my fingers touched the soft flesh above my collarbone, a phantom charge of fear rippled through me.

"He assaulted you. And worse, you were never able to protest. Because you didn't know what happened. Do you remember if you told anyone about how frightened you were? How much pain you were in from that night?"

I shook my head. "No one would have believed me. I was a nervous child. I had bad dreams. That was 'just how Amanda was.'" I reached for a Kleenex and impatiently swabbed my nose.

Suddenly, I couldn't sit still another second. I lurched to my feet and paced up and down the room, boiling with rage. "I was alone. I've been left alone with this all my life." I picked up a pillow resting against the wall and threw it at my chair. I sat back down and ground my fingers into my eyes.

"You know how you've often said Adrian was your worst nightmare, maybe you're his as well." Helen spoke quietly, but she leaned toward me as if ready to support me if I slumped over onto the floor.

"I'm okay." Then her words registered. "Really? You think he fears me?"

"It's very possible. You saw something he most likely didn't want anyone to see. You *know* him in a way perhaps no one else ever has."

I reached up and kneaded my left shoulder, which was slightly tender. The knifelike sensation was gone. I sat up straight, stretching my spine. "I can't believe the pain has changed."

"You're not frozen anymore. And neither is your body." Helen took off her tortoiseshell frames. Her blue eyes had a triumphant sheen.

"Thank you for saying that." I felt my face flush, but for once I didn't mind. "You know Teresa and I keep talking about what happened that night in Chicago when she was trapped in Adrian's car. How Adrian and Sarah were both in a rage. I tried desperately at first to figure out their motives. But then my thinking shifted. What if there is no reason or logic to how they behave? What if they're both caught in a script of their own that no one else can figure out? I think I finally see that giving up on trying to decipher a mystery is all right."

I looked at the courtyard outside Helen's window. "It feels like a victory of sorts." In the trees was a birdbath. A yellow-rumped warbler was perched at the edge, tipping its head to take a drink. Its simple beauty tore at my heart. "You know all these years I thought Adrian had a plan. That he was the most premeditated person I knew. I'm not sure that's true."

Helen leaned back in her chair. "It's possible that much of what happened in your childhood between the two of you was not personal—but of course as a child you would have taken everything personally. Your brother didn't control his impulses. He just flailed at anything in his path that he viewed as obstructive. You were in his way. Hence, you were hurt. What happened may not have been premeditated at all."

She thought a moment. "And I'm sure you infuriated him as well. He couldn't control you and he was furious when you crossed him or thwarted his desires. For instance, you didn't open the door when he was cold. He knocked and knocked and then lost his temper. In his mind, you'd struck out at him. He had to strike back."

I listened to this carefully. "I was more than in his way. I *watched* him. I was a witness to many things he did. And to the person he was. I saw his impulsive, rage-filled self, how he struck at anyone smaller than he was."

"What will you do with that?" Helen put her glasses back on. "Now that you're no longer in the tower."

I looked down to see my hands lying limp in my lap. For a moment I felt divorced from them, as if observing someone else's hand. I noticed how much the long fingers and broad palms resembled Adrian's. I shook my head. "I don't know."

Helen's voice was careful. "The image of this younger Adrian lives inside you as a predatory figure. But perhaps if you met him now, you would find that he is much less frightening, more ordinary. As you said earlier, when you saw him in Chicago he had no power over you."

I looked up and hesitated. "Are you saying that the Adrian who haunts my thoughts and dreams is separate from the Adrian who exists now as a mature person?" I nodded. "Yes, he'd have to be. The past is past. I don't know my brother anymore."

"The old Adrian did have power over you. But he doesn't now. Your life is your own." Helen waited and then said, "He has Sarah now. I imagine they will keep each other very occupied. Does that make you feel safer?"

"I think so. I'm not sure." I crossed my legs and studied my hands again, the hands of a middle-aged woman who had lived at least half her life. I clenched my fists and vowed I would not spend another year of the time I had left living in fear.

The round black clock was approaching the end of my hour. I listened to its ticking, wondering if for me this room would always be filled with the sense of lost time. "Do you know what I regret the most?"

"What?"

"That a part of me has remained focused on childhood and didn't really grow up. I've wasted so much time. You once loaned me a book that made a big impression on me—*Prisoners of Childhood*. Looking back, that's been my life."

"Amanda, listen to me." Helen's voice was blunt, without sentiment. "Nothing is wasted. You of all people know that. Your experience has given you knowledge and an empathy many people will never attain. Thank God you've come to this place in your life. You've been granted grace of a sort."

"You mean be grateful?"

"If that's what you want to call it. Make peace with it, however you can."

"Everyone's lessons are hard," I finally said. "I know that. Sometimes I just get tired of my own."

Helen looked up and we both smiled. "Amen to that," she said.

We sat together in silence for a bit. The afternoon light was changing, deepening, and the birdbath was entirely in shadow. And empty. "You know, I've measured much of my life by how Adrian will react, what Adrian will do or has done. It's hard to imagine letting all that go. I wonder . . . how do you change the habit of a lifetime?"

29

B abs called that night before Teresa came home from teaching her evening class. "I can't stop thinking about Marta."

It was as if no time had passed since we were all in Chicago, as if we
were still heatedly discussing what Babs called "the case" at every waking
moment. "I didn't tell you. That night in the theater, at the reception, I
noticed that she was wearing the opal ring you reminded me about. But it
wasn't on her middle finger. It was on her ring finger."

Babs sighed. I knew the workings of her mind so well that I sensed my
old friend was examining this detail from every angle before she spoke.
"Strange that Sarah would make that mistake."

"I remember you telling me that when you thought you saw Sarah at
the 7-Eleven that night, she was wearing the ring as Marta always did and
that's how you knew who it really was."

I heard the clink of ice cubes. "Yes. You know, I've been thinking. Sarah
and Adrian were testing us. They wanted us to know. Especially you. And
Teresa."

"But why?"

At the sound of swallowing, I took a sip of my scotch. Babs went on, a
leisurely note in her voice, a sign she'd been spinning possibilities in her
mind for some time. "Maybe it was a warning."

I felt a chill. "Of what?"

"Oh, that they have a long reach. That they're very, very smart. They
wanted us to know they'd outwitted the police. Faking Sarah's death and
so forth. After all, they made the scene of Marta's death so clear-cut there

was never an autopsy. Never a way of being absolutely sure whose body was lying in that bed."

"We knew they were smart before. I don't get it."

Babs sighed. I heard the scrape of glass against wood. "Neither do I. Let's hope they just congratulate each other forever and leave us out of it. How's Teresa?"

"Still exhausted from the trip. But she's moving on. She's stopped looking over her shoulder if you know what I mean."

"Ah. I'm glad to hear it but I'd like to know her secret. I'm still jittery, still spilling coffee, tripping on level surfaces, that sort of thing. I'm even putting Mister on tiptoe."

"Babs, there is one thing . . ."

"Hmm?"

"They were both injured when Adrian hit the tree. And Sarah had already hit her head. They could be seriously impaired."

"We may never know. Can you live with that?"

"Funny. Helen, my therapist, keeps asking me that question about most things pertaining to Adrian."

Babs cleared her throat and then spoke deliberately. "He's such a benchmark for you. Such a presence in your life. I often wonder—who would you be without Adrian?"

"Are you saying that Adrian made me who I am?"

"That's one way of putting it."

30

Teresa placed an envelope on my desk a week later. She pulled a chair up next to mine and sat, her head arcing forward gently, her hands twining in her lap as if she were meditating or praying.

"Can I read it?" I touched the open flap.

Teresa nodded. "It's from Connie Stephen. The old theater friend in Chicago I told you about."

Inside the envelope was a short obituary from the *Chicago Tribune* that announced Marta Conway's death from a subdural hematoma. She had died five days after we returned from Chicago.

I read through it twice. "I wonder if it was the second injury or the first."

"Five days. That means it was a very slow bleed. She might have thought she was okay, except for a slight disorientation. And she might have expected that was just natural from the impact she'd had and thought it would go away."

My eyes blurred as I stared at the small print in the obituary. The article was impossibly short—such a small thing to end so much. "She and Adrian never went to a hospital that night. That's why we couldn't find a record of them. Somehow they talked the paramedics out of admitting them."

"Somehow."

"So it's over." I dropped the paper on my lap and smoothed it out. "In one short paragraph."

Teresa's neck was still bowed, her hair falling gently around her face;

she reminded me of a swan, its head unmoving as it floats in the current. "At least now I can stop agonizing whether or not to go to the police."

I nodded. "There's no point in going now. But I don't think they would have reopened the investigation into Sarah's death all those years ago no matter what you'd told them. They would have just thought you were crazy."

"Yes, I suppose they would have. Babs was quite persuasive on that point." But as she raised her head, Teresa appeared troubled, not certain at all. "I don't know what to feel."

"It feels as if Marta died twice, doesn't it?" I folded the sheet of paper and put it back on the desk. "Poor Marta. But it's almost as if she got a revenge of sorts. Even though it took fourteen years for it to happen."

"Sarah didn't get away with it. I can take some solace in that." Teresa leaned her head on my shoulder as if it was too heavy for her to support. "What about Adrian? What do you think has happened to him?"

"I've been sitting here wondering that very thing. Part of me is sure he's alive and perfectly well. He is the kind of person Sarah once was—he has many more than nine lives."

"And the other part of you?" Teresa's voice sounded cloudy, obscured by tears.

"It's just waiting for the other shoe to drop. Whatever that is."

"That could take a long time," Teresa said.

———

Fourteen months later, in late December, I met Adrian at a small hospital in Moorhead, Minnesota. Eva had developed congestive heart failure over the last two years and recently contracted pneumonia. When I arrived, I found Adrian sitting at Eva's bedside. From the doorway our mother's body under the layers of thin white blankets looked very small and still.

Adrian greeted me with, "Manda." He smiled then, an almost sweet smile. "It's been a long time." He didn't look uncomfortable seeing me. Oddly, I sensed relief in his face.

Our gaits awkward, we walked toward each other and half hugged, each putting one arm around the mid-back of the other. Our bodies didn't touch.

"Still managing other people's money?" Adrian asked once he retreated back to his chair.

"No, I gave that up. I have a gallery again."

His gray eyes looked eager. "You're painting?"

"I'm doing a series, in pastel, of our farm. I think it's one of the best things I've ever done."

Adrian smoothed a strand of hair back from his temple. The gesture, slightly self-conscious, stirred me. "I . . . I hope I get to see them," he said.

I looked away, not sure if he meant what he'd said. I wondered whether he'd ever really come to Austin to see the paintings or to see me. Just then the blips and beeps above our mother's head reminded me why we were in that room together after so long. As the hospice nurse came in and checked the equipment, I moved aside.

———

Five days later, cars filled both sides of the block for the reception after the funeral. The streets glittered with ice, and piles of sooty snow lined the sidewalks by Eva's managed care complex. Winter came early this year to the northern plains, and the snowfall from a vicious snowstorm the week before remained. Teresa and I picked our way along the slick sidewalk. Our small, cautious steps contrasted with my memory of my young self gliding along the ice with long, sure strides. Someone said that every child at seven is a Cézanne. In our imaginations we are also a gymnast or an acrobat at that age, a Mikhail Baryshnikov soaring through space.

In the blank, square community events room, Adrian and I stood stiffly on one side of the piano, greeting cousins, our aged great-aunt, our mother's old friends.

The wall opposite us was painted a pale shell pink. It contained only a large print of a seacoast and a large calendar. I couldn't read the print, but I didn't have to. It was December 29, eight days past the anniversary of Duncan's death. The space between Adrian and me was large enough to hold Duncan, if he'd been there. I closed my eyes, and as easily as if the decades hadn't passed, sensed the quiet presence of my twin. I imagined the whisper of his hand touching mine, the echo of his voice in my ear.

I opened my eyes, startled, as Great-Aunt Agnes's bony fingers, the skin as thin as a whisper, enfolded my hands.

"You do know, sweetheart, your mother never recovered from what happened to Duncan. I don't think she ever had a peaceful moment again." The face with its pleated skin and sad brown eyes peered earnestly up at me.

My eyes began to spill over as I looked into my aunt's aged face. The unsettled soul of Eva weighed upon me, yet I couldn't help saying, "She wasn't the most peaceful person at the best of times."

To my surprise, Aunt Agnes didn't disagree. Her smile turned wistful, the left side of her mouth tilting down. "No. She was an anxious child. Poor thing. Took everything very hard."

It was hard to imagine my restless, purposeful mother as small and vulnerable. "She loved you," I told Agnes, and that much at least was true.

"I always made her cake, almond cake. She adored sweets." Aunt Agnes squeezed my hand, a small dry pressure, and then moved on, her back still erect, to speak to Adrian.

Eva died a month after turning seventy-six. At ninety-six, Aunt Agnes had survived her niece by twenty years. Unlike the astute Agnes, Eva's mind began its decline early, flaming out years before her death. In fact, the last time I visited her when she was still conscious, one month before her death, Eva hadn't recognized me. I wondered if Eva had roused herself one last time for Adrian. I hoped she was able to have that comfort.

My brother's broad shoulders leaned forward as he chatted with Agnes. At almost fifty, his hair was mostly silver; he wore it severely brushed back from his forehead. The short, sleek hair on the lean face gave him an almost military look.

By late afternoon, the crowd at the reception began to dissipate. Across the room, by the table under the calendar, Teresa checked the wine supplies, consolidated the food. She glanced at her watch in a discreet gesture I knew well, barely turning the inside of her wrist. Soon, only the three of us would remain.

Two of Eva's friends stayed on briefly to help us clean up. One of them volunteered to take Aunt Agnes back to her apartment. Agnes hugged me in a tight grip, and I assured her that I'd come to see her before I went back to Texas.

Around six o'clock, Teresa, Adrian, and I walked the short distance to Eva's ground-floor apartment, where Adrian was staying.

As Adrian fitted a key into the lock, Teresa put a hand on my arm. "Look, I have a splitting headache. I think I'll go back to the hotel."

I kissed her cheek. "Put your feet up. I'll join you soon."

Teresa's eyes flitted to Adrian, who opened the exterior door and slid a hand inside to switch on a light, and then back to me. "Call if you need me."

The shelves in Eva's living room looked even more crowded with china figurines and souvenir plates than the last time I'd been there. Once inside, Adrian collapsed sidewise into the BarcaLounger in the living room, his long limbs dangling across the chair's arm. "God, I need a drink."

"I have just the thing." I rummaged in the black canvas tote I'd dropped by the door and brought out a bottle of Glenlivet. "I brought this along for Teresa. She doesn't usually drink wine."

In the kitchen I discovered a whole cupboard packed with what Eva used to call "highball glasses," some with hairline cracks. In the back of another cabinet I found two rock glasses and managed to free a few cubes of ice from a sclerotic plastic ice tray. As I rinsed off the discolored ice for good measure, I faced the fact that the reception had used up every ounce of social energy I'd had on reserve.

I walked back into the living room and handed Adrian a glass, which he accepted without looking up. For a moment I considered leaving. Unless we really talked, there was nothing to say. I decided to be bold. "Do you want to talk about Sarah?"

Adrian's eyes fluttered shut. His voice sounded ambiguous. "That chapter is closed."

I couldn't stop myself from thinking that this "chapter," as he put it, made three—Adrian had presided three times at the death of someone close to him.

I sat across from him on an antique maroon loveseat, the same one our parents had in their bedroom in North Dakota. Eva used to sit on it when she put on her stockings.

Saying Sarah's name aloud had awakened my old curiosity, "the old itch" as a character in Betrayal put it. A barrage of questions filled my mind, but I forced myself to focus on the one thing I really needed to know. I wasn't sure when I'd have the opportunity again, for Adrian's facade had seemed to crack open the slightest bit from the emotion of losing Eva. I knew there were risks in pushing against that crack. This small chink in Adrian's armor made me think of the cellar door on the farm, how it opened barely a sliver, just enough to slide through its opening. Once inside, though, there was always the danger the door might get stuck and not allow for the return trip out of the root cellar's dank confines.

I drank down the single malt, refilled my glass, and took a long breath. "Eva's gone. We can talk now."

Adrian seemed at ease as he put his glass to his lips. But I knew from past interactions that the apparently languid motion of his arm could exist in inverse proportion to his inner tension. He swung his legs down from the arm of the chair to rest on the carpet and took off his shoes. He loosened his tie, red silk shot with tiny threads of gold. The fineness of the fabric reminded me of our father who often fussed over his choice of a tie.

"If you like," he said. "But I can't imagine you want to hear about the state of my research, or the house I'm renovating, or any number of things that occupy me."

He was so smug—always the eldest son and certain of his importance, even without Eva in this world backing him up. Even now I could almost see Eva standing behind his chair, ready to support him if he needed her. This was her place, after all, and Eva wouldn't let a small thing like the membrane that divided life from death separate her from her beloved Adrian.

Seeing how little had changed—aware of my lingering bitterness about our mother's attachment to Adrian even while the vision of Eva's ghost at his back seized my imagination—I wished I could laugh. But I was too edgy, poised for flight.

Summoning the courage to speak took all of my will. Rather than the commanding tone I'd imagined when thinking about this moment, my utterance came out subdued and breathy. "Adrian. I want to know about Duncan. About the day he died."

Adrian's head turned slowly toward me. His lips tightened into a straight line as he held out his glass for a refill.

I poured another two inches into his glass, distracted by how the amber liquid sloshed heavily and then settled into the glass. "There's no one else left, don't you see? No one else will ever know."

I had the strange sensation that Adrian was about to say something like, *And what will you give me if I tell you?* or that favorite response of children, *It's mine to know and yours to find out,* or even, *Make me.* I passed a hand over my face and willed myself not to cry, not to crumble in the face of Adrian's obstinate stare.

He sipped at his fresh drink. Then he glanced quickly over his shoulder, toward Eva's bedroom, and leaned in closer. "There's not much to tell."

My hope was like a fragile piece of glass in my chest and I breathed shallowly so as not to crack it. "Whatever there is, I need to know it."

"So that you can forgive me?" Adrian's voice sounded ironic, but he dipped his head; one hand drifted to his stomach as if it burned. "God, it's so long ago. Can it even matter after all this time?"

I squeezed my eyes shut. I wanted to scream at him how much it mattered, how much it surely mattered to him as well. But I couldn't afford to start a fight and silence him. "Yes."

I felt dizzy with my eyes closed; white dots flickered in front of my eyes. I was glad to be sitting down. I heard Adrian's breathing quicken and then he sucked in air. I looked up to find him doubled over in his chair.

"Manda . . . in the bathroom, in the medicine cabinet. There's a bottle of pills. Get them for me." Adrian's face looked grayish white.

"What is it?"

"Just get them. Now."

I did as I was told. I flew down the narrow hallway and into the bathroom. The cabinet held Eva's old medications and I fumbled around spilling the bottles into the sink until I found one with Adrian's name on it. I thought it odd that he'd put his pills here, and wondered how long he planned on staying.

I sloshed water into a glass resting by the faucet and brought it to him with the pills. But Adrian ignored the water and slid one tablet under his tongue. I wondered whether Adrian had heart trouble, at only forty-nine.

He waved me away as I hovered by his chair. "I'm fine." He cleared his throat. "A little angina. It's nothing."

I returned to the loveseat and perched on the edge of the cushion, ready to get up again and fetch something else. "I'm sorry."

Adrian shook his head as if impatient. Human frailty, I suspected particularly his own, had always annoyed him. I thought he'd ask me to leave him alone. But instead the twinge in his chest appeared to encourage him to speak. Perhaps Eva's funeral had reminded him of how time was shortening for both of us.

"That day. You remember how cold it had been and then almost warm, for December." He stopped, overcome by an extended fit of coughing. He drew out a handkerchief and passed it over his lips and forehead. After this, his color looked a little better.

"I remember."

Adrian began again, and as the words spilled out of him a little faster, I thought about the relief that telling a long-held secret brings, the exquisite release of it. "Duncan and I were skating. The ice seemed fine. But you know what a little sprite he was. How fast and what a daredevil he could be. He wanted to race me across the pond."

Adrian took a deep breath and held it as if to hold back the memory. Then he went ahead. "'No,' I told him. 'It's too dangerous after the thaw we had. Dad said we had to promise to stay on the outskirts.' Duncan laughed at me then. '*Dad said.* You're such a scaredy-cat, Adrian. Come on.' And he pushed off and swooped toward the center, flying with that red scarf of his spooling behind him like a flag." Adrian's voice dropped. "He was so beautiful. So graceful. He was the best skater of us all."

"So you skated after him?" I couldn't resist asking even though it was easy to imagine the scene, Duncan gliding across the ice, and Adrian annoyed that even with his superior strength he was stilted on his skates compared to Duncan.

"He had wings." Adrian's voice sounded wistful. "I couldn't catch him but I hustled after him."

In the dim living room Adrian's gray eyes looked dark, like the glaring ice under an iron-gray sky, the kind of sky that marked the day Duncan died. I sensed something cold in the room, something harsh, but instead of fear I felt infinitely sad. No matter what Adrian told me now, I'd lose something precious.

"Duncan flew and flew and then suddenly he broke through the ice right in front of me." Adrian sighed, and a bubble of sound popped out from between his lips. Tears filled his eyes.

Sitting erect, I found the strength to nod. I felt my body swaying slightly as I listened, sensing the shock a body goes through as the ground breaks away beneath you. "And you couldn't go near him. It was too dangerous. Too risky."

"No!" Adrian's voice turned harsh. "That's not true! I did go. I went in. I crashed through the ice just like he did. I wanted to pull him out. I tried. I reached for him. My arms were like lead and I was sinking . . . but still, I reached for him. 'Duncan! I'm begging you. Come to me! Please . . .'" Adrian cried, his voice breaking, shattering over and over like the ice on the pond.

"It was hopeless. I was sure we were both finished. And then it felt all right. At least I wouldn't be standing by while my little brother drowned. Let it go, I thought. Just let go."

Adrian leaned forward, his head in his hands. "And just then, I was so cold I was beginning to get hot, my head was still above the water, but barely. Just then, a branch came toward me over the ice."

I stiffened. I tried to imagine a figure at the end of the makeshift pole, and just when it began to materialize into a familiar shape, Adrian spoke.

"Mother was there. She was out of breath; her clothes looked torn as if she'd tumbled down the hill. But she was very, very focused. She pushed the branch at me; she was lying on the ice, spread-eagled to balance her weight. 'Take it,' she said. 'Here. I can get you out.'

"'No,' I said, 'give it to Duncan.' And I reached out and I found him! I don't know, I guess he'd floated over to me, I'm not sure, but I grabbed his coat and I pulled him over to the pole."

"'No,' she said. 'I have you—let's get you out first. Then I'll get Duncan. Quick, quick, there's no time to lose.' I couldn't think. I couldn't feel anymore, I was so cold. So I did what she told me, I grasped the pole and I don't know how we did it. I scrambled and scraped, always forward, an inch at a time. I was choking. I was drowning, I had water in my lungs, and still she held on and kept pulling me out and away. The ice was breaking around us but somehow she hauled me out of there. I was soaked and we were both freezing. I thought we'd all die."

Adrian stared down at his hands, turned them slowly around like they were useless to him. "And then it was too late. By the time we had Duncan clear of the water, his heart had given out. He'd never said a word. He looked so peaceful. I don't know, maybe he was still skating, moving in that perfect stride of his. When he hit that frigid water maybe his heart stopped right away. I never saw him struggle."

Adrian looked beseechingly at me. "That's what happened."

"You didn't kill Duncan." The words sounded brittle to my ear. "It was Eva. All this time. It was Eva."

"No, no, no. She didn't kill him. She rescued me first and then she'd have saved Duncan . . ."

I stood up, my body rocked forward, and I grabbed the arm of the love-seat. "But she didn't save Duncan. She let him die. She delivered you, only you."

"Yes." Adrian's face was a mask of misery. "She saved me."

I took one step. Then another. I reached Adrian and placed a hand on his shoulder. "You should have told me a long time ago. All this time . . . the agony of not knowing, thinking that it was you. It was wrong."

"But I couldn't tell you. You never would have believed me. You would have hated me, never forgiven me . . ."

He reached for the bottle of pills but I placed my hand over them and picked them up. My body felt far away and numb as if it had been submerged in the frozen water along with Duncan. "Forgiveness. How do we forgive, I wonder. . . . How could I forgive when I didn't have the knowledge that would have let me forgive? You knew, and Eva knew. And neither of you had the courage to tell me."

"I was ashamed that she chose me," Adrian said.

"But she gave you life. Twice."

"And she let Duncan go."

"You both let him go." The pill bottle grew warm in my hand. I felt an urge to drop it before it burned me. "I'm not saying I blame you for wanting to live. I can't say that. But you let him go. I never would have let him go."

I picture myself by the pond, screaming, calling out for someone to let us go back and try again to save my brother. Then the scene shifts. I see only Duncan floating in the water. I feel the paralyzing cold of the water seep over every inch of my body as I go to him.

Either we'd both have made it out or we'd both have stayed.

Adrian's eyes searched my face. "How? What could I have done?"

I shook my head, hard, from side to side. "You're not hearing me. I would not have let him go." Adrian didn't understand—leaving Duncan behind would have meant losing myself.

Eva's living-room clock chimed eight times, an improbably musical sound. "Adrian, there are so many other things that I know about you. How you've lived your life. The things you've done. The things you've done to me. What all of it has cost."

The clock clicked as if resetting itself. My chest ached; a sharp pain sliced through my belly. I pressed my hand against my stomach. I wondered if I'd make it out of the room intact. "The cost, Adrian. That is something you can't imagine."

I tried to draw myself together, to straighten my back, but my body just wanted to fold around its emptiness. A thought came to me as I stared at Adrian, one I didn't think I'd had before. "I know who you are."

Adrian's forehead creased as he raised his head, then his eyes darted back to the bottle in my hand.

"I believe that Eva rescued you." I wanted to speak with strength but my throat felt so tight that I barely managed a whisper. "I'm not sure I believe that you couldn't have saved Duncan."

"But you have to believe me. I knew you wouldn't forgive me. I was right about that, wasn't I?"

Adrian *didn't* understand. This wasn't about what I thought of him. At stake was how each of us had to find a way to live without Duncan, with the knowledge of how he'd died. We had to live with the fact that we'd survived, and he hadn't. "You have to forgive yourself that Eva saved only you. I have other things to live with. And to live without."

He reached toward the pills in my hand. "I need one of those. Right now." His lips looked pale on his lean face, his eyes bright. "Manda, please, I ask you to think what my life has been like because of this."

"I will. I'll think about it. I'll think about it as I try to live my life. A life I am very lucky to have."

My eyes traced the knifelike part on the top of his silvery-blond hair. His head was still fine, still elegant. I wanted to reach out and touch his beautiful face.

I gathered my coat from the back of the loveseat. The pills in the bottle I held rattled as I turned toward the door. I read the few words on the label over and over, turned the container over and closed my fingers tightly around it. I stood still for a moment, feeling only grief. For Duncan and for Eva. For Adrian and my father. A deep sigh escaped from my mouth, a sound with force behind it. Then I placed the bottle on the table within

Adrian's reach. "You've escaped before, Adrian. You will again. It's your gift."

"Don't go. Not yet," Adrian said, unscrewing the cap on the bottle. "I need to talk to you some more." To my surprise, he sounded scared.

My canvas bag, crumpled by the door, looked far away. I walked across the room and picked it up. Its weight over my shoulder anchored me, reminded me of my own life. I put my hand on the doorknob and scanned the room. "The last of Eva." My eyes lingered on my brother. "That's what you are."

I turned the knob and pulled. Swollen from a recent storm, the door caught on the frame and didn't budge. I pulled harder until it cracked open wide enough to let me slide into the space, and I slipped through.

ACKNOWLEDGMENTS

I am very fortunate to have writer friends who were my perceptive early readers for this novel: Christie Logan, Laura Furman, Elisabeth McKetta, Lee Potts, Chris Newbill, Laurie Haus, Anne Cooper, Phyllis Skoy, Jill Root, Tina Carlson, Lisa Lenard-Cook, and Sue Hallgarth.

Special thanks go to my friend Hilda Raz and to my editor, Elise McHugh, at the University of New Mexico Press for their insight and enthusiasm about this project. I am also grateful to Marsha Keener, Charlotte McClure, and Linda MacNeilage for teaching me about EMDR, Jungian therapy, and the psychological process.

And, as always, I truly appreciate my spouse, Lynda Miller, for her unfailing support as editor, friend, and muse.